# Getting
# OFF

# Getting OFF

## A NOVEL OF SEX AND VIOLENCE

## by Lawrence Block

### WRITING AS JILL EMERSON

A HARD CASE CRIME NOVEL

**A HARD CASE CRIME BOOK**
(HCC-101)

*First Hard Case Crime edition: September 2011*

Published by

Titan Books

A division of Titan Publishing Group Ltd

144 Southwark Street

London SE1 0UP

in collaboration with Winterfall LLC

*This book is a work of fiction. Names, characters, places, and incidents either are the products of the author's imagination or are used fictitiously, and any resemblance to actual events or persons, living or dead, is entirely coincidental.*

Print edition ISBN 978-0-85768-287-1
E-book ISBN 978-0-85768-599-5

Design direction by Max Phillips
*www.maxphillips.net*

Typeset by Swordsmith Productions

The name "Hard Case Crime" and the Hard Case Crime logo are trademarks of Winterfall LLC. Hard Case Crime books are selected and edited by Charles Ardai.

Printed in the United States of America

*Visit us on the web at www.HardCaseCrime.com*

BLOCK,
LAWRENCE

*for* CHARLES ARDAI

# Getting
# OFF

# ONE

Pronouns suited her.

*She, her, herself.* These worked just fine. Names came and went, you were out the door and on a plane or a train or a bus, and your name stayed behind, along with whatever else you didn't need anymore.

Once, in a man's apartment, a book caught her eye. The title was *She*, by H. Rider Haggard, and she plucked it from the shelf and opened it at random. She read this passage:

> *Oh, how beautiful she looked there in the flame! No angel out of heaven could have worn a greater loveliness. Even now my heart faints before the recollection of it, as naked in the naked fire she stood and smiled at our awed faces, and I would give half my remaining time upon this earth thus to see her once again.*

She might have read more, but she had to get out of there. The book's owner was in the bedroom, as naked as the woman in the story, sprawled on his back with his sightless eyes staring at the ceiling. So she couldn't stick around, and she wasn't interested enough in the book to take it away with her. She'd take money, that was different, but she wouldn't take a book, and she wiped her fingerprints from this one and returned it to its spot on the shelf.

When she was born her parents named her Katherine Anne Tolliver, and she grew up with seemingly endless variations of Katherine. Kathy, Katie, Kath, Kate.

Cat.

Kitty.

For a time, her father called her Kitten. The world shortened that to Kit, and somehow it stuck, and so he called her that as well.

Kit. Kit Tolliver.

The trouble with that, though, was that one name ran into the other, with her first name ending with the same letter that started her last name. So that someone hearing her name might think her surname was Oliver.

She still had the name when she graduated from high school. It was on her diploma, but some idiot misspelled it, left the E off her middle name. Katherine Ann Tolliver, it read, and that bothered her for about fifteen seconds. Then she realized she wouldn't be keeping the diploma. Or the name, either.

All the same, she packed the diploma and took it with her when she moved to the Cities. She went first to a motel in Red Cloud, just to be out of Hawley, and nine days later she signed Katherine Tolliver to the lease of an apartment in St. Paul. It was a perfectly fine apartment, and she had a two-year lease, but she was gone after ten weeks. Done with the Cities, done with Minnesota altogether. Done with being Kit Tolliver.

There were plenty of other places to go, and when one was used up she never had trouble finding another. There were plenty of names, too, an endless supply of names, and she'd keep one for an hour or an evening or a week or a month.

And then get another one.

Once she took a man's name along with his cash.

He'd given it as Les. "Les is more," he'd told her, and laughed heartily, and it had been clear she was not the first woman to receive this assurance. And, when this particular Les was no more, she went through his wallet and discovered that his name was not Lester, as she'd more or less assumed, but Leslie. Leslie Paul Hammond was the name on his driver's license, but on his credit cards the middle name was conveniently reduced to an initial.

Well, why not? The sexual ambiguity of the name made it easy enough, so why not let his AmEx card pay for a plane ticket, why not use his Visa to pay for a nice hotel room? It would be a while before anybody found him, and by then she'd have doubled back on her own trail, so anyone looking for her would be looking in the wrong places.

By then she'd be somewhere else. And by then she'd be *somebody* else.

Nothing to it.

*She*, by H. Rider Haggard.

She might have looked for a copy later on, but she never did. Instead she forgot about it, even as she forgot about the dead man in the other room. And all the men, and all the other rooms.

And moved on.

# TWO

She felt his eyes on her just about the time the bartender placed a Beck's coaster on the bar and set her dry Rob Roy on top of it. She wanted to turn and see who was eyeing her, but remained as she was, trying to analyze just what it was she felt. She couldn't pin it down physically, couldn't detect a specific prickling of the nerves in the back of her neck. She simply knew she was being watched, and that the watcher was a male.

It was, to be sure, a familiar sensation. Men had always looked at her. Since adolescence, since her body had begun the transformation from girl to woman? No, longer than that. Even in childhood, some men had looked at her, gazing with admiration and, often, with something beyond admiration.

In Hawley, Minnesota, thirty miles east of the North Dakota line, they'd looked at her like that. The glances followed her to Red Cloud and St. Paul, and other places after that, and now she was in New York, and, no surprise, men still looked at her.

She lifted her glass, sipped, and a male voice said, "Excuse me, but is that a Rob Roy?"

He was standing to her left, a tall man, slender, well turned out in a navy blazer and gray trousers. His shirt was a button-down, his tie diagonally striped. His face, attractive but not handsome, was youthful at first glance, but she could see he'd lived some lines into it. And his dark hair was lightly infiltrated with gray.

"A dry Rob Roy," she said. "Why?"

"In a world where everyone orders Cosmopolitans," he said, "there's something very pleasingly old-fashioned about a girl who drinks a Rob Roy. A woman, I should say."

She lowered her eyes to see what he was drinking.

"I haven't ordered yet," he said. "Just got here. I'd have one of those, but old habits die hard." And, when the barman moved in front of him, he ordered Jameson on the rocks. "Irish whiskey," he told her. "Of course this neighborhood used to be mostly Irish. And tough. It was a pretty dangerous place a few years ago. A young woman like yourself wouldn't feel comfortable walking into a bar unaccompanied, not in this part of town. Even accompanied, it was no place for a lady."

"I guess it's changed a lot," she said.

"It's even changed its name," he said. His drink arrived, and he picked up his glass and held it to the light, admiring the amber color. "They call it Clinton now. That's for DeWitt Clinton, not Bill. DeWitt was the governor a while back, he dug the Erie Canal. Not personally, but he got it done. And there was George Clinton, he was the governor, too, for seven terms starting before the adoption of the Constitution. And then he had a term as vice president. But all that was before your time."

"By a few years," she allowed.

"It was even before mine," he said. "But I grew up here, just a few blocks from here, and I can tell you nobody called it Clinton then. You probably know what they called it."

"Hell's Kitchen," she said. "They still call it that, when they're not calling it Clinton."

"Well, it's more colorful. It was the real estate interests who plumped for Clinton, because they figured nobody would want to move to something called Hell's Kitchen. And that may have been true then, when people remembered what a bad neighborhood this was, but now it's spruced up and gentrified and yuppified to within an inch of its life, and the old name gives it a little added cachet. A touch of gangster chic, if you know what I mean."

"If you can't stand the heat—"

"Stay out of the Kitchen," he supplied. "When I was growing up here, the Westies pretty much ran the place. They weren't terribly efficient, like the Italian mob, but they were colorful and blood-thirsty enough to make up for it. There was a man two doors down the street from me who disappeared, and they never did find the body. Except one of his hands turned up in somebody's freezer on Fifty-third Street and Eleventh Avenue. They wanted to be able to put his fingerprints on things long after he was dead and gone."

"Would that work?"

"With luck," he said, "we'll never know. The Westies are mostly gone now, and the tenement apartments they lived in are all tarted up, with stockbrokers and lawyers renting them now. Which are you?"

"Me?"

"A stockbroker? Or a lawyer?"

She grinned. "Neither one, I'm afraid. I'm an actress."

"Even better."

"Which means I take a class twice a week," she said, "and run around to open casting calls and auditions."

"And wait tables?"

"I did some of that in the Cities. I suppose I'll have to do it again here, when I start to run out of money."

"The Cities?"

"The Twin Cities. Minneapolis and St. Paul."

"That's where you're from?"

They talked about where she was from, and along the way he told her his name was Jim. She was Jennifer, she told him. He related another story about the neighborhood—he was really a pretty good storyteller—and by then her Rob Roy was gone and so was his Jameson. "Let me get us another round," he said, "and then why don't we take our drinks to a table? We'll be more comfortable, and it'll be quieter."

He was talking about the neighborhood.

"Irish, of course," he said, "but that was only part of it. You had blocks that were pretty much solid Italian, and there were Poles and other Eastern Europeans. A lot of French, too, working at the restaurants in the theater district. You had everything, really. The UN's across town on the East River, but you had your own General Assembly here in the Kitchen. Fifty-seventh Street was a dividing line; north of that was San Juan Hill, and you had a lot of blacks living there. It was an interesting place to grow up, if you got to grow up, but no sweet young thing from Minnesota would want to move here."

She raised her eyebrows at *sweet young thing,* and he grinned at her. Then his eyes turned serious and he said, "I have a confession to make."

"Oh?"

"I followed you in here."

"You mean you noticed me even before I ordered a Rob Roy?"

"I saw you on the street. And for a moment I thought—"

"What?"

"Well, that you were on the street."

"I guess I was, if that's where you saw me. I don't…oh, you thought—"

"That you were a working girl. I wasn't going to mention this, and I don't want you to take it the wrong way—"

What, she wondered, was the right way?

"—because it's not as though you looked the part, or were dressed like the girls you see out there. See, the neighborhood may be tarted up, but that doesn't mean the tarts have disappeared."

"I've noticed."

"It was more the way you were walking," he went on. "Not swinging your hips, not your walk per se, but a feeling I got that you weren't in a hurry to get anywhere, or even all that sure where you were going."

"I was thinking about stopping for a drink," she said, "and not sure if I wanted to, or if I should go straight home."

"That would fit."

"And I've never been in here before, and wondered if it was decent."

"Well, it's decent enough now. A few years ago it wouldn't have been. And even now, a woman alone—"

"I see." She sipped her drink. "So you thought I might be a hooker," she said, "and that's what brought you in here. Well, I hate to disappoint you—"

"What brought me in here," he said, "was the thought that you might be, and the hope that you weren't."

"I'm not."

"I know."

"I'm an actress."

"And a good one, I'll bet."

"I guess time will tell."

"It generally does," he said. "Can I get you another one of those?"

She shook her head. "Oh, I don't think so," she said. "I was only going to come in for one drink, and I wasn't even sure I wanted to do that. And I've had two, and that's really plenty."

"Are you sure?"

"I'm afraid so. It's not just the alcohol, it's the time. I have to get home."

"I'll walk you."

"Oh, that's not necessary."

"Yes, it is. Whether it's Hell's Kitchen or Clinton, it's still necessary."

"Well…"

"I insist. It's safer around here than it used to be, but it's a long way from Minnesota. And I suppose you get some unsavory characters in Minnesota, as far as that goes."

"Well, you're right about that," she said. And at the door she said, "I just don't want you to think you have to walk me home because I'm a lady."

"I'm not walking you home because you're a lady," he said. "I'm walking you home because I'm a gentleman."

The walk to her door was interesting. He had stories to tell about half the buildings they passed. There'd been a murder in this one, a notorious drunk in the next. For all that some of the stories were unsettling, she felt completely secure walking at his side.

At her door he said, "Any chance I could come up for a cup of coffee?"

"I wish," she said.

"I see."

"I've got this roommate," she said. "It's impossible, it really is. My idea of success isn't starring on Broadway, it's making enough money to have a place of my own. There's just no privacy when she's home, and the damn girl is always home."

"That's a shame."

She drew a breath. "Jim? Do you have a roommate?"

He didn't, and if he had the place would still have been large enough to afford privacy. A large living room, a big bedroom, a good-sized kitchen. Rent-controlled, he told her, or he could never have afforded it. He showed her all through the apartment before he took her in his arms and kissed her.

"Maybe," she said, when the embrace ended, "maybe we should have one more drink after all."

She was dreaming, something confused and confusing, and then her eyes snapped open. For a moment she did not know where she was, and then she realized she was in New York, and realized the dream had been a recollection or reinvention of her childhood in Hawley.

In New York, and in Jim's apartment.

And in his bed. She turned, saw him lying motionless beside her, and slipped out from under the covers, moving with instinctive caution. She walked quietly out of the bedroom, found the bathroom. She used the toilet, peeked behind the shower curtain. The tub was surprisingly clean for a bachelor's apartment, and looked inviting. She didn't feel soiled, not exactly that, but something close. Stale, she decided. Stale, and very much in need of freshening.

She ran the shower, adjusted the temperature, stepped under the spray.

She hadn't intended to stay over, had fallen asleep in spite of her intentions. Rohypnol, she thought. Roofies, the date-rape drug. Puts you to sleep, or the closest thing to it, and leaves you with no memory of what happened to you.

Maybe that was it. Maybe she'd gotten a contact high.

She stepped out of the tub, toweled herself dry, and returned to the bedroom for her clothes. He hadn't moved in her absence and lay on his back beneath the covers.

She got dressed, checked herself in the mirror, found her purse, put on lipstick but no makeup, and was satisfied with the results. Then, after another reflexive glance at the bed, she began searching the apartment.

His wallet, in the gray slacks he'd tossed over the back of a chair, held almost three hundred dollars in cash. She took that but left the credit cards and everything else. She found just over a thousand dollars in his sock drawer, and took it, but left the mayonnaise jar full of loose change. She checked the refrigerator, and the set of brushed aluminum containers on the kitchen counter, but the fridge held nothing but food and drink, and one container held tea bags while the other two were empty.

That was probably it, she decided. She could search more thoroughly, but she'd only be wasting her time.

And she really ought to get out of here.

But first she had to go back to the bedroom. Had to stand at the side of the bed and look down at him. Jim, he'd called himself. James John O'Rourke, according to the cards in his wallet. Forty-seven years old. Old enough to be her father, in point of fact, although the man in Hawley who'd sired her was his senior by eight or nine years.

He hadn't moved.

Rohypnol, she thought. The love pill.

"Maybe," she had said, "we should have one more drink after all."

I'll have what you're having, she'd told him, and it was child's play to add the drug to her own drink, then switch glasses with him. Her only concern after that had been that he might pass out before he got his clothes off, but no, they kissed and petted and found their way to his bed, and got out of their clothes and into each other's arms, and it was all very nice, actually, until he yawned and his muscles went slack and he lay limp in her arms.

She arranged him on him on his back and watched him sleep. Then she touched and stroked him, eliciting a response without waking the sleeping giant. Rohypnol, the wonder drug, facilitating date rape for either sex. She took him in her mouth, she mounted him, she rode him. Her orgasm was intense, and it was hers alone. He didn't share it, and when she dismounted his penis softened and lay upon his thigh.

In Hawley her father took to coming into her room at night. "Kitten? Are you sleeping?" If she answered, he'd kiss her on the forehead and tell her to go back to sleep.

Then half an hour later he'd come back. If she was asleep, if she didn't hear him call her name, he'd slip into the bed with her. And touch her, and kiss her, and not on her forehead this time.

She would wake up when this happened, but somehow knew to feign sleep. And he would do what he did.

Before long she pretended to be asleep whenever he came into the room. She'd hear him ask if she was asleep, and she'd lie there silent and still, and he'd come into her bed. She liked it, she didn't like it. She loved him, she hated him.

Eventually they dropped the pretense. Eventually he taught her how to touch him, and how to use her mouth on him. Eventually, eventually, there was very little they didn't do.

It took some work, but she got Jim hard again, and this time she made him come. He moaned audibly at the very end, then subsided into deep sleep almost immediately. She was exhausted, she felt as if she'd taken a drug herself, but she forced herself to go to the bathroom and look for some Listerine. She couldn't find any, and wound up gargling with a mouthful of his Irish whiskey.

She stopped in the kitchen, then returned to the bedroom.

And, when she'd done what she needed to do, she decided it wouldn't hurt to lie down beside him and close her eyes. Just for a minute…

And now it was morning, and time for her to get out of there. She stood looking down at him, and for an instant she seemed to see his chest rise and fall with his slow even breathing, but that was just her mind playing a trick, because his chest was in fact quite motionless, and he wasn't breathing at all. His breathing had stopped forever when she slid the kitchen knife between two of his ribs and into his heart.

He'd died without a sound. *La petite mort,* the French called orgasm. The little death. Well, the little death had drawn a moan from him, but the real thing turned out to be soundless. His breathing stopped, and never resumed.

She laid a hand on his upper arm, and the coolness of his flesh struck her as a sign that he was at peace now. She thought, almost wistfully, how very serene he had become.

In a sense, there'd been no need to kill the man. She could have robbed him just as effectively while he slept, and the drug would ensure that he wouldn't wake up before she was out the door. She'd used the knife in response to an inner need, and the need had in fact been an urgent one; satisfying it had shuttled her right off to sleep.

Back in Hawley, her mother's kitchen had held every kind of knife you could imagine. A dozen of them jutted out of a butcher-block knife holder, and others filled a shallow drawer. Sometimes she'd look at the knives, and think about them, and the things you could do with them. Cutting, piercing. Knife-type things.

"You're my little soldier," her father used to say, and she felt like a soldier the night of her high school graduation, marching when her name was called, standing at attention to receive her diploma. She could feel the buzz in the audience, men and women telling each other how brave she was. The poor child, with all she'd been through.

She never touched her mother's knives, and for all she knew they were still in the kitchen in Hawley. But a few weeks later she left her apartment in St. Paul and went bar-hopping across the river in Minneapolis, and the young man she went home with had a set of knives in a butcher-block holder, just like her mother's.

Bad luck for him.

She let herself out of the apartment, drew the door shut and made sure it locked behind her. The building was a walk-up, four apartments to the floor, and she made her way down three flights and out the door without encountering anyone.

Time to think about moving.

Not that she'd established a pattern. The man last week, in the posh loft near the Javits Center, had smothered to death. He'd been huge, and built like a wrestler, but the drug rendered him helpless, and all she'd had to do was hold the pillow over his face. He didn't come close enough to consciousness to struggle. And the man before that, the advertising executive, had shown her why he'd feel safe in any neighborhood, gentrification or no. He kept a loaded handgun in the drawer of the bedside table, and if any burglar was unlucky enough to drop into his place, well—

When she was through with him, she'd retrieved the gun, wrapped his hand around it, put the barrel in his mouth, and squeezed off a shot. They could call it a suicide, even as they could call the wrestler a heart attack, if they didn't look too closely. Or they could call all three of them murders without ever suspecting they were all the work of the same person.

Still, it wouldn't hurt her to move. Find another place to live before people started to notice her on the streets and in the bars. She liked it here, in Clinton or Hell's Kitchen, whatever you wanted to call it. It was a nice place to live, whatever it may have been in years past. But, as she and Jim had agreed, the whole of Manhattan was a nice place to live. There weren't any bad neighborhoods left, not really.

Wherever she went, she was pretty sure she'd feel safe.

# THREE

She woke up abruptly—*click!* Like that, no warmup, no transition, no ascent into consciousness out of a dream. She was just all at once awake, brain in gear, all of her senses operating but sight. Her eyes were closed, and she let them remain that way for a moment while she picked up what information her other senses could provide.

She felt the cotton sheet under her, smooth. A good hand, a high thread count. Her host, then, wasn't a pauper, and had the good taste to equip himself with decent bed linen. She didn't feel a top sheet, felt only the air on her bare skin. Cool, dry air, air-conditioned air.

Whisper-quiet, too. Probably central air-conditioning, because she couldn't hear it. She couldn't hear much, really. A certain amount of city noise, through windows that were no doubt shut to let the central air do its work. But less of it than she'd have heard in her own Manhattan apartment.

And the energy level here was more muted than you would encounter in Manhattan. Hard to say what sense provided this information, and she supposed it was probably some combination of them all, some unconscious synthesis of taste and touch and smell and hearing, that let you know you were in one of the outer boroughs.

Memory filled in the rest. She'd taken the 1 train clear to the end of the line, following Broadway up into the Bronx, and she'd gone to a couple of bars in Riverdale, both of them nice preppy places where the bartenders didn't look puzzled when you ordered a Dog's Breakfast or a Sunday Best. And then…

Well, that's where it got a little fuzzy.

She still had taste and smell to consult. Taste, well, the taste in her mouth was the taste of morning, and all it did was make her want to brush her teeth. Smell was more complicated. There would have been more to smell without air conditioning, more to smell if the humidity were higher, but nevertheless there was a good deal of information available. She noted perspiration, male and female, and sex smells.

He was right there, she realized. In the bed beside her. If she reached out a hand she could touch him.

For a moment, though, she let her hand stay where it was, resting on her hip. Eyes still closed, she tried to bring his image into focus, even as she tried to embrace her memory of the later portion of the evening. She didn't know where she was, not really. She'd managed to figure out that she was in a relatively new apartment building, and she figured it was probably in Riverdale. But she couldn't be sure of that. He might have had a car, and he might have brought her almost anywhere. Westchester County, say.

Bits and pieces of memory hovered at the edge of thought. Shreds of small talk, but how could she know what was from last night and what was bubbling up from past evenings? Sense impressions: a male voice, a male touch on her upper arm.

She'd recognize him if she opened her eyes. She couldn't picture him, not quite, but she'd know him when her eyes had a chance to refresh her memory.

Not yet.

She reached out a hand, touched him.

She had just registered the warmth of his skin when he spoke.

"Sleeping beauty," he said.

Her eyes snapped open, wide open, and her pulse raced.

"Easy," he said. "My God, you're terrified, aren't you? Don't be. Everything's all right."

He was lying on his side facing her. And yes, she recognized him. Dark hair, arresting blue eyes under arched brows, a full-lipped mouth, a strong jawline. His nose had been broken once and imperfectly reset, and that saved him from being male-model handsome.

Early thirties, maybe eight or ten years her senior. A good body. A little chest hair, but not too much. Broad shoulders. A stomach flat enough to show a six-pack of abs.

No wonder she'd left the bar with him.

And she remembered leaving the bar. They'd walked, so she was probably in Riverdale. Unless they'd walked to his car. Could she remember any more?

"You don't remember, do you?"

Reading her mind. And how was she supposed to answer that one?

She tried for an ironic smile. "I'm a little fuzzy," she said.

"I'm not surprised."

"Oh?"

"You were hitting the Cosmos pretty good. I had the feeling, you know, that you might be in a blackout."

"Really? What did I do?"

"Nothing they'd throw you in jail for."

"Well, that's a relief."

"You didn't stagger or slur your words, and you were able to form complete sentences. Grammatical ones, too."

"The nuns would be proud of me."

"I'm sure they would. Except…"

"Except they wouldn't like to see me waking up in a strange bed."

"I'm not sure how liberal they're getting these days," he said. "That wasn't what I was going to say."

"Oh."

"You didn't know where you were, did you? When you opened your eyes."

"Not right away."

"Do you know now?"

"Well, sure," she said. "I'm here. With you."

"Do you know where 'here' is? Or who I am?"

Should she make something up? Or would the truth be easier?

"I don't remember getting in a car," she said, "and I do remember walking, so my guess is we're in Riverdale."

"But it's a guess."

"Well, couldn't we call it an educated guess? Or at least an informed one?"

"Either way," he said, "it's right. We walked here, and we're in Riverdale."

"So I got that one right. But why wouldn't the nuns be proud of me?"

"Forget the nuns, okay?"

"They're forgotten."

"Look, I don't want to get preachy. And it's none of my business. But if you're drinking enough to leave big gaps in your memory, well, how do you know who you're going home with?"

*Whom*, she thought. *The nuns wouldn't be proud of you, buster.*

She said, "It worked out all right, didn't it? I mean, you're an okay guy. So I guess my judgment was in good enough shape when we hooked up."

"Or you were lucky."

"Nothing wrong with getting lucky."

She grinned as she spoke the line, but he remained serious. "There are a lot of guys out there," he said, "who aren't okay. Predators, nut cases, bad guys. If you'd gone home with one of those—"

"But I didn't."

"How do you know?"

"How do I know? Well, here we are, both of us, and…what do you mean, how do I know?"

"Do you remember my name?"

"I'd probably recognize it if I heard it."

"Suppose I say three names, and you pick the one that's mine."

"What do I get if I'm right?"

"What do you want?"

"A shower."

This time he grinned. "It's a deal. Three names? Hmmm. Peter. Harley. Joel."

"Look into my eyes," she said, "and say them again. Slowly."

"What are you, a polygraph? Peter. Harley. Joel."

"You're Joel."

"I'm Peter."

"Hey, I was close."

"Two more tries," he said, "and you'd have had it for sure. You told me your name was Jennifer."

"Well, I got that one right."

"And you told me to call you Jen."

"And did you?'

"Did I what?"

"Call me Jen."

"Of course. I can take direction."

"Are you an actor?"

"As sure as my name is Joel. Why would you…oh, because I said I could take direction? Actually I had my schoolboy ambitions, but by the time I got out of college I smartened up. I work on Wall Street."

"All the way downtown. What time is it?"

"A little after ten."

"Don't you have to be at your desk by nine?"

"Not on Saturday."

"Oh, right. Uh, Peter…or do I call you Pete?"

"Either one."

"Awkward question coming up. Did we…"

"We did," he said, "and it was memorable for one of us."

"Oh."

"I felt a little funny about it, because I had the feeling you weren't entirely present. But your body was really into it, no matter where your mind was, and, well—"

"We had a good time?"

"A very good time. And, just so that you don't have to worry, we took precautions."

"That's good to know."

"And then you, uh, passed out."

"I did?"

"It was a little scary. You just went out like a light. For a minute I thought, I don't know—"

"That I was dead," she supplied.

"But you were breathing, so I ruled that out."

"That keen analytical mind must serve you well on Wall Street."

"I tried to wake you," he said, "but you were gone. So I let you sleep. And then I fell asleep myself, and, well, here we are."

"Naked and unashamed." She yawned, stretched. "Look," she said, "I'm going to treat myself to a shower, even if I didn't win the right in the *Name That Stud* contest. Don't go away, okay?"

The bathroom had a window, and one look showed that she was on a high floor, with a river view. She showered, and washed her hair with his shampoo. Then she borrowed his toothbrush and brushed her teeth diligently, and gargled with a little mouthwash.

When she emerged from the bathroom, wrapped in his big yellow towel, the aroma of fresh coffee led her into the kitchen, where he'd just finished filling two cups. He was wearing a white terry robe with a nautical motif, dark blue anchors embroidered on the pockets. His soft leather slippers were wine-colored.

Gifts, she thought. Men didn't buy those things for themselves, did they?

"I made coffee," he said.

"So I see."

"There's cream and sugar, if you take it."

"Just black is fine." She picked up her cup, breathed in the steam that rose from it. "I might live," she announced. "Do you sail?"

"Sail?"

"The robe. Anchors aweigh and all that."

"Oh. I suppose I could, because I don't get seasick or anything. But no, I don't sail. I have another robe, if you'd be more comfortable."

"With anchors? Actually I'm comfortable enough like this."

"Okay."

"But if I wanted to be even more comfortable…" She let the towel drop to the floor, noted with satisfaction the way his eyes widened. "How about you? Wouldn't you be more comfortable if you got rid of that sailor suit?"

❖

Afterward she propped herself up on an elbow and looked down at him. "I feel much much better now," she announced.

"The perfect hangover cure?"

"No, the shower and the coffee took care of the hangover. This let me feel better about myself. I mean, the idea of hooking up and not remembering it…"

"You'll remember this, you figure?"

"You bet. What about you, Peter? Will you remember?"

"Till my dying day."

"I'd better get dressed and head on home."

"And I can probably use a shower," he said. "Unless you want to—"

"You go ahead. I'll have another cup of coffee while you're in there."

Her clothes were on the chair, and she dressed quickly, then picked up her purse and checked its contents. She opened the little plastic vial, and counted the little blue pills.

Six of them, which was the same number she'd had at the start of the evening. Six little Roofies, so she hadn't slipped one into his drink, as she'd planned.

Nor had she fucked up big time and taken Rohypnol herself, which was what she'd begun to suspect. Because she hadn't been hitting the Cosmos anywhere near hard enough to account for the way the evening had turned out. It would have added up if she'd dosed his drink and then chosen the wrong glass, but she still had all her pills left.

Unless…

Oh, Peter, she thought. Peter Peter, pussy eater, what a naughty young man you turned out to be.

She returned the vial of blue pills to her purse and drew out the small glassine envelope instead. It was unopened, and held perhaps half a teaspoonful of a crystalline white substance. Not so fast as Rohypnol, according to her information, but rather more permanent.

She went into the kitchen, poured herself more coffee, and considered what was left in the pot. *No, leave it*, she thought, and turned her attention to the bottle of vodka on the sinkboard.

He must have fed her the Roofie at the bar. Otherwise she'd remember coming here. But there were two unwashed glasses next to the bottle, so they'd evidently had a nightcap before she lost it completely.

What a shock he'd given her! The touch, the unexpected warmth of his skin. And then his voice.

She hadn't expected that.

She uncapped the bottle, opened the glassine envelope, poured its contents in with the vodka. The crystals dissolved immediately. She replaced the cap on the bottle, returned the empty envelope to her purse.

She made her cup of coffee last until he was out of the shower and dressed in khakis and a polo shirt, which was evidently what a Wall Street guy wore on the weekend. "I'll get out of your hair now," she told him. "And I'm sorry about last night. I'm going to make it a point not to get quite that drunk again."

"You've got nothing to apologize for, Jen. You were running a risk, that's all. For your own sake—"

"I know."

"Hang on and I'll walk you to the subway."

She shook her head. "Really, there's no need. I can find it."

"You're sure?"

"Positive."

"If you say so. Uh, can I have your number?"

"You really want it?"

"I wouldn't ask if I didn't."

"Next time I won't pass out. I promise."

He handed her a pen and a notepad, and she wrote down her area code, 212, and picked seven digits at random to keep it company. And then they kissed, and he said something sweet, and she said something clever in response, and she was out the door.

The streets were twisty and weird in that part of Riverdale, but she asked directions and somebody pointed her toward the subway. She waited on the elevated platform and thought about how shocked she'd been when she opened her eyes.

Because he was supposed to be dead. That was how it worked, you put the crystals in the guy's drink and it took effect one or two hours later. After they'd had sex, after he'd dozed off or not. His heart stopped, and that was that.

It worked like a charm. But it only worked if you put the crystals in the guy's drink, and if you were too drunk to manage that, well, you woke up and there he was.

Bummer.

Sooner or later, she thought, he'd take the cap off the vodka bottle. Today or tomorrow or next week, whenever he got around to it. And he'd take a drink, and one or two hours later he'd be cooling down to room temperature. She wouldn't be there to scoop up his cash or go through his dresser drawers, but that was all right. The money wasn't really the point.

Maybe he'd have some other girl with him. Maybe they'd both have a drink before hitting the mattress, and they could die in each other's arms. Like Romeo and Juliet, sort of.

Or maybe she'd have a drink and he wouldn't. That would be kind of interesting, when he tried to explain it all to the cops.

A pity she couldn't be a fly on the wall. Would she ever find out what happened? Sooner or later, there'd be something in the papers. But by then she could well be a thousand miles away.

Because it felt as though it might be time to get out of New York. She felt at home here, but she had the knack of feeling at home just about anywhere. And a girl didn't want to overstay her welcome.

# FOUR

He was wearing a Western-style shirt, scarlet and black with a lot of gold piping, and one of those bolo string ties, and he should have topped things off with a broad-brimmed Stetson, but that would have hidden his hair. And it was the hair that had drawn her in the first place. It was a rich chestnut with red highlights, and so perfect she'd thought it was a wig. Up close, though, you could see that it was homegrown and not store bought, and it looked the way it did because he'd had one of those $400 haircuts that cost John Edwards the Iowa primary. This barber had worked hard to produce a haircut that appeared natural and effortless, so much so that it wound up looking like a wig.

He was waiting his turn at the craps table, betting against the shooter, and winning steadily as the dice stayed cold, with one shooter after another rolling craps a few times, then finally getting a point and promptly sevening out.

She didn't know dice, didn't care about gambling. Something about this man had drawn her, something about the wig that was not a wig, and she stood beside him and breathed in his after-shave—an inviting lemon-and-leather scent, a little too insistent but nice all the same. The string tie, she saw, had a Navaho slide, a thunderbird accented in turquoise.

Here in Michigan, the slide and its owner were a long way from home.

"Seven," the stickman announced. "New shooter coming out."

And the dice passed to the man with the great haircut.

He cradled them in his palm, held them in front of her face. Without looking at her he said, "Warm these up, sweet thing."

He'd given no indication that he was even aware of her presence, but she wasn't surprised. Men generally noticed her.

She took hold of his wrist, leaned forward, blew warm breath on the dice.

"Now that's just what was needed," he said, and dropped a black chip on the table, then gave the dice a shake and rolled an eleven. A natural, a winner, and that doubled his stake and he let it ride and rolled two sevens before he caught a point, an eight.

Now it became hard for her to follow, because she didn't know the game, and he was pushing his luck, betting numbers, scattering chips here and there, and rolling one combination after another that managed to be neither an eight nor a seven. He made the point, eventually, and the one after that, and by the time he finally sevened out he'd won thousands of dollars.

"And that's that," he said, stepping away from the table, turning to take his first good long look at her. He wasn't shy about letting his eyes travel the length of her body, then return to her face. "When you get lucky," he said, "you got to ride it and push your luck. That's half of it, and the other half is knowing when to stop."

"And you're stopping?"

"For now. You stay at the table long enough, you're sure to give it all back. Luck goes one way and then it goes the other, like a pendulum swinging, and the house has always got more money than you do and it can afford to wait you out. Any casino'll break you in the long run, even a pissant low-rent Injun casino way the hell up in the Upper Peninsula." He grinned. "But in the long run we're all dead, so the hell with the long run. In the short run a person can get lucky and do himself some good, and it might never have happened if you didn't come along and blow on my dice. You're my lucky charm, sweet thing."

"It was exciting," she said. "I don't really know anything about dice—"

"You sure know how to blow on 'em, darlin'."

"—but once you started rolling everything happened so fast, and everybody got excited about it—"

"Because the ones who followed my play got to win along with me."

"—and I got excited, too."

He looked at her. "Excited, huh?"

She nodded.

"And now," he said, "I suppose it's passed, and you're not excited anymore."

"Not in the same way."

"Oh?"

She allowed herself a smile.

"C'mon," he said. "Why don't we sit down and have ourselves some firewater."

They took a table in a darkened corner of the lounge, and a dark-skinned girl with braids brought their drinks. He'd ordered a Dirty Martini, and she'd followed his lead.

"Olive juice," he explained. "Gives a little salty taste to the vodka. But I have to say what I like most about it is just saying the name of it. 'A Dirty Martini, please. Straight up.' Don't you like the sound of it?"

"And the taste."

"Did you ever tell me your name? Because I can't remember it."

"It's Lucky."

"You're kidding, right?"

"It says Lucky on my driver's license," she said. "On my birth certificate it says Lucretia, but my parents didn't realize they'd opened the door for a lifetime of Lucretia Borgia jokes."

"I can imagine."

"You can't, because you don't know the whole story. Lucretia is bad enough, but when you attach it to Eagle Feather it becomes really awful, and—"

"That's your last name? Eagle Feather?"

"Used to be. I chopped the Lucretia and dropped the Feather and went in front of a judge to make it legal. Lucky Eagle's what I wound up with, and it's still pretty dopey."

"You're Indian."

God, he was quick on the uptake, wasn't he? You just couldn't keep anything from this dude.

"My father's half Chippewa," she improvised, "and my mother's part Apache and part Blackfoot, and some Swedish and Irish and I don't know what else. I worked it all out one time, and I'm one-third Indian."

"A third, huh?"

"Uh-huh."

"Lucky Eagle Feather," he said. She liked that he was willing to skip the Lucretia part, but still wanted to hold on to that Feather. Made her a little bit more exotic, that's how she figured it. A little more Indian. And hadn't he just finished screwing a bunch of Indians out of a few thousand dollars? So why not screw a genuine Indian for dessert?

His name, she learned, was Hank Walker. Short for Henry, but he'd been Hank since childhood. Seemed to suit him better, he told her, but it still said Henry on his driver's license. And he'd been born in New Jersey, the southern part of the state, near Philadelphia, but he'd moved west as soon as he could, because that seemed to suit him better, too. He indicated the Western shirt, the string tie. "Sort of a uniform," he said, and grinned.

"It suits you," she agreed.

He lived in Nevada now, outside of Carson City. And right now he was driving across the country, seeking out casinos wherever he went.

"I guess you like to play."

"When I'm on a roll," he said. "But these out-of-the-way places, I come here for the chips as much as the action."

"The chips?"

"Casino chips. People collect them."

"You sure collected a batch at the crap table."

What people collected, he explained, just as others collected coins and stamps, were the small-denomination chips the casinos issued, especially the one-dollar chips. At each casino he visited he'd buy twenty or thirty or fifty of the dollar chips, and they'd be added to his stock when he got back home. He had a collection of his own, of course, but he also had a business, selling chips to collectors at chip shows—who knew there were chip shows?—and on his website.

"Ever since the government decided the tribes have the right to run casinos," he told her, "they've been popping up like mushrooms. And they come and they go, because not all of the tribes know a whole lot about running a gaming operation. You belong to the tribe that's operating this place?"

She didn't.

"Well, nothing against them, and I hope they make a go of it, but there are a few things they're doing wrong." She half-listened while he took the casino's inventory, took another sip of her Dirty Martini (which, all things considered, sounded better than it tasted), and breathed in his aftershave and an undertone of perspiration.

He finished his casino critique and reached across the table to put his hand on hers. "Now it seems to me we've got a decision to make. Do we have another round of drinks before we go to my room?"

For answer she picked up his hand, lowered her head and blew her warm breath into his palm. "For luck," she said without looking up, and then her tongue darted out and she licked his palm. His sweat, she noticed, tasted not all that different from the Dirty Martini.

He had a nice body. Barrel-chested, with a little more of a gut than she might have preferred, and a lot of chest hair. No hair on his back, though, and she supposed he got it waxed at the same salon that provided his million-dollar haircuts.

Muscular arms, muscular shoulders, and that meant regular gym workouts, because he couldn't have gotten those muscles simply by throwing his own weight around. An all-over tan, too, that probably came from a tanning bed. You could shake your head at the artifice, or you could go with the result—a fit, good-looking man in his late forties, who, it had to be said, was as impressive in the sack as he'd been at the crap table. And if he owed some of that to Viagra, well, so what? He got her hot and he got her off, and what more could a poor girl desire?

And the best was yet to be.

*Optima futura*—that was the Latin for it, and she knew it because it had been her high school's motto. It was, she'd always thought, singularly apt, because anything the future held had to be better than high school.

Somewhere along the way, after high school was just a blur, she'd come across some lines from Robert Browning, and perhaps it was the high school motto that made her commit them to memory, but it had worked, because she remembered them still:

*Grow old along with me*
*The best is yet to be*
*The last of life, for which the first was made…*

"Part Indian, huh? I bet I know which part is Indian."

And he reached out a hand and touched the part he had in mind. She put her hand on top of his hand, rubbed his fingers against her.

"A third Indian," she reminded him.

"So you said. You know, I was wondering—"

She put her hand on him, curled her fingers around him. She worked him artfully, and he sighed.

"Lucky," he said. "Man, I'd say I got Lucky, didn't I? But I think I'm tapped out for this evening."

"You think so?"

"You drained me to the dregs, babe. About all I can do right now is sleep."

"I bet you're wrong."

"Oh?"

"What we did so far," she said, "was just a warmup."

"Yeah, right."

"Can I ask you something?"

He raised his eyebrows.

"Have you ever been tied up?"

"Jesus," he said.

"Just imagine," she said, her hands still busy. "You're tied up, you can't move, and the entire focus is giving you pleasure. I'll do things to you nobody's ever done to you before, Hank. You think this has been your lucky night? You just wait."

"Uh—"

"I've got all the gear in my bag," she said. "Everything we could possibly need. You're gonna love this."

❋

Handcuffs, silk scarves, nylon cords. She had everything she needed, and she knew just how to employ them.

The last time she'd done this she'd given her partner a couple of the blue pills first, and let them knock him out before she trussed him up. That had worked fine, but she'd been stuck with a two-hour wait for the son of a bitch to wake up, and who needed that?

This was much simpler. And he cooperated, putting his hands where she told him, spread-eagling himself on the bed. And making little jokes while she did what she had to do.

By the time she was done, he was already semi-erect. She wrapped the base with an elastic band. "Sort of a roach motel," she said. "The blood gets in and it can't get out, so you stay firm."

"Is it safe?"

"Absolutely," she said. "It's an old Indian trick. And now you can do something for me, and after that everything will be entirely one hundred percent for you." And she sat on his face and he did what he was supposed to do, and he was pretty good at it, too. He didn't have to be, she was so excited right now that great technique on his part was by no means required, but this made it even better.

"Now that was just wonderful," she said. She went to her bag, got out the duct tape, and cut off an eight-inch length. "And I wanted to do that first," she went on, "because that's our last chance for that particular activity."

And she slapped the tape over his mouth.

Oh, the look in his eyes! Worth the price of admission right there. He wasn't quite sure whether this was going to make it even more exciting for him, or whether it was maybe something he ought to worry about.

But why worry? What good would that do? What good would anything do?

"See, isn't this neat? You're harder than ever. And you're going to stay that way."

She mounted him, sat facing his feet in the reliable Reverse Cowgirl, felt him swelling impossibly larger inside her. "Mmmm, nice," she said. "Oh, yes. Very nice."

She rode him for a long time. Her climaxes came one after the other, and all they did was pitch her excitement higher. After a few of them she changed position so that she could watch his face while she rode him, and that was a treat, because the wide-eyed desperation was something to see. At last she fell forward, her breasts crushed against his chest. A smooth chest would have been nice, but a hairy chest was nice, too. Everything was nice when you could do whatever you wanted, and when you knew just how it was going to end.

She got up because she wanted to be able to see his eyes now. "I told you some lies," she said. "My name's not Lucky. Or Lucretia, or any of that. My last name's not Eagle, or Eagle Feather, and don't ask me how I came up with all of that on the spur of the moment. As far as I know, I haven't got a drop of Indian blood in me. A third Indian! How could anybody be a third anything? I mean, you've got two parents, four grandparents, eight great-grandparents—I mean, do the math. You're the one who knows all the odds on the crap table, so you would have to know that you can only be half or a fourth or an eighth or three-sixteenths or whatever you are of anything."

She wagged a finger at him. "You weren't paying attention, Hank. Little Henry there was doing your thinking for you. And that's another lie I told you, incidentally. That it's safe to wrap you up like that. If you don't loosen it in time, you can do permanent damage."

She left the bed, reached into her purse, found the knife. She let him see the blade. She let the tip of the blade graze his cheek as she mounted him one more time.

"God, it's bigger than ever," she told him. "You're in pain now, aren't you? Oh, dear, I'm afraid that's going to get worse. Well, more intense, anyway. *Optima futura*, you know. That's Latin. It means the best is yet to be. For me, that is. For you, well, maybe not."

She left with close to five thousand dollars in cash and chips, and stopped downstairs at the cashier's cage to turn the chips into currency. Then she got in her car and started driving.

She'd left his one-dollar chips in the room. She'd left his credit cards, too, and a gold signet ring that had to be worth a few hundred dollars. She took the slide from his string tie, just because she liked it, and she took her cuffs and cords and scarves, because it would be a nuisance to replace them. But she left the elastic band in place.

And she took the scalp, tucked away in a plastic bag. It was just such good theater to scalp him, what with having been drawn to his hair in the first place, and then the whole Indian motif of their encounter. Before she was halfway done with the process she regretted having begun it in the first place, because even minor scalp cuts bleed like crazy, and when you scalp a person altogether—well, the Indians probably waited to scalp people until they were safely dead, and disinclined to bleed, but she went ahead and finished what she'd started, and it was almost worth it when she shook the scalp in front of him and let him gape at it.

She'd cleaned up her fingerprints, but she knew she'd left plenty of DNA evidence, and people at the casino could furnish a description of her. But she'd been working variations on this theme for a good long while now, and she always got away with it, and she figured all she could do was play out the string. And she'd ditch his scalp where it wouldn't be found, and the scalping would guarantee a lot of press, and a manhunt for some unforgiving Indian seeking vengeance for Wounded Knee.

Yes, she'd just go ahead and play out the string. Because it kept getting better, didn't it? *Optima futura.* That pretty much said it all.

# FIVE

Toledo. What did she know about Toledo?

Like, Holy Toledo. The original city, in Spain, was famous for fine swords, and the newspaper here in Ohio called itself *The Toledo Blade*. That was a better name than the Mud Hens, which was what they called the baseball team.

And here she was in Toledo.

There was a Starbucks just across the street from the building where he had his office, and she settled in at a window table a little before five. She thought she might be in for a long wait. In New York, young associates at law firms typically worked until midnight and took lunch and dinner at their desks. Was it the same in Toledo?

Well, the cappuccino was the same. She sipped hers, making it last, and was about to go to the counter for another when she saw him.

But was it him? He was tall and slender, wearing a dark suit and a tie, clutching a briefcase, walking with purpose. His hair when she'd known him was long and shaggy, a match for the jeans and T-shirt that was his usual costume, and now it was cut to match the suit and the briefcase. And he wore glasses now, and they gave him a serious, studious look. He hadn't worn them then, and he'd certainly never looked studious.

But it was Douglas. No question, it was him.

She rose from her chair, hit the door, quickened her pace to catch up with him at the corner. She said, "Doug? Douglas Pratter?"

He turned, and she caught the puzzlement in his eyes. She helped him out. "It's Kit," she said. "Katherine Tolliver." She smiled softly. "A voice from the past. Well, a whole person from the past, actually."

"My God," he said. "It's really you."

"I was having a cup of coffee," she said, "and looking out the window and wishing I knew somebody in this town, and when I saw you I thought you were a mirage. Or that you were just somebody who looked the way Doug Pratter might look eight years later."

"Is that how long it's been?"

"Just about. I was fifteen and I'm twenty-three now. You were two years older."

"Still am. That much hasn't changed."

"And your family picked up and moved right in the middle of your junior year of high school."

"My dad got a job he couldn't say no to. He was going to send for us at the end of the term, but my mother wouldn't hear of it. We'd all be too lonely is what she said. It took me years before I realized she just didn't trust him on his own."

"Was he not to be trusted?"

"I don't know about that, but the marriage failed two years later anyway. He went a little nuts and wound up in California. He got it in his head that he wanted to be a surfer."

"Seriously? Well, good for him, I guess."

"Not all that good for him. He drowned."

"I'm sorry."

"Who knows? Maybe that's what he wanted, whether he knew it or not. Mom's still alive and well."

"In Toledo?"

"Bowling Green."

"*That's* it. I knew you'd moved to Ohio, and I couldn't remember the city, and I didn't think it was Toledo. Bowling Green."

"I've always thought of it as a color. Lime green, forest green, and bowling green."

"Same old Doug."

"You think? I wear a suit and go to an office. Christ, I wear glasses."

"And a wedding ring." And, before he could tell her about his wife and kiddies and adorable suburban house, she said, "But you've got to get home, and I've got plans of my own. I want to catch up, though. Have you got any time tomorrow?"


*It's Kit. Katherine Tolliver.*

Just saying her name had taken her back in time. She hadn't been Kit or Katherine or Tolliver in years. Names were like clothes, she'd put them on and wear them for a while and then let them go. The analogy only went so far, because you could wash clothes when you'd soiled them, but there was no dry cleaner for a name that had outlived its usefulness.

Katherine "Kit" Tolliver. That wasn't the name on the ID she was carrying, or the one she'd signed on the motel register. But once she'd identified herself to Doug Pratter, she'd become the person she'd proclaimed herself to be. She was Kit again—and, at the same time, she wasn't.

Interesting, the whole business.

Back in her motel room, she surfed her way around the TV channels, then switched off the set and took a shower. Afterward she spent a few minutes studying her nude body and wondering how it would look to him. She was a little fuller in the breasts than she'd been eight years before, a little rounder in the butt, a little closer to ripeness overall. She had always been confident of her attractiveness, but she couldn't help wondering what she might look like to those eyes that had seen her years ago.

Of course, he hadn't needed glasses back in the day.

She had read somewhere that a man who has once had a particular woman somehow assumes he can have her again. She didn't know how true this might be, but it seemed to her that something similar applied to women. A woman who had once been with a particular man was ordained to doubt her ability to attract him a second time. And so she felt a little of that uncertainty, but willed herself to dismiss it.

He was married, and might well be in love with his wife. He was busy establishing himself in his profession, and settling into an orderly existence. Why would he want a meaningless fling with an old girlfriend, who'd had to say her name before he could even place her?

She smiled. *Lunch*, he'd said. *We'll have lunch tomorrow.*

Funny how it started.

She was in Kansas City, sitting at a table with six or seven others, a mix of men and women in their twenties. And one of the men mentioned a woman she didn't know, though most of the others seemed to know her. And one of the women said, "That slut."

And the next thing she knew, the putative slut was forgotten while the whole table turned to the question of just what constituted sluttiness. Was it a matter of attitude? Of specific behavior? Was one born to slutdom, or was the status acquired?

Was it solely a female province? Could you have male sluts?

That got nipped in the bud. "A man can take sex too casually," one of the men asserted, "and he can consequently be an asshole, and deserving of a certain measure of contempt. But as far as I'm concerned, the word *slut* is gender-linked. Nobody with a Y chromosome can qualify as a genuine slut."

And, finally, was there a numerical cutoff? Could an equation be drawn up? Did a certain number of partners within a certain number of years make one a slut?

"Suppose," one woman suggested, "suppose once a month you go out after work and have a couple—"

"A couple of men?"

"A couple of drinks, you idiot, and you start flirting, and one thing leads to another, and you drag somebody home with you."

"Once a month?"

"It could happen."

"So that's twelve men in a year."

"When you put it that way," the woman allowed, "it seems like a lot."

"It's also a hundred and twenty partners in ten years."

"Except you wouldn't keep it up for that long, because sooner or later one of those hookups would take."

"And you'd get married and live happily ever after?"

"Or at least live together more or less monogamously for a year or two, which would cut down on the frequency of hookups, wouldn't it?"

Throughout all of this, she barely said a word. Why bother? The conversation buzzed along quite well without her, and she was free to sit back and listen, and to wonder just what place she occupied in what someone had already labeled "the saint–slut continuum."

"With cats," one of the men said, "it's nice and clear-cut."

"Cats can be sluts?"

He shook his head. "With women and cats. A woman has one cat, or even two or three cats, she's an animal lover. Four or more cats and she's a demented cat lady."

"That's how it works?"

"That's exactly how it works. With sluts, it looks to be more complicated."

Another thing that complicated it, someone said, was if the woman in question had a significant other, whether husband or boyfriend. If she didn't, and she hooked up half a dozen times a year, well, she certainly wasn't a slut. If she was married and still fit in that many hookups on the side, well, that changed things, didn't it?

"Let's get personal," one of the men said to one of the women. "How many partners have you had?"

"Me?"

"Well?"

"You mean in the past year?"

"Or lifetime. You decide."

"If I'm going to answer a question like that," she said, "I think we definitely need another round of drinks."

The drinks came, and the conversation slid into a game of Truth, though it seemed to Jennifer—these people knew her as Jennifer, a name she seemed to have picked up again, after having left it behind months ago in New York—it seemed to her that the actual veracity of the responses was moot.

And then it was her turn.

"Well, Jen? How many?"

Would she ever see any of these people again? Probably not. Kansas City was all right, but she was about ready for a change of venue. So it really didn't matter what she said.

And what she said was, "Well, it depends. How do you decide what counts?"

"What do you mean? Like blow jobs don't count?"

"Isn't that what Clinton said?"

"As far as I'm concerned, blow jobs count."

"And hand jobs?"

"They don't count," one man said, and there seemed to be general agreement on that point. "Not that there's anything wrong with them," he added.

"So what's your criterion here, exactly? Something has to be inside of something?"

"As far as the nature of the act," one man said, "I think it has to be subjective. It counts if you think it counts. So, Jen? What's your count?"

"Suppose you passed out, and you know something happened, but you don't remember any of it?"

"Same answer. It counts if you think it counts."

The conversation kept going, but she was detached from it now, thinking, remembering, working it out in her mind. How many men, if gathered around a table or a campfire, could compare notes and tell each other about her? That, she thought, was the real criterion, not what part of her anatomy had been in contact with what portion of his. Who could tell stories? Who could bear witness?

And, when the table quieted down again, she said, "Five."

"Five? That's all? Just five?"

"Five."


She had arranged to meet Douglas Pratter at noon in the lobby of a downtown hotel not far from his office. She arrived early and sat where she could watch the entrance. He was five minutes early himself, and she saw him stop to remove his glasses, polishing their lenses with a breast-pocket handkerchief. Then he put them on again and stood there, his eyes scanning the room.

She got to her feet, and now he caught sight of her, and she saw him smile. He'd always had a winning smile, optimistic and confident.

Years ago, it had been one of the things she liked most about him.

She walked to meet him. Yesterday she'd been wearing a dark gray pants suit; today she'd paired the jacket with a matching skirt. The effect was still business attire, but softer, more feminine. More accessible.

"I hope you don't mind a ride," he told her. "There are places we could walk to, but they're crowded and noisy and no place to have a conversation. Plus they rush you, and I don't want to be in a hurry. Unless you've got an early afternoon appointment?"

She shook her head. "I had a full morning," she said, "and there's a cocktail party this evening that I'm supposed to go to, but until then I'm free as the breeze."

"Then we can take our time. We've probably got a lot to talk about."

As they crossed the lobby, she took his arm.

The fellow's name in Kansas City was Lucas. She'd taken note of him early on, and his eyes had shown a certain degree of interest in her, but his interest mounted when she told the group how many sexual partners she'd had. It was he who'd said, "Five? That's all? Just five?" When she'd confirmed her count, his eyes grabbed hers and held on.

And now he'd taken her to another bar, the lounge of the Hotel Phillips, a nice quiet place where they could really get to know each other. Just the two of them.

The lighting was soft, the décor soothing. A pianist played show tunes unobtrusively, and a waitress with an indeterminate accent took their order and brought their drinks. They touched glasses, sipped, and he said, "Five."

"That really did it for you," she said. "What, is it your lucky number?"

"Actually," he said, "my lucky number is six."

"I see."

"You were never married."

"No."

"Never lived with anybody."

"Only my parents."

"You don't still live with them?"

"No."

"You live alone?"

"I have a roommate."

"A woman, you mean."

"Right."

"Uh, the two of you aren't…"

"We have separate beds," she said, "in separate rooms, and we live separate lives."

"Right. Were you ever, uh, in a convent or anything?"

She gave him a look.

"Because you're remarkably attractive, you walk into a room and you light it up, and I can imagine the number of guys who must hit on you on a daily basis. And you're how old? Twenty-one, twenty-two?"

"Twenty-three."

"And you've only been with five guys? What, were you a late bloomer?"

"I wouldn't say so."

"I'm sorry, I'm pressing and I shouldn't. It's just that, well, I can't help being fascinated. But the last thing I want is to make you uncomfortable."

The conversation wasn't making her uncomfortable. It was merely boring her. Was there any reason to prolong it? Was there any reason not to cut to the chase?

She'd already slipped one foot out of its shoe, and now she raised it and rested it on his lap, massaging his groin with the ball of her foot. The expression on his face was reward enough all by itself.

"My turn to ask questions," she said. "Do you live with your parents?"

"You're kidding, right? Of course not."

"Do you have a roommate?"

"Not since college, and that was a while ago."

"So" she said. "What are we waiting for?"

# SIX

The restaurant Doug had chosen was on Detroit Avenue, just north of I-75. Walking across the parking lot, she noted a motel two doors down and another across the street.

Inside, it was dark and quiet, and the décor reminded her of the cocktail lounge where Lucas had taken her. She had a sudden memory of her foot in his lap, and the expression on his face. Further memories followed, but she let them glide on by. The present moment was a nice one, and she wanted to live in it while it was at hand.

She asked for a dry Rob Roy, and Doug hesitated, then ordered the same for himself. The cuisine on offer was Italian, and he started to order the scampi, then caught himself and selected a small steak instead. Scampi, she thought, was full of garlic, and he wanted to make sure he didn't have it on his breath.

The conversation started in the present, but she quickly steered it back to the past, where it properly belonged. "You always wanted to be a lawyer," she remembered.

"Right, I was going to be a criminal lawyer, a courtroom whiz. The defender of the innocent. So here I am doing corporate work, and if I ever see the inside of a courtroom, that means I've done something wrong."

"I guess it's hard to make a living with a criminal practice."

"You can do okay," he said, "but you spend your life with the scum of the earth, and you do everything you can to keep them from getting what they damn well deserve. Of course I didn't know any of that when I was seventeen and starry-eyed over *To Kill a Mockingbird*."

"You were my first boyfriend."

"You were my first real girlfriend."

She thought, Oh? And how many unreal ones were there? And what made her real by comparison? Because she'd slept with him?

Had he been a virgin the first time they had sex? She hadn't given the matter much thought at the time, and had been too intent upon her own role in the proceedings to be aware of his experience or lack thereof. It hadn't really mattered then, and she couldn't see that it mattered now.

And, she'd just told him, he'd been her first boyfriend. No need to qualify that; he'd truly been her first boyfriend, real or otherwise.

But she hadn't been a virgin. She'd crossed that barrier two years earlier, a month or so after her thirteenth birthday, and had had sex in one form or another perhaps a hundred times before she hooked up with Doug.

Not with a boyfriend, however. I mean, your father couldn't be your boyfriend, could he?

Lucas lived alone in a large L-shaped studio apartment on the top floor of a new building. "I'm the first tenant the place has ever had," he told her. "I've never lived in something brand spanking new before. It's like I've taken the apartment's virginity."

"Now you can take mine."

"Not quite. But this is better. Remember, I told you my lucky number."

"Six."

"There you go."

And just when, she wondered, had six become his lucky number?

When she'd acknowledged five partners? Probably, but never mind. It was a good enough line, and one he was no doubt feeling proud of right about now, because it had worked, hadn't it?

As if he'd had any chance of failing…

He made drinks, and they kissed, and she was pleased but not surprised to note that the requisite chemistry was there. And, keeping it company, there was that delicious surge of anticipatory excitement that was always present on such occasions. It was at once sexual and non-sexual, and she felt it even when the chemistry was not present, even when the sexual act was destined to be perfunctory at best, and at worst distasteful. Even then she'd feel that rush, that urgent excitement, but it was greatly increased when she knew the sex was going to be good.

He excused himself and went to the bathroom, and she opened her purse and found the little unlabeled vial she kept in the change compartment. She looked at it and at the drink he'd left on the table, but in the end she left the vial in her purse, left his drink untouched.

As it turned out, it wouldn't have mattered. When he emerged from the bathroom he reached not for his drink but for her instead, and it was as good as she'd known it would be, inventive and eager and passionate, and finally they fell away from each other, spent and sated.

"Wow," he said.

"That's the right word for it."

"You think? It's the best I can come up with, and yet it somehow seems inadequate. You're—"

"What?"

"Amazing. I have to say this, I can't help it. It's almost impossible to believe you've had so little experience."

"Because I'm clearly jaded?"

"No, just because you're so good at it. And in a way that's the complete opposite of jaded. I swear to God this is the last time I'll ask you, but were you telling the truth? Have you really only been with five men?"

She nodded.

"Well," he said, "now it's six, isn't it?"

"Your lucky number, right?"

"Luckier than ever," he said.

"Lucky for me, too."

She was glad she hadn't put anything in his drink, because after a brief rest they made love again, and that wouldn't have happened otherwise.

"Still six," he told her afterward, "unless you figure I ought to get extra credit."

She said something, her voice soft and soothing, and he said something, and that went on until he stopped responding. She lay beside him, in that familiar but ever-new combination of afterglow and anticipation, and then finally she slipped out of bed, and a little while later she let herself out of his apartment.

All by herself in the descending elevator, she said out loud, "Five."

A second round of Rob Roys arrived before their entrees. Then the waiter brought her fish and his steak, along with a glass of red wine for him and white for her. She'd only had half of her second Rob Roy, and she barely touched her wine.

"So you're in New York," he said. "You went there straight from college?"

She brought him up to date, keeping the responses vague for fear of contradicting herself. The story she told was all fabrication; she'd never even been to college, and her job résumé was a spotty mélange of waitressing and office temp work. She didn't have a career, and she worked only when she had to.

If she needed money—and she didn't need much, she didn't live high—well, there were other ways to get it besides work.

But today she was Connie Corporate, with a job history to match her clothes, and yes, she'd gone to Penn State and then tacked on a Wharton MBA, and ever since she'd been in New York, and she couldn't really talk about what had brought her to Toledo, or even on whose behalf she was traveling, because it was all hush-hush for the time being, and she was sworn to secrecy.

"Not that there's a really big deal to be secretive about," she said, "but, you know, I try to do what they tell me."

"Like a good little soldier."

"Exactly," she said, and beamed across the table at him.

"You're my little soldier," her father had told her. "A trooper, a little warrior."

In the accounts she sometimes found herself reading, the father (or the stepfather, or the uncle, or the mother's boyfriend, or even the next-door neighbor) was a drunk and a brute, a bloody-minded savage, forcing himself upon the child who was his helpless and unwilling partner. She would get angry, reading those case histories. She would hate the male responsible for the incest, would sympathize with the young female victim, and her blood would surge in her veins with the desire to even the score, to exact a cruel but just vengeance. Her mind supplied scenarios—castration, mutilation, disembowelment, all of them brutal and heartless, all richly deserved.

But her own experience was quite unlike what she read.

Some of her earliest memories were of sitting on her father's lap, his hands touching her, patting her, petting her. Sometimes he was with her at bath time, making sure she soaped and rinsed herself thoroughly. Sometimes he tucked her in at night, and sat by the side of the bed stroking her hair until she fell asleep.

Was his touch ever inappropriate? Looking back, she thought that it probably was, but she'd never been aware of it at the time. She knew that she loved her daddy and he loved her, and that there was a bond between them that excluded her mother. But it never consciously occurred to her that there was anything wrong about it.

He would put her to bed and tuck her in. One night a dream woke her, and without opening her eyes she realized that he was in bed with her. She felt his hand on her shoulder and slipped back beneath the cover of sleep.

She'd lie awake, pretending to be asleep, and at last her door would ease open and he'd be in her room, and he'd stand there while she pretended to be asleep, then get into bed with her. He'd hold her and pet her, and his presence would somehow give her permission to fall genuinely asleep.

Then, when she was thirteen, when her body had begun to change, there was a night when he came to her bed and slipped beneath the covers. "It's all right," he murmured. "I know you're awake." And he held her and touched her and kissed her.

The holding and touching and kissing was different that night, and she recognized it as such immediately, and somehow knew that it would be a secret, that she could never tell anybody. And yet no enormous barriers were crossed that night. He was very gentle with her, always gentle, and his seduction of her was infinitely gradual. She had since read how the Plains Indians took wild horses and domesticated them, not by breaking their spirit but by slowly, slowly, winning them over, and the description resonated with her immediately, because that was precisely how her father had turned her from a child who sat so innocently on his lap into an eager and spirited sexual partner.

He never broke her spirit. What he did was awaken it.

He came to her every night for months, and by the time he took her virginity she had long since lost her innocence, because he had schooled her quite thoroughly in the sexual arts. There was no pain on the night he led her across the last divide. She had been well prepared, and was entirely ready.

Away from her bed, they were the same as they'd always been.

"Nothing can show," he'd explained. "No one would understand the way you and I love each other. So we must not let them know. If your mother knew—"

He hadn't needed to finish that sentence.

"Someday," he'd told her, "you and I will get in the car, and we'll drive to some city where no one knows us. We'll both be older then, and the difference in our ages won't be that remarkable, especially when we've tacked on a few years to you and shaved them off of me. And we'll live together, and we'll get married, and no one will be the wiser."

She tried to imagine that. Sometimes it seemed like something that could actually happen, something that would indeed come about in the course of time. And other times it seemed like a story an adult might tell a child, right up there with Santa Claus and the Tooth Fairy.

"But for now," he'd said more than once, "for now we have to be soldiers. You're my little soldier, aren't you? Aren't you?"

"I get to New York now and then," Doug Pratter said.

"I suppose you and your wife fly in," she said. "Stay at a nice hotel, see a couple of shows."

"She doesn't like to fly."

"Well, who does? What they make you go through these days, all in the name of security. And it just keeps getting worse, doesn't it? First they started giving you plastic utensils with your in-flight meal, because there's nothing as dangerous as a terrorist with a metal fork. Then they stopped giving you a meal altogether, so you couldn't complain about the plastic utensils."

"It's pretty bad, isn't it? But it's a short flight. I don't mind it that much. I just open up a book, and the next thing I know I'm in New York."

"By yourself."

"On business," he said. "Not that frequently, but every once in a while. Actually, I could get there more often, if I had a reason to go."

"Oh?"

"But lately I've been turning down chances," he said, his eyes avoiding hers now. "Because, see, when my business is done for the day I don't know what to do with myself. It would be different if I knew anybody there, but I don't."

"You know me," she said.

"That's right," he agreed, his eyes finding hers again. "That's right. I do, don't I?"

Over the years, she'd read a lot about incest. She didn't think her interest was compulsive, or morbidly obsessive, and in fact it seemed to her as if it would be more pathological if she were not interested in reading about it.

One case imprinted itself strongly upon her. A man had three daughters, and he had sexual relations with two of them. He was not the artful Daughter Whisperer that her own father had been, but a good deal closer to the Drunken Brute end of the spectrum. A widower, he told the two older daughters that it was their duty to take their mother's place. They felt it was wrong, but they also felt it was something they had to do, and so they did it.

And, predictably enough, they were both psychologically scarred by the experience. Almost every incest victim seemed to be, one way or the other.

But it was their younger sister who wound up being the most damaged of the three. Because Daddy never touched her, she figured there was something wrong with her. Was she ugly? Was she insufficiently feminine? Was there something disgusting about her?

Jeepers, what was the matter with her, anyway? Why didn't he want her?

After the dishes were cleared, Doug suggested a brandy. "I don't think so," she said. "I don't usually drink this much early in the day."

"Actually, neither do I. I guess there's something about the occasion that feels like a celebration."

"I know what you mean."

"Some coffee? Because I'm in no hurry for this to end."

She agreed that coffee sounded like a good idea. And it was pretty good coffee, and a fitting conclusion to a pretty good meal. Better than a person might expect to find on the outskirts of Toledo.

How did he know the place? Did he come here with his wife? She somehow doubted it. Had he brought other women here? She doubted that as well. Maybe it was something he'd picked up at the office water cooler. *"So I took her to this Eye-tie place on Detroit Avenue, and then we just popped into the Comfort Inn down the block, and I mean to tell you that girl was good to go."*

Something like that.

"I don't want to go back to the office," he was saying. "All these years, and then you walk back into my life, and I'm not ready for you to walk out of it again."

You were the one who walked, she thought. Clear to Bowling Green.

But what she said was, "We could go to my hotel room, but a downtown hotel right in the middle of the city—"

"Actually," he said, "there's a nice place right across the street."

"Oh?"

"A Holiday Inn, actually."

"Do you think they'd have a room at this hour?"

He managed to look embarrassed and pleased with himself, all at the same time. "As a matter of fact," he said, "I have a reservation."

# SEVEN

She was four months shy of her eighteenth birthday when every-thing changed.

What she came to realize, although she hadn't been consciously aware of it at the time, was that things had already been changing for some time. Her father came a little less frequently to her bed, sometimes telling her he was tired from a hard day's work, sometimes explaining that he had to stay up late with work he'd brought home, sometimes not bothering with an explanation of any sort.

Then one afternoon he invited her to come for a ride. Sometimes rides in the family car would end at a motel, and she thought that was what he planned on this occasion. In anticipation, no sooner had he backed the car out of the driveway than she'd dropped her hand into his lap, stroking him, awaiting his response.

He pushed her hand away.

She wondered why, but didn't say anything, and he didn't say anything, either, not for ten minutes of suburban streets. Then abruptly he pulled into a strip mall, parked opposite a shuttered bowling alley, and said, "You're my little soldier, aren't you?"

She nodded.

"And that's what you'll always be. But we have to stop. You're a grown woman, you have to be able to lead your own life, I can't go on like this…"

She scarcely listened. The words washed over her like a stream, a babbling stream, and what came through to her was not so much the words he spoke but what seemed to underlie those words: *I don't want you anymore.*

After he'd stopped talking, and after she'd waited long enough to know he wasn't going to say anything else, and because she knew he was awaiting her response, she said, "Okay."

"I love you, you know."

"I know."

"You've never said anything to anyone, have you?"

"No."

"Of course you haven't. You're a soldier, and I've always known I could count on you."

On the way back, he asked her if she'd like to stop for ice cream. She just shook her head, and he drove the rest of the way home.

She got out of the car and went up to her room. She sprawled on her bed, turning the pages of a book without registering their contents. After a few minutes she stopped trying to read and sat up, her eyes focused on a spot on one wall where the wallpaper was misaligned.

She found herself thinking of Doug, her first real boyfriend. She'd never told her father about Doug; of course he knew that they were spending time together, but she'd kept their intimacy a secret. And of course she'd never said a word about what she and her father had been doing, not to Doug or to anybody else.

The two relationships were worlds apart in her mind. But now they had something in common, because they had both ended. Doug's family had moved to Ohio, and their exchange of letters had trickled out. And her father didn't want to have sex with her anymore.

Something really bad was going to happen. She just knew it.

✿

A few days later, she went to her friend Rosemary's house after school. Rosemary, who lived just a few blocks away on Covington, had three brothers and two sisters, and anybody who was still there at dinner time was always invited to stay.

She accepted gratefully. She could have gone home, but she just didn't want to, and she still didn't want to a few hours later. "I wish I could just stay here overnight," she told Rosemary. "My parents are acting weird."

"Hang on, I'll ask my mom."

She had to call home and get permission. "No one's answering," she said. "Maybe they went out. If you want I'll go home."

"You'll stay right here," Rosemary's mother said. "You'll call right before bedtime, and if there's still no answer, well, if they're not home, they won't miss you, will they?"

Rosemary had twin beds, and fell asleep instantly in her own. Kit, a few feet away, had this thought that Rosemary's father would let himself into the room, and into her bed, but of course this didn't happen, and the next thing she knew she was asleep.

In the morning she went home, and the first thing she did was call Rosemary's house, hysterical. Rosemary's mother calmed her down, and then she was able to call 911 to report the deaths of her parents. Rosemary's mother came over to be with her, and shortly after that the police came, and it became pretty clear what had happened. Her father had killed her mother and then turned the gun on himself.

"You sensed that something was wrong," Rosemary's mother said. "That's why it was so easy to get you to stay for dinner, and why you wanted to sleep over."

"They were fighting," she said, "and there was something different about it. Not just a normal argument. God, it's my fault, isn't it? I should have been able to do something. The least I could have done was to say something."

Everybody told her that was nonsense.

After she'd left Lucas's brand-new high-floor apartment, she returned to her own older, less imposing sublet, where she brewed a pot of coffee and sat up at the kitchen table with a pencil and paper. She wrote down the numbers one through five in descending order, and after each she wrote a name, or as much of the name as she knew. Sometimes she added an identifying phrase or two. The list began with 5, and the first entry read as follows:

*Said his name was Sid. Pasty complexion, gap between top incisors. Met in Philadelphia at bar on Race Street (?), went to his hotel, don't remember name of it. Gone when I woke up.*

Hmmm. Sid might be hard to find. How would she even know where to start looking for him?

At the bottom of the list, her entry was simpler and more specific. *Douglas Pratter. Last known address Bowling Green. Lawyer? Google him?*

She booted up her laptop.

Their room in the Detroit Avenue Holiday Inn was on the third floor in the rear. With the drapes drawn and the door locked, with their clothes hastily discarded and the bedclothes as hastily tossed aside, it seemed to her for at least a few minutes that she was fifteen years old again, and in bed with her first boyfriend. She tasted a familiar sweetness in his kisses, a familiar raw urgency in his ardor.

But the illusion didn't last. And then it was just lovemaking, at which each of them had a commendable proficiency. He went down on her this time, which was something he'd never done when they were teenage sweethearts, and the first thought that came to her was that he had turned into her father, because her father had done that all the time.

Afterward, after a fairly long shared silence, he said, "I can't tell you how many times I've wondered."

"What it would be like to be together again?"

"Well, sure, but more than that. What life would have been like if I'd never moved away in the first place. What would have become of the two of us, if we'd had the chance to let things find their way."

"Probably the same as most high school lovers. We'd have stayed together for a while, and then we'd have broken up and gone separate ways."

"Maybe."

"Or I'd have gotten pregnant, and you'd have married me, and we'd be divorced by now."

"Maybe."

"Or we'd still be together, and bored to death with each other, and you'd be in a motel fucking somebody new."

"God, how'd you get so cynical?"

"You're right, I got off on the wrong foot there. How about this? If your father hadn't moved you all to Bowling Green, you and I would have stayed together, and our feeling for each other would have grown from teenage hormonal infatuation to the profound mature love it was always destined to be. You'd have gone off to college, and as soon as I finished high school I'd have enrolled there myself, and when you finished law school I'd have my undergraduate degree, and I'd be your secretary and office manager when you set up your own law practice. By then we'd have gotten married, and by now we'd have one child with a second on the way, and we would remain unwavering in our love for one another, and as passionate as ever." She gazed wide-eyed at him. "Better?"

His expression was hard to read, and he appeared to be on the point of saying something, but she turned toward him and ran a hand over his flank, and the prospect of a further adventure in adultery trumped whatever he might have wanted to say. Whatever it was, she thought, it would keep.

"I'd better get going," he said, and rose from the bed, and rummaged through the clothes he'd tossed on the chair.

She said, "Doug? Don't you think you might want to take a shower first?"

"Oh, Jesus. Yeah, I guess I better, huh?"

He'd known where to take her to lunch, knew to make a room reservation ahead of time, but he evidently didn't know enough to shower away her spoor before returning to home and hearth. So perhaps this sort of adventure was not the usual thing for him. Oh, she was fairly certain he tried to get lucky on business trips—those oh-so-lonely New York visits he'd mentioned, for instance—but you didn't have to shower after that sort of interlude, because you were going back to your own hotel room, not to your unsuspecting wife.

She started to get dressed. There was no one waiting for her, and her own shower could wait until she was back at her own motel. But she changed her mind about dressing, and was still naked when he emerged from the shower, a towel wrapped around his middle.

"Here," she said, handing him a glass of water. "Drink this."

"What is it?"

"Water."

"I'm not thirsty."

"Just drink it, will you?"

He shrugged, drank it. He went and picked up his undershorts, and kept losing his balance when he tried stepping into them. She took his arm and led him over to the bed, and he sat down and told her he didn't feel so good. She took the undershorts away from him and got him to lie down on the bed, and she watched him struggling to keep a grip on consciousness.

She put a pillow over his face, and she sat on it. She felt him trying to move beneath her, and she watched his hands make feeble clawing motions at the bedsheet, and observed the muscles working in his lower legs. Then he was still, and she stayed where she was for a few minutes, and an involuntary tremor, a very subtle one, went through her hindquarters.

And what was that, pray tell? Could have been her coming, could have been him going. Hard to tell, and did it really matter?

When she got up, well, duh, he was dead. No surprise there. She put her clothes on, cleaned up all traces of her presence, and transferred all of the cash from his wallet to her purse. A few hundred dollars in tens and twenties, plus an emergency hundred-dollar bill tucked away behind his driver's license. She might have missed it, but she'd learned years ago that you had to give a man's wallet a thorough search.

Not that the money was ever the point. But they couldn't take it with them and it had to go somewhere, so it might as well go to her. Right?

How it happened: That final morning, shortly after she left for school, her father and mother had argued, and her father had gone for the handgun he kept in a locked desk drawer and shot her mother dead. He left the house and went to his office, saying nothing to anyone, although a coworker did say that he'd seemed troubled. And sometime during the afternoon he returned home, where his wife's body remained undiscovered. The gun was still there (unless he'd been carrying it around with him during the intervening hours) and he put the barrel in his mouth and blew his brains out.

Except that wasn't really how it happened, it was how the police figured it out. What did in fact happen, of course, is that she got the handgun from the drawer before she left for school, and went into the kitchen where her mother was loading the dishwasher.

She said, "You knew, right? You had to know. I mean, how could you miss it?"

"I don't know what you're talking about," her mother said, but her eyes said otherwise.

"That he was fucking me," she said. "You know, Daddy? Your husband?"

"How can you say that word?"

How indeed? So she shot her mother before she left for school, and called her father on his cell as soon as she got home from school, summoning him on account of an unspecified emergency. He came right home, and by then she might have liked to change her mind, but how could she with her mother dead on the kitchen floor? So she shot him and arranged the evidence appropriately, and then she went over to Rosemary's.

Di dah di dah di dah.


You could see Doug's car from the motel room window. He'd parked in the back and they'd come up the back stairs, never going anywhere near the front desk. So no one had seen her, and no one saw her now as she went to his car, unlocked it with his key, and drove it downtown.

She'd have preferred to leave it there, but her own rental was parked near the Crowne Plaza, so she had to get downtown to reclaim it. You couldn't stand on the corner and hail a cab, not in Toledo, and she didn't want to call one. So she drove to within a few blocks of the lot where she'd stowed her Honda, parked his Volvo at an expired meter, and used the hanky with which he'd cleaned his glasses to wipe away any fingerprints she might have left behind.

She redeemed her car and headed for her own motel. Halfway there, she realized she had no real need to go there. She'd packed that morning and left no traces of herself in her room. She hadn't checked out, electing to keep her options open, so she could go there now with no problem, but for what? Just to take a shower?

She sniffed herself. She could use a shower, no question, but she wasn't so rank that people would draw away from her. And she kind of liked the faint trace of his smell coming off her flesh.

And the sooner she got to the airport, the sooner she'd be out of Toledo.

She managed to catch a 4:18 flight that was scheduled to stop in Cincinnati, on its way to Denver. She'd stay in Denver for a while, until she'd decided where she wanted to go next.

She hadn't had a reservation, or even a set destination, and she took the flight because it was there to be taken. The leg from Toledo to Cincinnati was more than half empty, and she had a row of seats to herself, but she was stuck in a middle seat from Cincinnati to Denver, wedged between a fat lady who looked to be scared stiff of something, possibly the flight itself, and a man who tapped away at his laptop and invaded her space with his elbows.

Not the most pleasant travel experience she'd ever had, but nothing she couldn't live through. She closed her eyes, let her thoughts turn inward.

         ✿

After her parents were buried and the estate settled, after she'd finished the high school year and collected her diploma, after a realtor had listed her house and, after commission and closing costs, netted her a few thousand over and above the outstanding first and second mortgages, she'd stuffed what she could into one of her father's suitcases and boarded a bus.

She'd never gone back. And, until her brief but gratifying reunion with Douglas Pratter, Esq., she'd never been Katherine Tolliver again.

On the tram to Baggage Claim, a businessman from Wichita told her how much simpler it had been getting in and out of Denver before they built Denver International Airport. "Not that Stapleton was all that wonderful," he said, "but it was a quick cheap cab ride from the Brown Palace. It wasn't stuck out in the middle of a few thousand square miles of prairie."

It was funny he should mention the Brown, she said, because that's where she was staying. So of course he suggested she share his cab, and when they reached the hotel and she offered to pay half, well, he wouldn't hear of it. "My company pays," he said, "and if you really want to thank me, why don't you let the old firm buy you dinner?"

Tempting, but she begged off, said she'd eaten a big lunch, said all she wanted to do was get to sleep. "If you change your mind," he said, "just ring my room. If I'm not there, you'll find me in the bar."

She didn't have a reservation, but they had a room for her, and she sank into an armchair with a glass of water from the tap. The Brown Palace had its own artesian well, and took great pride in their water, so how could she turn it down?

"Just drink it," she'd told Doug, and he'd done what she told him. It was funny, people usually did.

"Five," she'd told Lucas, who'd been so eager to be number six.

But he'd only managed it for a matter of minutes, because the list was composed of men who could sit around that mythical table and tell each other how they'd had her, and you had to be alive to do that. So Lucas had dropped off the list when she'd chosen a knife from his kitchen and slipped it right between his ribs and into his heart. He fell off her list without even opening his eyes.

After her parents died, she didn't sleep with anyone until she'd graduated and left home for good. Then she got a waitress job, and the manager took her out drinking after work one night, got her drunk, and performed something that might have been date rape; she didn't remember it that clearly, so it was hard to say.

When she saw him at work the next night he gave her a wink and a pat on the behind, and something came into her mind, and that night she got him to take her for a ride and park on the golf course, where she took him by surprise and beat his brains out with a tire iron.

There, she'd thought. Now it was as if the rape—if that's what it was, and did it really matter what it was? Whatever it was, it was as if it had never happened.

A week or so later, in another city, she quite deliberately picked up a man in a bar, went home with him, had sex with him, killed him, robbed him, and left him there. And that set the pattern.

Four times the pattern had been broken, and those four men had joined Doug Pratter on her list. Two of them, Sid from Philadelphia and Peter from Wall Street, had escaped because she drank too much. Sid was gone when she woke up. Peter was there, and in the mood for morning sex, after which she'd laced his bottle of vodka with the little crystals she'd meant to put in his drink the night before. She never did find out how that played out, so she didn't really know whether Peter deserved a place on her list.

It wouldn't be hard to find out, and if he was still on the list, well, she could deal with it. It would be a lot harder to find Sid, because all she knew about him was his first name, and that might well have been improvised for the occasion. And she'd met him in Philadelphia, but he was already registered at a hotel, so that meant he was probably from someplace other than Philadelphia, and that meant the only place she knew to look was the one place where she could be fairly certain he didn't live.

She knew the first and last names of the two other men on her list. Graham Weider was a Chicagoan she'd met in New York; he'd taken her to lunch and to bed, then jumped up and hurried her out of there, claiming an urgent appointment and arranging to meet her later. But he'd never turned up, and the desk at his hotel told her he'd checked out.

So he was lucky, and Alvin Kirkaby was lucky in another way. He was an infantry corporal on leave before they shipped him off to Iraq, and if she'd realized that she wouldn't have picked him up in the first place, and she wasn't sure what kept her from doing to him as she did to the other men who entered her life. Pity? Patriotism? Both seemed unlikely, and when she thought about it later she decided it was simply because he was a soldier. That gave them something in common, because weren't they both military types? Wasn't she her father's little soldier?

Maybe he'd been killed over there. She supposed she could find out. And then she could decide what she wanted to do about it.

Graham Weider, though, couldn't claim combatant status, unless you considered him a corporate warrior. And while his name might not be unique, neither was it by any means common. And it was almost certainly his real name, too, because they'd known it at the front desk. Graham Weider, from Chicago. It would be easy enough to find him, when she got around to it.

Of them all, Sid would be the real challenge. She sat there going over what little she knew about him and how she might go about playing detective. Then she treated herself to another half-glass of Brown Palace water and flavored it with a miniature of Johnny Walker from the minibar. She sat down with the drink and shook her head, amused by her own behavior. She was dawdling, postponing her shower, as if she couldn't bear to wash away the traces of Doug's lovemaking.

But she was tired, and she certainly didn't want to wake up the next morning with his smell still on her. She undressed and stood for a long time in the shower, and when she got out of it she stood for a moment alongside the tub and watched the water go down the drain.

Four, she thought. Why, before you knew it, she'd be a virgin all over again.

# EIGHT

Four.

Four men who'd been with her. Four men, each of whom could see her walking down the street, nudge a friend, and say, "You see that one? Nice, huh? Well, I had her once."

There'd been others, of course, who could have made that claim. You couldn't say there'd been too many to count, but it was true that she could no longer count them, because they weren't there to be counted. They no longer existed. They were dead, and their successes with her—if you wanted to call them that—had been expunged from the record books.

Her pattern for a few years now had been simple enough. She found a man, or was found by one; she went to his bed or took him to hers; she left, and left him dead. If he had money, she took it with her. It let her live with a degree of comfort and paid her way from one hunting ground to the next. She'd take a job now and then, but she worked only when she wanted to.

And the jobs never lasted. Because sooner or later she'd hook up with one of nature's noblemen, and she'd give him what he wanted, and then take it all back with interest. And then, of course, it would be time to get out of Dodge. Or Philadelphia, or Toledo, or Louisville, or Kansas City, or—well, wherever. The places all tended to merge in her memory. So did the men. And why make an effort to bring their images into focus? They were gone, and once they were gone it was as if they had never existed.

In Toledo she'd erased a man from her past, and even as his

body was approaching room temperature she was on her way to Denver. She stayed a few days at the Brown Palace, where she flirted with a few suits—a corporate lawyer, a real estate guy, a venture capitalist—but didn't let any of them get any further than a little conversational double entendre.

She flew from Denver to Phoenix, checked into a Courtyard by Marriott, and was walking down a street near the hotel when a sign in a diner window caught her eye. WAITRESS WANTED. The place was unprepossessing, and none of the handful of customers struck her as a potential big tipper. Could she even take home enough to cover her hotel room?

Still, it might be interesting, slinging hash at the Last Chance Café, or whatever it called itself. And what did it call itself? She looked up above the window, where a sign read STAVRO'S DINER.

She went in, unfastened the Scotch tape that held the WAIT-RESS WANTED sign in place, took it down and carried it to the counter, where a stocky man with a moustache raised his abundant eyebrows and watched her from beneath them. "You must be Stavro," she said. "You can put this away. I'm your new waitress."

"Just like that? How you know I wanna hire you?"

"What do you want, references from Delmonico's? A letter of recommendation from Wolfgang Puck? You need a waitress and I need a job. So?"

He gave her a look, and then a look-over. His eyes were a sort of muddy brown, and she could feel them on her breasts. Their expression said it was his place and his eyes could go where they wanted. And so could his hands.

"Steve," he said.

"Steve?"

"My name was Stavros," he said. "Not Stavro. Idiot who made the sign, thinks if you put an S you gotta put an apostrophe in front of it."

"Couldn't you make him do it over?"

" 'I ain't payin' you,' I told him. He said he'd do it over. 'I still ain't payin' you,' I said, and that's where we left it. Stavros, Stavro, what's the difference? Everybody calls me Steve anyway. You can call me Steve."

"Okay."

"What do I call you?"

What indeed? She hadn't bothered to figure out that part, and didn't want to use the same name she'd written on the registration card at the hotel.

"Carol," she said.

"Like a Christmas Carol? You probably hear that all the time."

"You're the first."

"Yeah, I bet. You wanna start now? There's an apron on the peg. It'll fit you. Last girl worked here, she was about your size, but I gotta say she didn't have your shape. You got a real nice shape to you."

She'd drawn a few cups of coffee, served a couple of Blue Plate Specials, and had Steve brush up against her a few times, with an apology each time, always with an inflection to belie the words. And the next time she passed through the kitchen he dropped the accidentally-on-purpose pretense and ran a hand appraisingly over her bottom.

"Very nice," he said.

Well, she'd thought she might stay a while in Phoenix, and that didn't seem likely now, did it? Oh, she could deflect his pass and make it clear she wasn't willing to play, but she didn't get the impression Steve would take no for an answer. She sensed that making herself available to him was part of the job description, which might explain why the vacancy had existed.

She could quit, of course. Take off the apron, throw it in his face, and tell him to save it for the next girl with a nice shape to come along.

But the son of a bitch got her motor running. He was crude and crass, and you couldn't call him good-looking, but there was a sexual magnetism about him that she couldn't deny. Even the rank smell of him, all musk and sweat and a shirt that had gone too long between washings, was part of the package; she might wrinkle her nose when she breathed in his scent, but that didn't keep her from getting wet.

Now? Or later?

Either course held its attractions. She could hurry the two customers at the counter, then turn the sign on the door from OPEN to CLOSED and return to the kitchen. Look at him through half-lidded eyes, part her lips a little and run her tongue around them. It wouldn't be all that difficult to give him the idea, given that he already had the idea, had had it the moment he laid those muddy brown eyes on her and let them linger.

She'd take off her panties before she went in there. Then just pull up her skirt and bend over the counter, and he'd be on her like a mongoose on a cobra. She imagined his hands on her, his cock deep inside her, her nostrils filled with the raw smell of him.

And in the afterglow, while he was catching his breath and thinking of all the things he'd soon get to do with his hot new waitress, she'd be well placed to finish what she'd started. It was a kitchen, there were knives and cleavers all over the place, and she'd grab one and put it where it would do the most good, and he'd be dead and she'd be gone. Back to her room and under the shower—God, she'd need a shower—and then goodbye Phoenix.

But what was her hurry? He'd want her even more if she gave

him a taste and made him wait for the rest of it. Why strike while the iron was hot when all it could do was get hotter?

In the end, it was he who turned the sign from OPEN to CLOSED. "Okay, time to go," he said to one old lag sitting with an empty cup of coffee and a newspaper another customer had left behind. And, as the old fellow got to his feet, "Hey, Joe, don't be a cheap bastard. This is Carol's first day, ain't you gonna leave her a tip?"

Shamed into it, the man put a pair of quarters on the table. "Last of the big spenders," Steve said, and scooped up the coins, presenting them to her like a cat depositing a dead mouse at its owner's feet. And, with the window sign turned and the door bolted, he gave her a grin and motioned her into the kitchen.

She didn't have to pretend to be excited when he handled her breasts and buttocks and ran a hand up between her legs. There was nothing artful about his technique, but the crudeness itself was exciting. Oh, one would tire of it soon enough, but for now—

"Not tonight," she said.

He was a man who would indeed take no for an answer, but not until the fourth or fifth time he heard it. She'd fend him off and he'd go at her again, until at last he realized that no meant no. He let out a sigh and leaned back against the counter.

"Tomorrow," she said. "Tonight, it, uh, it wouldn't be good. God, you're exciting. I can't wait until tomorrow, Steve."

"So why wait?" He looked at her, then shrugged. "Never mind. I guess you got your reasons."

He'd need her working noon to eight, he told her. He opened at 6:30 for breakfast, but his sister helped him out mornings. Maybe she might like to get there a little earlier tomorrow, he suggested. So they could go over some things together before the lunch crowd showed up. Say eleven?

Back at the hotel, she didn't shower right away. Her room had two beds, and she stripped and got in one of them and pulled the covers all the way up, trapping his smell. She breathed it in while she touched herself, giving her fantasies free rein, holding herself back from the edge, then finally allowing herself the release of orgasm.

She'd have showered afterward, but sleep took her by surprise, and she slept deeply until dawn and woke up ravenous. She'd made herself a sandwich midway through her shift, but had gone to bed without supper. First, though, she needed that shower.

But was there any point? In a matter of hours she'd be smelling of him all over again.

She took the shower anyway. Nothing lasted, so why expect a shower to endure?

In a sense, the effects of the shower were gone by the time she got dressed. She put on the same skirt and blouse she'd worn the day before, not wanting to get his scent on a second outfit. She'd wear the same clothes, even if it meant walking around all morning with that musky odor on her, and after it was over she'd throw everything out.

Should she check out now? Take her bag to the bus station, stash it in a locker? That would get her out of town faster, but you couldn't always find those coin-operated lockers. They'd been disappearing for a while now, to thwart dope dealers. And, she supposed, terrorists.

So should she take the suitcase to the diner? Or would that be suspicious? He might see it and think she was leaving town.

And if he did? Like, so what? It's not as though the prospect of her imminent departure would make him any less eager to fuck her.

So that would work. She'd bring the bag along, stash it in the kitchen. And during the slow time before the lunch crowd showed up, she'd go in back and let him do what he wanted. And then she'd do what *she* wanted, and she'd retrieve her bag and be out the door with the CLOSED sign hanging in the window.

With his smell all over her.

She'd need the room so she could shower and change. And she could afford to pay for a second night, but it went against the grain. She picked up the phone, rang the front desk, asked about a late checkout.

No problem, Ms. Perkins. Two o'clock all right?

Perfect, she said, and went out for breakfast.

She knew she didn't want to eat at the diner, but she had to walk past it to get to the other nearby restaurants, and that gave her a chance for a look at Steve's putative sister. The woman she saw through the window, carrying plates of eggs and bacon as if she'd been doing this since childhood, was short and stocky and dark-complected, with black hair and thick eyebrows. So she certainly might have been a sister, but she hadn't believed it when he said it and was no more inclined to believe it now. She'd bet anything this beauty queen was Steve's wife.

She walked on, found a place to eat with better lighting and a reassuring commitment to hygiene. She settled into a booth with a copy of the morning paper, ate a big breakfast, and drank two cups of coffee.

And smelled him on her clothes.

"Right on time," he said.

There were two customers in the place, and one of them was the same man he'd run off the night before. Did the old fart live here? He looked to be wearing the same clothes, too—a forest-green work shirt worn through at one elbow, with a pair of baggy trousers that must have started life as the bottom half of a business suit.

Well, what else did she expect? She hadn't changed her outfit, and neither, she was unsurprised to see, had Steve. Classy joint, the Stavro's Diner. Everybody wears the same clothes forever, and nobody bathes, and they all smell about the same. Be a shame to say goodbye to a place like this.

And damned if Steve didn't run the old boy off again, and the shrunken blue-haired woman at the corner table along with him. "Gotta close for a few minutes," he told them. "Gotta go over a thing or two with Carol here."

He ushered them out. And bolted the door, and fixed the sign. And, with a wolfish grin, beckoned her to the kitchen.

It smelled of eggs and grease and bacon, and of course of Steve himself. His hand cupped her shoulder and turned her toward him, and she hoped he wouldn't kiss her. Some hookers, she knew, drew the line at kissing, objecting to it because it was somehow too intimate to be available for a price. She had never minded kissing men regardless of what she might have planned for them, and her objection now was purely aesthetic; she didn't want to kiss him because she found him revolting.

But she definitely wanted to fuck him. He might disgust her, but he also turned her on something fierce.

His hands, clumsy but confident, touched and patted and stroked and squeezed. She realized with some relief that he was no more interested in kissing than she was. Maybe it was an intimacy he reserved for his wife, maybe he didn't like to kiss a woman without a moustache.

And then, as she had fantasized earlier, he turned her around and pushed her face down toward the counter. It was topped with a butcher-block cutting board, and she smelled blood and meat, along with the musky sweat smell, the Steve smell.

He pulled up her skirt, bunched it around her hips, then reached to lower her panties. They fell to her ankles, and she would have stepped out of them but she couldn't because he was holding her by the hips.

She thought, *Greek foreplay. Brace yourself, Athena!* And then he was inside her.

She had to wait at the bus station for an hour and ten minutes, and tried to will the time to pass and the bus to come. She wasn't anxious about the time it was taking, because it would be hours before the authorities found out about Steve. She'd found a set of keys on a peg by the entrance to the kitchen, and one of them fit the outer door. With the lights out and the door locked, and the CLOSED sign already in place, there was every chance that nobody would find him before morning.

As it was, she'd missed the bus to Tucson by less than ten minutes. She could have been on it with time to spare if she hadn't insisted on spending a full half hour in the shower, soaping and rinsing and soaping and rinsing. *I'm gonna wash that man right out of my hair*—the song ran through her mind as she used up Marriott's entire mini-bottle of shampoo. It left her hair smelling of orange and ginger, and wasn't that an improvement on *eau de Stavros?*

And now she was dressed in clean clothes from head to toe, and a plastic bag on the bench beside her held everything she'd been wearing: skirt, blouse, panties, socks, even her shoes. And it was the bag and its contents that made her wish the bus would come, because the plastic was no barrier to that godawful smell.

There was a trash receptacle in her line of sight, and the impulse to drop the clothes into it was almost irresistible. *Bad idea*, she told herself, over and over. There were bloodstains on her skirt and blouse, and she could imagine what trace evidence her shoes and panties would yield. Not that an investigating officer would need a microscope, or any of the battery of tools they used on *CSI*. The sniff test would be plenty for anyone who'd ever been within ten yards of Steve, living or dead.

The bus would take her north, to Flagstaff. She'd stay there long enough to get rid of the bag of dirty clothes, then take another bus and get across a state line or two. She could take buses all the way to her ultimate destination, but Chicago was a long ways off, and by the time she got there she'd need a long shower just to get rid of her own smell.

Crazy the way she couldn't stop thinking about smells. Gross, really.

She thought about Chicago, and Graham Weider. Of the four living members of her personal alumni association, he had to be the softest target. Alvin Kirkaby, if he was still alive, could still be in Iraq, on another tour of duty. Or maybe his unit had been dispatched to Afghanistan. Or maybe he'd lived and returned home, wherever home might be. She didn't know where he hailed from, and couldn't guess where he might be now.

She'd met Graham Weider in New York, where he bought her a good lunch before taking her back to his hotel room for their quickie, the details of which had long since faded from her mind. They arranged to meet later for a good dinner, to be followed by a not-so-quickie. When he didn't show up, she went back to his hotel, where he'd left a note at the desk. *Sorry, business meeting necessitated immediate departure. Rushing to airport and flight to L.A. Call me, love to see you again.*

And there'd been a phone number, but she had neither called it nor kept it. At the time she felt a little regret at having failed to close the books on Graham Weider, but not so much that she was going to hop on a plane and hunt him down. It hadn't seemed all that important.

It did now.

Once again she managed to get a seat all to herself, toward the front but not too close to the driver. There was room in the overhead for her suitcase, and for the bag of clothes as well. She could still smell the clothes, even in their new location, but she had the feeling that she'd still be smelling them if she'd chanced leaving them in the trash can. Her nose was full of his scent, and it would take more than distance to clear them. It would take time as well.

She'd bought a novel at the newsstand in the station, but never looked at it again until she was on the bus. Even then she waited until they'd cleared the Phoenix city limits before she switched on the overhead light.

The book was a paperback thriller. Some wild-eyed eco-terrorist, crazy as a bedbug and twice as charming, had raided a secret government laboratory, killed half a dozen scientists, and made off with enough anthrax, plague bacteria, and smallpox virus to depopulate an already troubled planet. And, astonishingly enough, the only person in the world with even a slim chance of stopping this lunatic was a beautiful young FBI agent, the identical twin sister of one of the murdered scientists.

*Well, sure,* she thought. *These things happen.*

She read for a while, dozed for a while, opened her eyes when the bus pulled to a stop in Sedona. Three people got off, two got on. Next stop, Flagstaff.

*

She'd had one genuine oh-shit moment in the Phoenix bus station. She'd been sitting there, the suitcase at her feet, the bag of clothes beside her, the paperback unopened on her lap, when the room went dead silent, jarring her out of her reverie.

When she turned her head to find out what everyone was looking at, what she saw was a pair of uniformed police officers striding through the entrance. One had a hand on the butt of his holstered pistol.

Time, which had been crawling to begin with, came to a dead stop. She tried to think of something to do, some action to take, and came up empty.

And then the cops walked straight over to a gaunt and hollow-eyed young man, his jeans out at the knee, his arms and neck and who knew what else heavily tattooed. He evidently couldn't think of anything to do either. She'd thought earlier that he looked like a fugitive, and evidently he was, and his days on the run were over, because he didn't even protest, just stood up and turned around to be handcuffed.

After they'd led him out, the silence held for an instant. Then almost everybody started talking at once, and the ones who weren't talking were hauling out their cell phones. This would make a good story for all of them, she thought. It would make an even better story for her, but one she wasn't likely to tell.

On the last leg of the trip, she remembered what had taken place in the kitchen, with her cheek against the cutting board and her panties around her ankles. As she'd anticipated, Steve was one of those piledriver types, hammering away at her, thrusting hard and fast, like John Henry determined to beat the steam drill or die trying.

*When John Henry was a little baby*
*Just a settin' on his mammy's knee*
*He picked up a hammer an' a little piece of steel*
*Said, Gonna be the death of me*
*Lord, Lord,*
*Gonna be the death of me…*

The John Henry approach had never been a favorite of hers, but she was far too excited to demand finesse. Her response was immediate and unqualified, and she didn't see how it could have been otherwise. And that would have been the case even if he'd been true to ethnic stereotype and chosen a narrower passage than the conventional one. It might have proved painful, given the thickness of his cock and the lack of foreplay, but that wouldn't have been enough to keep her from enjoying it.

The hammering continued, and she writhed and twisted in response, and he tightened his grip on her hindquarters, as if any movement on her part was an unwelcome diversion. Her orgasm came on anyway, and it was strong enough but somehow incomplete, as if it was just an interim stop on the way to release.

Then, with a great cry and a final powerful thrust, he finished.

*Five*, she thought.

And he tore himself off her and out of her, spun around, collapsed against the stainless steel triple sink. And she couldn't wait, she just couldn't, and so what if he didn't see it coming? So what if she didn't get to see his face? There were knives everywhere, and the one she grabbed was long enough and heavy enough, and she buried it in his back. And stabbed him again and again and again, five times at least, maybe more, as she was too much in the moment to keep track.

And then he stopped making noises, and stopped moving, and

lay on the floor. She was pretty sure he was dead, but she stabbed him one final time, making sure the blade found the heart. She bent down and stepped out of her panties, using them to wipe the handle of the knife, the counter where she'd gripped it, and anything else she thought she might have touched.

And snatched his keys from the peg, and turned off lights, and locked the door once she was through it.

On the way to her hotel, she dropped his keys in a storm drain.

*Four.*

In Flagstaff she wanted to get a hotel room and bed down for the night. She was tired, and not at all eager to set off on another bus ride. But she weighed that against her desire to get out of Arizona, and decided she ought to cross a state line as soon as possible. She thought about heading north and west to Vegas, but decided to go east instead. There was a bus for Albuquerque in two hours and change, and that would give her more than enough time for a proper meal, her first food since breakfast.

The bus station in Flagstaff was really just a large gas station and mini-mart where they kept schedules and sold tickets. She used the rest room to freshen up, and wanted to drop her plastic bag full of dirty clothes in the trash can. There wasn't any risk in that, was there? She was a long ways from Phoenix, and the Phoenix police had already missed one chance at her, choosing instead to grab the crystal freak with all the ink.

But it was the bus station, or as close as Flagstaff came to having a bus station. If they traced her to the bus, mightn't they check out the trash in the ladies room?

Why take a chance?

So she walked in a direction that struck her as most likely to yield a decent place to eat, and on the way she passed a parking lot, and toward the rear of the lot she spotted a corrugated steel bin the size of a privy, with a sign next to it reading GOODWILL. She was a few yards past it when she realized what it was—a collection box for Goodwill Industries.

She lowered the little door and emptied her plastic bag into the bin, then tossed the bag in after it. And hoisted her suitcase and walked on.

The restaurant she found was Mexican. She had salsa and chips and a combination plate with a taco and two enchiladas and something else she couldn't identify. The food and service were good, and the only aggravation was the three-piece mariachi band, which insisted on serenading her. They probably knew another song in addition to "Cielito Lindo," but you couldn't prove it by her.

She made her bus with time to spare. In Albuquerque she stayed the night in an inexpensive downtown hotel. She took a shower when she got there and another before she went to bed. In the morning she took another shower, then walked around the corner for a bowl of red at an unprepossessing café on Gold Street. She wiped the bowl with the last tortilla, finished her coffee, and took a cab to the airport.

She caught a direct flight to O'Hare and let public transportation convey her to the Near North Side, where she'd spent enough time over the years to know her way around. She picked a mostly residential hotel on North Wells and took a shower right away, because she always preferred to sluice away that stale airplane energy once she was off a flight. But this shower felt less urgent than the others she'd taken recently, because somewhere between Albuquerque and Chicago she'd stopped smelling Steve. His reek had outlived him, but only for a little while.

# NINE

There was no Graham Weider listed in the Chicago white pages.

That was annoying, but couldn't be said to amount to a dead end. He was some sort of corporate executive, and she seemed to remember a wedding ring, so he'd be more likely to live in a suburb than within the city limits.

A branch library had all the suburban phone books. No Graham Weider there, either. But there were two G. Weiders, one in Lake Forest, the other in Naperville. *"Hello, is Graham there?"* And he wasn't, and neither party knew anything about a Graham Weider. The G in Naperville stood for Gloria, and the one in Lake Forest wasn't saying.

Hmmm.

Well, all that meant was that his number was unlisted. Or listed in his wife's name, as there were plenty of Weiders scattered throughout Chicagoland. Should she call them all?

The library had computers available, but you had to sign up, and there was a long list ahead of her. She found an Internet café and searched for *Graham Weider Illinois* and came up empty.

A guy hit on her in the Internet café. Her frustration must have been showing, because his approach was, "You know, whatever you're looking for, I bet I could help you find it." He had a couple of piercings, along with a rattlesnake flag tattoo with the traditional *Don't Tread On Me* updated to *Don't Y'all Fuck With Me.* Not an improvement, she thought, but maybe it was supposed to be ironic.

He was the sort of young man for whom irony was a sort of default setting.

"We'll never know," she said, and his expression suggested that he enjoyed the put-down more than anything an acceptance might have led to. That was almost enough to make her change her mind, but not really. Better to take the tattoo's advice.

If only she knew something about Graham Weider besides his name.

His employer, for instance. It was a corporation, and he must have mentioned its name, but if it had ever registered on her memory, time had long since pressed the Delete key.

And she couldn't just call firms at random. Even if she limited herself to Fortune 500 corporations, how many of them had Chicago offices? Four hundred? Four-fifty?

No, that wouldn't work. But his New York hotel would probably have his business address on file, and *that* would let her know where he worked.

If only she could remember the hotel.

Well, it was somewhere in New York, specifically somewhere in midtown Manhattan. And it was a first-rate hotel, not some budget bargain spot. But which one?

Why the hell couldn't she remember? She'd been there, for God's sake, and not once but twice—once when he took her to his room and fucked her, and another time when he stood her up and she went to the front desk looking for him. And he'd left a note for her, on a piece of hotel stationery, but of course she hadn't kept it.

Dammit anyway. She could remember standing in the lobby, reading the note. She could even recall the supercilious look on the face of the desk clerk.

Or was that some other snotty clerk, in some other hotel on

some other occasion? Or was it all just her imagination trying to fill in the blanks?

Graham Weider, she thought. Graham Weider from Chicago, not Joe Blow from Kokomo. Why was he giving her so much trouble?

She tried the phone again, working her way through the Weiders. More often than not she'd get a machine, and rang off without leaving a message. The Weiders she managed to reach had never heard of a Graham Weider. "How does he spell it?" one of them asked her, and she started in: "G, R, A—" and was interrupted. "No, Weider," the woman said. "There are different spellings, you know."

And that sent her off on a whole new tangent, checking all the area phone directories, looking for Wieder and Wheider and Weeder and Weidter and every other permutation she could think of. A couple of them had the initial G, which triggered some fruitless phone calls, but nothing led anywhere useful.

She gave up on the Weiders, however they spelled their names, and thought about giving up on Graham altogether. Then she remembered something she'd read about Thomas Edison, and how he'd invented the lightbulb. It didn't just form over his head, as in a cartoon; it took hundreds upon hundreds of experiments, in which the inventor and his assistants employed one material after another in an effort to find a workable filament, one that would glow when electric current ran through it without burning up or out in the process.

At one point, someone consoled Edison for his lack of progress. And he replied that he was making wonderful progress, that he had already discovered umpteen hundred substances that would not work.

That was inspiring, all right, but she couldn't see that it led anywhere. She went out and walked for a while, stopped for a late-afternoon cappuccino at a little coffeehouse that billed itself as "the anti-Starbucks," and sat there wondering how she'd come upon the Edison anecdote, and whether or not he'd actually ever said it.

And then, remarkably, a lightbulb, complete with tungsten filament, formed above her own head.

There were a great many Weiders, spelled one way or another, living in or near Chicago, and most of them didn't answer the phone, and the ones who did were no help at all. And how many Fortune 500 companies were there? That question was right up there with *Who's buried in Grant's Tomb?* and *What color is orange juice?* There were 500 of them, far too many to call, and there was no guarantee that Graham Weider's employer was on that list in the first place.

But there were far fewer A-list hotels in midtown Manhattan. And, no matter what time of day she called, there'd be somebody there to answer the phone.

She went back to the Internet café and pulled all the midtown four-star hotels from the hotels.com site, then found a quiet bench in Lincoln Park and worked her way down the list from the top. *"Hi, my name's Susan Richardson and I'm on the organizing committee for the upcoming class reunion for Oak Park High. It's my job to track down the graduates we've lost track of, and one of our class members, well, about the only thing anyone could come up with was that he always stays at your establishment on business trips to New York. So I was wondering—"*

The people she talked to were remarkably cooperative. Maybe it was the wholly frivolous nature of her request; she had the feeling they'd have made less of an effort if she'd claimed an urgent business reason to establish contact with Graham Weider, but how could they resist something as pointless as a high school reunion?

And perhaps it was their positive attitude that sustained her when the first ten hotels were unable to find Graham Weider in their records. *Ten more failed filaments*, she thought. *Ten steps closer to success.*

Her eleventh call was to the Sofitel on West 44th, and this time the lightbulb blazed like the sun.

It took her an hour to pack and check out of her hotel, and most of another hour to get through traffic to O'Hare. She ate a Caesar salad and drank a bottle of iced green tea while she waited for her flight to Seattle, which was just as well, because all they gave her on the plane was a cup of truly bad coffee and a tiny packet of trail mix.

It was early evening when they landed at Sea-Tac. She picked up her suitcase at Baggage Claim and caught a cab to the Heathman Hotel in Kirkland, right across from the library and a block from Peter Kirk Park.

She'd booked a room earlier, and it was ready for her. It was spacious and tastefully appointed, and you could see the park from her window. She'd stayed at the Heathman in Portland once, so she wasn't surprised at how nice it was, but her enjoyment was tempered somewhat by the knowledge that she couldn't afford a long stay. Even a single night was a questionable luxury, and you could say the same for the cab ride from the airport. There was almost certainly a bus that would have made the trip for thirty dollars less, not even counting the tip, and it wasn't as though it hadn't occurred to her. But she'd been worn out from the travel and keyed up at the prospect of finally finding Graham Weider, and she couldn't be bothered by the need to watch the pennies.

But she'd have to start doing just that.

She'd had a lot of expenses lately and zero income. She usually paid cash for everything, wanting to avoid a paper trail, and that included airline tickets and hotels. She'd had what seemed like plenty of cash when she left Denver, but it was going fast, and she'd missed an opportunity in Phoenix. Stenchful Steve was the sort of man who'd keep a lot of cash on his person, and she'd never even checked his pants for a wallet. That was a mistake, and so was her failure to clean out the cash register. Between the two, she'd left hundreds of dollars behind, maybe even thousands.

A hell of a price to pay, just because she'd felt in urgent need of a shower.


"Graham Weider, Graham Weider, Graham Weider," said Bob, the cheerful fellow at Sofitel New York. "Now he was a regular a few years ago, wasn't he? And then he stopped coming. I hope we didn't do anything to alienate his affections."

"I understand he was based in Chicago then," she ventured.

"Let's just see. Willoughby & Kessel, State Street, in the heart of the Windy City. So-called not because of the wind from the lake but the legendary verbosity of its politicians. But you'd know that, wouldn't you? Oak Park High and all that."

She actually hadn't known that, nor did she know if there really was an Oak Park High.

"Oh, lookie here! If he got ticked off at us, he must have gotten over it, because here he is just four months ago for three days, and again for three days the following month. But he's no longer with Willoughby & Kessel."

"I hope he didn't do anything to alienate *their* affections."

"If so, the aftershocks sent him clear out of Chicago. His current employer is Barling Industries, whoever they may be, in Kirkland, Washington."

*

Barling Industries, whoever they might be, housed their opera-
tions in a concrete-block cube set in an industrial park on the
eastern edge of Kirkland. And Graham Weider, whoever *he* might
be these days, lived in a modest ranch house on a skimpily land-
scaped half-acre lot less than a mile from his office. She obtained
both addresses from the phone book in her hotel room, and filled
in the descriptions by spending some more of her cash on a taxi.
The taciturn driver, an Asian immigrant with a much better grasp
of the local geography than the English language, returned her at
length to the Heathman, where she packed up and checked out.

She sat in the park with a PennySaver and checked the rental
classifieds against a street map. Some of the more promising list-
ings were a ways to the south, near Northwest University, but she
found a woman with a room to rent within walking distance of both
Barling Industries and Graham Weider's residence. She called
and made an appointment to come see the room, then studied the
map and figured out how to get there by bus. It was complicated,
but she didn't feel like springing for another cab.

The house, she discovered, was very much like the one Weider
inhabited, a compact ranch with a brick façade and white clap-
board siding. Weider's had black trim and shutters, while this
house was trimmed in forest green. And the shrubbery here had
had more time to establish itself.

Rita Perrin, whose house it was, appeared at first glance to be
as safely suburban as her house. If you looked a second time,
something in her eyes suggested there might be a little more to
her than that. She was a few years older than her prospective
tenant, and a little fuller in the breasts and hips. She was alone now,
she explained, and the house was really too big for one person.
There were three bedrooms, but she thought two housemates

would be too much, and besides she could use the smallest bedroom as a home office, and had in fact set it up that way.

The second bedroom was clean and airy, and looked out on the garden. A month's rent, with kitchen and living room privileges, would cost her a few dollars less than a two-night stay at the Heathman. "And the garage will hold a second car," Rita said, "as soon as we move some of my stuff out of the way."

She explained that she didn't have a car, and didn't plan to get one. She'd already established that she was in a doctoral program at the University of Washington, that she'd finished her course work and needed a quiet place to work on her thesis.

"And you didn't have a car at the U? You'll probably want one here."

She'd grown up in New York City, she explained, and had never learned to drive.

"I was going to say you could borrow mine until you get one of your own, but if you never learned—"

It might be handy to borrow Rita's car. She had a license, but it didn't match the name she'd already given Rita. Easier to let it go.

"You know what you could do, Kim? There's a bicycle in the garage. I never use it, I was planning on donating it to the next rummage sale. You're welcome to the use of it. Uh, I've never actually been to New York. Do people there ride bikes?"

Indeed they do, she thought. The wrong way on one-way streets, and on sidewalks, and sailing through red lights. "I can't remember the last time I was on a bike," she told Rita. "But I guess it's not something you forget how to do."

"Oh, that's what they say," Rita assured her. "Like swimming, isn't that what they say?"

Or drowning, she thought.

✼

A little after five she told Rita she was going for a walk to clear her head. She headed for Graham Weider's house, and passed a supermarket about halfway to her destination. Good—she would stop on her way home, so that she wouldn't have to walk a mile every time she wanted something to eat.

She didn't have any trouble finding her way, and got there by 5:30. If his workday was nine to five, and if he came straight home when he was done at the office, she would probably be on time to see him arrive. Unless he stopped for a drink, or visited a mistress, or was out of town altogether, staying at the equivalent of Sofitel New York in St. Louis or Detroit or Baltimore.

There were lights on in his house, and the picture window showed a TV screen, almost large enough for her to make out the images from across the street. That was where she stationed herself, and she would stand in one spot for a few minutes, then glance at her watch and walk a dozen yards in one direction, then return a few minutes later. The impression, she hoped, was one of a woman waiting for a friend to pick her up. That would do, although it would be even better if no one took any notice of her in the first place.

His lawn needed mowing. It wasn't wildly overgrown, but the grass in front of the Weider house was noticeably longer than the adjacent lawns. So Graham mowed his lawn, but not as frequently as he might. What else did her view tell her about him?

Well, duh, he was a daddy. Either that or he had curious taste in transportation for a grown man, because there was a child's tricycle at the side of the driveway.

That wasn't much. Maybe she'd know more when she got a look at him.

She searched her memory, couldn't picture the man. She wondered if he'd even look familiar.

❖

Graham Weider's suburban street didn't get a lot of traffic, and each time a car approached she took note of it, and waited to see if it would turn into his driveway. Shortly after six o'clock, when the metallic green Subaru squareback came into view, she knew immediately that it was him. And sure enough, the car slowed as it neared the driveway. There was an unaccompanied man at the wheel, but she couldn't make out his features, and when the garage door rose at his command she despaired of getting a better look at him.

The Subaru made the turn, then stopped halfway to the garage. The driver emerged to walk around the back of the car and wheel the tricycle into the garage. Then he returned to the Subaru, and a moment later it and its driver were out of sight behind the descending garage door.

That told her something about the man's character. He had plenty of clearance, he could have left the tricycle where it was and driven directly into the garage. She couldn't jump to any conclusions about his nature on the basis of that action because for all she knew he'd now enter the house screaming, "Mary, why can't you keep the little bastard's bike out of the fucking driveway?" But that seemed unlikely, given the air of calm acceptance he'd projected clear across the street.

But none of that really amounted to anything. The little bastard's bike had played a more important role from her own singular point of view. Because it had given her a good look at the little bastard's father, full face and profile, and she recognized him. Graham Weider, now of Kirkland, Washington, but once a Chicagoan in New York, who'd shared a bed with her for an hour or so and then been so inconsiderate as to skip town before she could finish what she'd started.

She stopped at the supermarket on the way home, careful not to buy more than she could carry, but the bag boy automatically placed her groceries in her shopping cart. No one came here on foot, she realized, and everybody wheeled their purchases to their cars.

She followed the cart all the way home.

# TEN

What they said seemed to be true: You didn't forget how to ride a bicycle.

She rode Rita's the next morning to Barling Industries. The parking lot was unattended, and she was able to stash her bike between a couple of minivans and walk around in search of Weider's Subaru. She'd had a good look at the license plate while he moved the tricycle, and made a point of memorizing the first three digits, so she knew his car when she came upon it.

So he was here. Somewhere within the concrete-block cube, doing whatever it was they paid him to do, so he in turn could go on paying the mortgage on the nice little suburban house and buy the kid a real bike when he was ready to step up from the tricycle.

Now what?

A thought, unbidden: What she could do, and it would be simplicity itself, was forget all about Graham Weider. What did the man who moved the tricycle have to do with the man who'd taken her to lunch and to bed? Why remain committed to this curious mission to purge the planet of her past and future lovers? He had a kid, he lived in the suburbs, and what did he have to do with her, or she with him?

She pushed the thought away. *This is what I do,* she told herself. *This is who I am.*

✿

She got on her bike, rode away, rode around. And was back in the Barling lot by noon. This time she stationed herself where she could see both his car and the employee entrance, and she spotted him right away when he left the building in the company of another man. They both wore shirts and ties, but they'd left their suit jackets inside.

They walked to the Subaru, got in, and drove off. Two fellow workers, she decided, on their way to a casual lunch. She could follow, but only if Rita's bike were jet-propelled.

So? What was she supposed to do now, hang around and wait for him to come back, then follow him home and watch him move the tricycle again?

She hopped on her bike, headed for home.

Saturday morning she took a bus to Seattle and found her way to Spy Shoppe, a retail firm with a showroom one flight above a sporting goods store. Spy Shoppe worked both sides of the espionage avenue, offering a wide range of eavesdropping gadgets and just as wide a range of devices made to foil them. Want to tap a phone? Want to know if your phone is tapped? They were like international arms dealers, she thought, cheerfully peddling weapons to opposing factions.

The gear they had on offer was so fascinating it was hard to stay focused on her reason for being there. The salesman was a prototypical geek, all Buddy Holly glasses and Adam's apple, perfectly happy to show off for her. There was a homing device to be attached to a car's bumper, and she asked about that, and learned how it worked.

But it was pretty expensive, and that was just the beginning. Then you'd need something to pick up the signal and locate it for you, and that was more expensive by the time you put the whole package together, and then where were you? You could find out where he and his friend were lunching, and if you pedaled like crazy on your bike, you might get there before they finished their second cup of coffee.

Pointless, really.

Of course, she could get everything she needed for free. All she had to do was date the geek.

That was something that didn't even occur to her until he cleared his throat and stammered and looked at his feet, and blurted out that his work day ended at six, and that maybe they could meet for coffee, his treat, and uh talk about things and uh—

"Well, I could meet you," she said, "but then I'd have to kill you."

He stared at her, puzzled, until he figured out that it was a joke. And laughed accordingly.

Sunday afternoon she went to a movie, and when she got home Rita had dinner on the table, with two places set. "It's easier cooking for two than for one," she said, "so I took a chance. I hope you haven't eaten."

The meal was meatloaf and mashed potatoes and creamed corn, comfort food, and she let herself enjoy it, and Rita's company. Afterward they sat in front of the TV and told stories of their childhoods. Her own were improvised, but she figured Rita's were probably true.

She wondered what Rita would do if she made a pass at her.

And wondered where that thought had come from. She'd never been with another woman herself, although she'd thought about it from time to time. Never very seriously, though, and she wasn't giving it serious consideration now, but it did raise some questions. For instance, would it count? Would she feel the same need to wipe the slate clean afterward?

✿

Monday morning she didn't get to the Barling lot until 11:45. It wasn't until 12:20 that she spotted him, and for a change he was all by himself. He headed for his car, and she began walking in that direction herself. *Oh, aren't you Graham Weider?* A chance meeting in a parking lot where she had no reason to be. No, she thought, maybe not.

She stopped walking and watched as he got into his car and drove off. He was wearing a jacket this time. It was at least as warm as it had been the other times she'd watched him head off to lunch, and previously he'd always gone in shirtsleeves, so what would Sherlock make of that?

A lunch date with someone from outside the company. A business associate? A golf or tennis partner? Or, just possibly, a lady friend?

If she had a car she could follow him. If someone had just left a key in their ignition—

Oh, please. What were the odds of that? No point in looking, and couldn't she come up with a better way?

She got out her phone, punched in numbers, found a way around voicemail. To the woman who answered she said, "Is Graham Weider there? I missed him? I was afraid of that. I've got something he needs for his meeting and I was supposed to drop it at the restaurant, but I can't remember…Yes, of course, that's it. Thanks, thanks so much, you've been very helpful. And could you please not tell him I had to call? He'll think I'm an idiot."

It took fifteen minutes of hard pedaling to get her to the Cattle Baron, a strip mall steak house that didn't look very baronial from the outside. Was she dressed for it? Could she leave her bike and expect it to be there later? And, after all that bicycling, did she smell?

She brushed the questions aside and entered the restaurant. She spotted Weider right away in a corner booth with three companions, all of them men in suits. Which made it easier, really, than if he were with a woman.

She told the maitre d' a friend would be joining her, and he put her at a table for two. She ordered a white wine spritzer, then went straight to the restroom to freshen up and put on lipstick. She checked, and her underarms passed the sniff test. While she didn't exactly feel like an Irish Spring commercial, neither was she likely to knock a buzzard off a slaughterhouse wagon.

She headed for her table, then did a take when she caught sight of the four men in the corner. She hesitated, then walked directly to their booth. They all looked at her, but she looked only at Weider.

"Excuse me," she said, "but aren't you Graham Weider?"

He hesitated, clearly not knowing who she was, and the man sitting next to him said, "If he's not, ma'am, then I am. I'm sure I'd make just as good a Graham Weider as he ever could."

"It's been a few years," she said. "And I only met you briefly, so you're forgiven if you don't remember my name." *Or, clearly, anything else about me.* "It's Kim."

She had no idea what name she might have used when she was with him. She'd become Kim when she moved into Rita's house, so it was simplest all around to remain Kim with Graham Weider. And it would be an easy name for him to remember. Though not, she trusted, for very long.

"Kim," he said, as if testing a foreign word on his tongue. He had a gratifying deer-in-the-headlights look.

"I don't want to take any more of your time," she said, "but do you have a card? I'd love to call you and catch up."

She gave each of them a smile, especially the one who'd volunteered to take Weider's place. He was cute, and he'd be about as hard to get as coffee at Starbucks. How tough would it be to fuck him in the restroom and leave him dead in a stall?

Without returning to her table, she caught up with her waitress and gave her enough money to cover the drink. She'd had a phone call, she explained, and her lunch partner had to cancel, so she was going straight on to her next meeting.

Her bike was right where she'd left it. There was a hardware store right there on the strip mall, and she went in and bought a bicycle lock. Just to be on the safe side.

She didn't really need his card. She already knew how to reach him at his office. But if she called him without having been given his number, she'd look for all the world like a stalker.

Which, come to think of it, she was.

She called him late that afternoon, caught him before he left for the day. "It's Kim," she said, "and I want to apologize. I never should have barged in while you were with other people. But it was such a surprise to run into you after all those years."

"I'd like to catch up," he said, "but I'm not sure—"

"That the phone's the best way to do it? I feel the same way, believe me. Why don't we have lunch tomorrow?"

"Lunch?"

"My treat," she said. "You bought me lunch last time. So it's my turn. But I'm new in the area. Can you suggest a place?"

The restaurant was Italian, its Mulberry Street décor of check-ered tablecloths and straw-covered Chianti bottles at odds with its strip mall location. She'd allowed herself half an hour to get there and made it with seven minutes to spare. After she'd stashed Rita's bike and locked it, she used the restroom at a convenience store, checked her makeup, freshened her lipstick. She entered the restaurant right on time, and he was at one of the three occupied tables, a cup of coffee at his elbow.

He got to his feet when he caught sight of her. He was wearing a jacket and tie, and—no surprise—a wary expression. A handsome man, she noted, and felt a little quiver of anticipatory excitement. This was going to be fun, she thought, and it would end well, too.

He had a hand extended, but instead of shaking it she gripped his forearm with both hands and leaned forward, giving him no real choice but to kiss her cheek and breathe in her scent.

"Well," she said, and held his eyes for a moment. Then she sat down, and so did he, and he asked her if she'd like a drink. "If you're having one," she said.

"Just coffee for me."

"That sounds good."

He signaled the waiter, and he asked if she'd had trouble finding the place. She said she hadn't, but managed to tell him she'd come by bicycle. *Isn't that crazy? Some idiot hit my car and I can't get a loaner while it's in the shop, so I've been getting around on a bicycle.*

Then the waiter brought her coffee and refilled Graham's cup and left them alone, and after a thoughtful silence he said, "When exactly did we—"

"It was a few years ago. I was living in New York, and you were there on business. You were with Willoughby & Kessel, and you were staying at the Sofitel."

"That's where I always stayed."

"I can see why," she said. "You had a lovely room."

"I guess we did more than have lunch."

"I'll say."

He took a sip of coffee. "I won't pretend I recognized you," he said, "but when I saw you I had the sense that we'd been, uh, intimate."

"We had lunch and went back to your room. Then you had to go to a meeting, and we arranged to meet again later that day. But you didn't show up, and left a note for me at the desk. You had to fly somewhere."

"Oh, God," he said. "I remember now."

"Well, good, Graham. I thought that might trigger your memory. I figured it was either that or show you my tits."

She thought that would get a smile. Instead his face darkened, and he reached again for his coffee cup, the way a person might reach for a real drink.

And, while she didn't realize it yet, that pretty much explained everything.

"In those days," he said, "I was doing a lot of drinking."

Was he? "I guess you had a drink or two with lunch," she said. "I don't think it affected you."

"Oh, it affected me."

"Not back at the Sofitel it didn't. Not in the performance department."

"Sometimes it did, sometimes it didn't. I guess that must have been a good day."

"A very good day," she said.

He colored. "This is hard for me," he said.

*It was certainly hard for me,* she thought. But she left the words unvoiced, sensing that double entendre was not what the situation called for.

"I was married then," he said.

She glanced at his ring. "So? You're married now."

"Different lady."

"Ah."

"See, I drank my way out of my first marriage."

"And into a second one?"

He shook his head. He hadn't even met his second wife until a full year after he'd stopped drinking. First his marriage ended, then his career went into the toilet, and eventually he found his way to rehab.

"To stop drinking," she said.

"Well, that was the first rehab. For drinking."

"There was a second?"

He nodded. "It turned out drinking was the symptom. The second rehab addressed the real problem."

"And what was that?"

"Sexual compulsivity. I was addicted to sex."

"Maybe that's why you were so good at it."

Most men would have taken that as a compliment, but he recoiled from it as if from a blow.

"It almost killed me," he said. "I was lucky. I went through rehab for it, and I joined SCA, and—"

"SCA?"

"Sexual Compulsives Anonymous."

After the waiter took their orders—pasta and a salad for both— he told her his story in more detail than she really required, and she found herself boiling it down to a single long sentence: *I used to drink and I used to smoke and I used to gamble and I used to fuck around and now I don't do any of these things but instead lead this glorious rich fulfilling life of fidelity and sobriety and moral decency and utter unremitting stifling boredom.*

"I guess that explains the coffee," she said.

"Uh-huh. But there's no reason you can't have a drink if you want one."

"And risk an arrest for drunken bicycling? No, I'm fine with coffee. SCA, huh? Are their meetings like AA? Do you tell each other all the things you used to do in the good old days?"

"We tell our stories," he said, "but it's a little different, because we have to guard against getting off on what we tell, or what we hear. So the stories are intentionally vague. 'I acted out with a partner, I acted out alone, I acted out with a group—' "

" 'I acted out with two nuns and a sheep.' I was thinking that the meetings might be fun, but you nipped that little fantasy in the bud. So you used to act out and now you don't, and I gather you're happily married, and did you say you've got a kid?"

He nodded. "And speaking of bicycles, he's learning to ride one."

*It's a tricycle, and he still hasn't learned to put it in the garage.* But of course she couldn't say that.

The food came, and he said he knew she'd offered to buy him lunch, but it was going to have to be on him. This, he said, would be a small way of making it up to her for the way he'd treated her in New York, back in the bad old days.

"You treated me fine," she said.

"I was acting out sexually, and I exploited you."

"Acting out? Whatever it was you were doing, I was doing it, too. And I must have enjoyed it, and felt just fine about it, or I wouldn't have hit on you yesterday."

"You weren't hitting on me."

"Yes I was," she said. "It's what I'm doing now, too. In case you hadn't noticed."

"Kim—"

"I know you're attracted to me. Aren't you?"

"You're a very attractive woman."

"And you're an extremely attractive man, and if there weren't other people around I'd be under the table with your cock in my mouth. You used to like that, and I'll bet you still do."

"We shouldn't be having this conversation."

"Why not? Graham, I *know* you, I know what you *like*. Are you going to try pretending you don't enjoy having your cock sucked?"

He just looked at her. He was getting hard, she could tell. And something came back to her, some rush of memory from out of nowhere.

"You wanted to fuck me in the ass! *That's* what you promised me, when you went off to your meeting. We'd meet for dinner and come back to the room, and you'd have plenty of lube on hand, and you'd fuck me up my ass." She looked at him levelly, licked her lips. "See? If you want to make it up to me, that'd be a good place to start. You owe me."

The son of a bitch was hopeless. He went to AA meetings and SCA meetings, so no wonder he didn't have time to mow his lawn. SCA might have been fun if there was a decent amount of back-sliding involved, but he took it seriously, the idiot, and he took his wedding vows seriously, especially the part about forsaking all others.

It infuriated her, and she was on the verge of losing it when she caught hold of herself. No point in cursing the fish when it wouldn't take the bait. More effective to reel in and try again.

"I'm sorry, Graham," she said. "I guess I'm not used to rejection. It's not something I get a lot of."

"I'm not rejecting *you*, Kim. It's just—"

"I understand. You'd actually love to fuck me, but you won't let yourself. Because it doesn't fit with your new life."

"I might not have phrased it quite that way. But that's close enough."

"So now we'll go our separate ways," she said. "Will you think about me when you masturbate?"

He flushed deeply.

"I get it," she said. "You don't do that anymore either, right?"

"It's a form of acting out," he said, "that we don't encourage."

"*We* meaning SCA?"

He nodded.

"I'm glad I'm not a member," she said, "because I have to tell you, Graham, I'm gonna have my hands full tonight. I'll put on some music and I'll get out my sex toys and I'll imagine all the things you and I aren't gonna do to each other. Oh, is this conversation making you uncomfortable?"

"I think you know it is."

"Well, if you get all worked up, you can go home and knock off a good one with Wifey. The two of you do have sex, don't you?"

"Of course we do."

"You'll be thinking of me," she said.

"That's not true."

"It's not? Oh, I think it is. You'll be inside your precious wife, in whatever position's ordinary enough so that it doesn't come under the heading of 'acting out,' but in your mind you'll be doing me in the ass. You'll be hotter than a forest fire and she'll wonder what got into you, and in the morning you'll be all racked with guilt and have to go to a meeting to confess your sins to your buddies. But you won't dare be too specific about it, or they'd all get hot and the meeting would turn into one big circle jerk. Which, now that I think about it, would be a big improvement all around."

Well, gee, she'd lost it after all, hadn't she?

# ELEVEN

Rita was cooking something. The aroma, richly inviting, caught her up when she opened the door.

She'd prowled around restlessly all afternoon. First a movie at a mall theater, where she kept changing her seat. That was easy enough, the theater was weekday-afternoon empty, but she couldn't find a seat that wasn't too near or too far from the screen, couldn't let herself get into the story, and finally couldn't remain in the theater for longer than forty minutes.

She stalked out, then roamed the mall, walking in and out of stores and up and down aisles. She didn't need anything, didn't want to buy anything, but she tried on a pair of jeans in one boutique and flirted with a cell-phone salesman in the Radio Shack. It occurred to her to take him in back, to an office or rest room, and scratch the itch that Graham Weider had inflicted. Blow him, fuck him, whatever. And then kill him, but with what? There might be something in the back, a pair of heavy-duty scissors, a letter opener, a heavy glass ashtray to hit him with. No, not an ashtray, because smoking wouldn't be allowed, but maybe a desk lamp, maybe a paperweight.

Could you count on finding something? No, of course you couldn't. And the guy was a doofus anyway, built full in the hips, and he waddled like a penguin, and she didn't really want to do him in the first place. She wanted to do Graham Weider, and she couldn't, the bastard had turned her down, and the way her luck was running today she'd get the same reception from the penguin, and she wasn't sure she could take it.

She got out of there. And found another store to walk into, and walk out of.

And now she was back home, and Rita was telling her that she hoped Kim hadn't eaten, because the only way the beef bourguignon recipe worked was if you cooked enough for four, so—

"It smells terrific," she said, "and no, I haven't eaten. In fact I didn't have much of a lunch. I'll be back in fifteen minutes, how's that?"

She hopped on her bike and rode to a liquor store she'd noted earlier. What did you drink with beef bourguignon? The clerk, who couldn't keep his eyes off her tits, recommended a Nuits-Saint-Georges or a Chateauneuf du Pape. The Nuits-Saint-Georges was two dollars cheaper, and that made the decision for her.

Pull the clerk into the back room? The look on his face suggested he wouldn't put up much of a struggle, and afterward the wine bottle would serve as a handy blunt instrument. He was all alone in the store, so she could go through the register on her way out, and very likely pocket a few hundred bucks for her trouble. And then she could take the murder weapon home and share its contents with her landlady, and that had a certain undeniable appeal.

*Oh, get over it; will you?*

She got on her bike and headed for home.

The wine made quite an impression on Rita. "Oh, I bought wine," she said, "but nothing anywhere near this good. I picked up a half-gallon of California red and used half of it in the stew, thinking we'd drink the rest with the meal. But we have to have yours, it's a Burgundy, it should be perfect with beef bourguignon."

As indeed it was. The meal was simple, just the main course and a salad, and she hadn't eaten since she stormed out of the Italian place in the middle of lunch, and Rita had prepared a superb meal. She had the radio tuned to an Easy Listening station, and the conversation stayed comfortably superficial until they were about halfway through the bottle of Nuits-Saint-Georges.

Then, complimenting the meal again, she said that this was turning out to be an acceptable day after all.

"You had a bad day, Kim?"

Could she talk about it? She'd have to drop the central element, but maybe it wouldn't hurt to talk around it a little.

"I've been running around like a bitch in heat," she said. "I've been so damned horny all day I could scream. I probably shouldn't be talking like that—"

"Oh, I've heard worse." Rita raised her wine glass. "And had days like that myself. A lot of them, actually."

"Maybe it's the bike," she said. "All that low-grade stimulation in that general area."

"The vibration and all."

She reached for the wine bottle, filled Rita's glass, then her own. "Here's to vibration," she said.

"You said it."

"Speaking of which," she said, "*that's* what I should have bought. I kept walking in and out of mall stores, and never buying a thing. Maybe that's what I was really looking for."

"A vibrator?"

"Uh-huh. The one I had gave up the ghost after years of loyal service. God, will you listen to me? This wine must be having an effect."

"It's the company," Rita said. "I have the feeling you and I can say things to each other that neither of us could say to anybody else."

That had to be the wine talking, she thought. On the other hand, wasn't there supposed to be truth in wine?

"Not that I absolutely have to have a vibrator," she found herself saying. She raised her hand, wiggled her fingers. "I come prepared. And, as far as that goes, I'm prepared to come."

"Kim, you're a riot!"

"Well, why pretend the evening's going to end with prayer and meditation? When the wine's gone I'm going to hole' up in my bedroom and treat myself to an orgasm that'll make the walls shake. And I might as well tell you about it, Rita, because you'll probably hear me. I tend to make a little noise when I get off."

"Oh? Did you hear me the night before last?"

"No."

"It's probably just as well."

"Oh?"

"Can I tell you? I probably shouldn't. But—"

"Oh, come on, Rita. Don't be a tease."

"Maybe if I have another glass of wine. Oh, the bottle's empty. Do you think we could switch to the jug wine? It'll be a disappointment after the Nooee—I don't know how to pronounce it."

"The French stuff."

"That's it, the French stuff."

"And at this point it'll taste fine, Rita. We're past the point of being able to tell the difference."

"I think you're right. Well, here's to the French, and the wonderful things they come up with."

"God, I'll drink to that." She did, and said, "This tastes fine to me. And now you can tell me about the night before last."

"Oh God. Well, okay. I was on the phone."

"With—?"

"Someone I met on the Internet, except I didn't ever actually meet him. I got his number, and I call him, and we give each other phone sex."

"How does that work?"

"Well, you know."

"Rita—"

"We talk dirty."

"Like 'I want to eat your pussy, I want to suck your cock'? Like that?"

"Some of that. More like telling stories."

"Things you did."

"Except they're partly made up. Mine are, anyway, and I'm pretty sure his are, too. Not over the top, like pornography, because it's more exciting if it's realistic enough so that you can believe it."

"And he'll tell you a story while you—"

"Pleasure myself. Pretty pathetic, huh?"

"It sounds hot."

"You think?"

"I'm getting hot thinking about it," she said. "You've got his voice in your ear and your fingers in your pussy. You bet it's hot."

Rita giggled. "One problem," she said. "Can you guess?"

"You can only use one hand."

"That's right! Omigod, how did you guess it so fast?"

"It just came to me. What's the matter with speakerphone?"

"I've only got it on the kitchen phone. Anyway, you wouldn't want the whole room echoing with it, would you?"

"I see what you mean."

"It's nicer to have his voice right there in my ear."

"And your finger right there in your cunt. Oops, I said the C word, didn't I?"

"I *love* the C word! It's supposed to be disgusting and demeaning to women, but I just don't get that at all. Cunt, cunt, *cunt*! Could anybody ever come up with a hotter word than that? Just saying it is getting me hot."

"I may not be the only one who ends the evening jilling off."

"Jilling—oh, like jacking off but for girls! God, I never heard that before. No, you won't be the only one, Kimmie."

*Kimmie?*

"In fact, I was trying to think of a way to offer you the use of my vibrator."

"But you're going to need it yourself."

"I'm going to need something."

"Will you call your friend?"

"My friend? Oh, Paul. If that's his name, which I'm sure it isn't, any more than mine is Justine. I wouldn't dream of giving him my real name, so why should he give me his?"

"And you call him?"

"In other words, can't he get my number and trace me that way? I bought one of those prepaid phones. Lots of luck tracing the number."

"You bought it just for phone sex?"

"God, doesn't that make me sound like a pervert."

"More like a femme fatale."

"A femme fatale! *Much* better. But no, I won't call him tonight. You know what he wanted me to do? Call him on Skype. It's like a phone call except you do it online, so you can see each other on your computers. No way I'm gonna do that."

"You don't want to see him?"

"On the phone," Rita said, "he looks just the way I want him to look. And I look however he wants to picture me. But it's more than that. I couldn't possibly say the things I want to say if I've got him looking me in the eye. So I'll stick to the phone, but not tonight, because I won't need him. My cunt's on fire already."

"I see what you mean about the C word."

"I know, isn't it just the cuntiest word there is? I can't believe it, we finished the wine."

"I don't feel drunk or anything."

"No, neither do I. I just feel good."

"Me too."

"And hot."

"Well, I told you what I've been like all day long. But then it just felt frustrating, and now it feels kind of nice."

"I know what you mean, Kimmie." A sigh. "So I guess we ought to go to our separate rooms and pretend we can't hear each other moaning."

"Unless—"

"Unless what?"

"We could give each other phone sex," she said, "but without the phone."

"How would that work?"

"It's not something I've ever done, Rita, and I can't imagine ever doing it with anybody else—"

"And?"

"Suppose instead of going into separate rooms," she said, "we both sat in the living room. And we could tell each other stories, but real ones, you know? Things we did that were hot."

"And touched ourselves."

"Right."

"Played with our cunts. Our *own* cunts, I mean. 'Cause I don't think—"

"No, I wouldn't be up for that myself."

"Good, because neither would I. Did you ever—?"

"With another girl? No, never."

"Neither did I."

"Though I'll admit there were times I thought about it."

"Oh, how could you help it? But thinking and doing—"

"Two different things."

"Exactly. But telling stories and getting each other off that way—Kimmie, we've just got to try it."

"I know."

"I can almost come just from the idea of it, you know? Kimmie—God, I should have asked, is it all right if I call you Kimmie?"

"Sure."

"Do lots of people call you that?"

"You're the first."

"Honestly? And you're sure you don't mind?"

"I kind of like it."

"Rhymes with gimme."

"I was thinking that."

" 'Gimme, Kimmie.' You know what let's do? Let's put on night-gowns, because I wouldn't want us to be naked, but we ought to have—"

"Access."

"Exactly!"

"Except I don't own a nightgown."

"You don't? So you'll wear one of mine. It'll be a little big on you, but that shouldn't be a problem."

"Not at all."

"And borrowing one of my nightgowns isn't quite like using my vibrator."

"And sticking it up my cunt."

"Oh, God, stop it! You're just saying that word because you know what it does to me."

❀

"After working there for one hour, I knew two things for certain. One, I couldn't stand the raw animal stink of that man. Every breath I took felt like I was putting something filthy in my lungs. And two, I was going to have sex with him. The smell might be making me sick to my stomach, but it was sending a message straight to my clit. Nothing on earth was going to keep me from fucking him."

They were in the living room, curled up in armchairs on opposite sides of the marble-topped coffee table. Their shortie nightgowns were identical except for color; Rita's was shell-pink, hers apricot. They'd sat there for a few minutes, lamenting that the wine was finished, agreeing that they didn't really need any more of it, and anticipating the rest of the evening with edgy excitement.

Rita's vibrator sat on the coffee table. Rita had switched it on to check the batteries, and it hummed softly for a few seconds before she silenced it. It was the exact color of its owner's nightie, a simple pink cylinder with nothing specifically penis-like about it aside from its overall shape. That made it less blatant than some anatomically correct device with a glans and veins, but it was right there where either of them could reach out and take hold of it.

Rita's legs showed clear to the tops of her thighs. They'd never hire her to model stockings, but they were nice legs all the same. And she'd already noted that Rita's full breasts were nicely shaped, but the sheer nightie gave her a much better view of them.

She took a breath and got the ball rolling.

And she told all about Steve, and the diner in Phoenix. Except, of course, she had to change things. She relocated the place from Phoenix to Denver, situating it on one of the side streets off Colfax Avenue. She changed Steve's name to George, and she made herself younger, putting the whole incident four years earlier, when she was a college student on summer break.

More to the point, she changed the ending. There was no knife, no feverish thrusting with the blade, no blood spattering her clothes, no blood pooling on the kitchen floor.

And it didn't feel as though she was holding anything back, because the story changed first in her mind, and all she had to do was recount what happened with George, and how he looked and smelled, and how he fucked her. The first time was as it had been with Steve, but in the telling now there was a second time as well, and then he reopened the diner for the noon rush and she worked all afternoon, smelling of him, while his bodily fluids leaked out of her vagina and trickled down her thighs. Except she didn't say vagina, she said cunt, just to make sure Rita stayed interested.

And then there was a third time, after he closed the place for the day, and he took her in the kitchen again and made her go down on him, with his dick reeking of both of them, and then he fucked her like a mad bull, and she went home and took a dozen showers and burned her clothes and never went back.

Early in the account, she'd seen Rita's hand slip under her nightgown. It stayed there, but it wasn't always busy, and she knew that Rita was holding back, keeping herself on the edge, wanting her own climax to coincide with the story's.

She almost made it. She held off until, during their final trip to the kitchen, she got off a few sentences before George did.

"You never went back."

"Rita, I wouldn't even walk down that block. I was afraid to walk past the diner."

"Like you'd be powerless to keep from going inside?"

"Sort of."

"Wow. I have to tell you, Kimmie, this is tons better than phone sex with Paul."

"Well, sure. This way you got to use both hands."

"Were you watching?"

"Of course."

"That made it hotter, somehow. Watching you watching me. But the main thing was you told it so well, Kimmie! It's like I was right there while it was happening. I could smell him myself."

"Whatever you imagined," she said, "the real George was worse."

"Gosh." Deep breath. "I guess it's my turn, huh?"

"Your turn to tell all," she said, and put her hand under her nightie. "My turn to play."

# TWELVE

Rita had married young. Her husband was her own age, and not much more experienced than she was, and their sex was all vanilla and white bread. He never went down on her, and when she demurred at his suggestion that she go down on him, he seemed almost relieved. So she never did, and he never brought it up again, and after half a dozen years during which they were unable to conceive a child— "And thank God for that!"—they were divorced.

Eventually she started dating again, and the next man she went to bed with introduced oral sex into the relationship. At first she didn't like it when he went down on her, but then she did. Like, a lot. So she couldn't really pull away when he steered her face toward his dick.

"But I didn't know what I was doing, you know? And I didn't have a lot in the way of natural aptitude. Maybe some girls are born knowing how, or these days with all the Internet porn you can at least see how it's done, and maybe that's a help. But whatever I was doing, he didn't like it much. He actually made me stop.

"And I thought, well, I'll try to do better next time. But there wasn't a next time, because he didn't call me again."

There were other men, and she began to enjoy giving head, and didn't wait for her partner to suggest it. She liked when it was small and soft and she could make it grow in her mouth. But when her mouth had worked its magic, transforming small-and-soft into big-and-hard, then she didn't know what to do with it.

Sometimes it worked anyway, sort of. "The first time a guy came in my mouth I loved it. Loved it! I was afraid I'd be disgusted, but I wasn't, not at all, and I wanted to gulp down every last drop. I swear I could feel all that energy going right into the cells of my body."

But she still wasn't good at it. What she needed was a course of instruction, and she was trying to build up her courage to hire a prostitute to give her lessons, when something better came along.

"What is it they say, Kimmie? *When the pupil is ready the master will appear?* That's exactly what happened."

The master was her hairdresser, Brian, a flamboyant queen who told the most outrageous stories and somehow invited confidences. "It's not that I don't *like* to do it," she told him, "it's that I don't know what I'm doing." And then, after they'd discussed the subject for a while, "I'll bet *you* could teach me."

He showed up the following night with a present for her, and she knew what it held before she got it unwrapped. "A dildo," she said, "and unlike my discreet vibrator, you could say it was anatomically correct, veins and all. They must have done a casting. Kimmie, if I ever meet the guy whose dick they used, I swear I'll be able to recognize him, because it'll be like running into an old friend."

Brian taught her what to do, and watched what she did, and commented on her technique. She was horribly self-conscious at first, but she got over it, and it began to seem natural enough, sucking on a rubber cock while her coach critiqued her performance. Then he left her to practice, and she sat up for hours fellating the dildo.

"Then I took it and stuck it in. In my *cunt*, Kimmie, and after I got off I took it out and sucked it some more. Before, the one thing wrong with it was it didn't taste like anything, and now it tasted like me."

She had a hand under the borrowed nightie, stroking herself

gently while Rita went on talking. This was no fabrication, no improvement on the truth, like her transformation of Steve into George. She could tell that Rita was recounting her education exactly as she remembered it, but at the same time it was very much a performance, designed to excite her good friend Kimmie.

And it was working. She'd been horribly frustrated, unable to seduce that moralistic moron Graham Weider, and thus unable to cross him off her list of unfinished business. And she'd have masturbated this evening, she'd have had to if she was going to get any sleep, but this was worlds different from fingering herself in the privacy of her bedroom.

This was kind of gay, actually.

She was listening to Rita, hearing how they'd had a second lesson, which concluded with Brian telling his pupil that she'd be able to make some lucky straight guy very happy. And she was watching Rita, watching her lick her lips, watching her put her own hand between her own legs and finger herself idly as she talked. And she was checking out the swell of Rita's breasts, and the shape of Rita's legs, and she could feel Rita's eyes on her own body, and without really thinking about it she whipped the nightie over her head and tossed it aside.

Rita's story stopped in mid-sentence.

"No, don't stop," she told Rita. "I was just feeling warm, you know? And if I'm going to sit here jilling off in front of you, it seems silly to hide my tits." She cupped a breast, and could feel Rita's gaze on it. "Or my cunt," she said, and opened her legs, holding the pose for a long moment before putting her hand back where it had been before. "Now tell me the rest," she said. "Once you got your diploma from the Academy of Brian, who was the lucky guy?"

*

The lucky guy, as it happened, turned out to be Brian.

It wasn't his idea. She had to suggest it, and then she had to talk him into it. "I'm *gay*," he kept insisting. "It's not as though I've never *been* with women. I have, on several occasions, but let's just say I've *been* there and *done* that, and it's just not *me*."

"I don't want to get married," she told him. "I don't even want you to kiss me goodnight later. I just want to blow you. What's so bad about that?"

Nothing, as it turned out.

He agreed, finally, and it turned out to be a lesson, because he offered suggestions and feedback as she went along. And somewhere along the way she graduated, because there was a shift in the energy and she was in command, she was in control, and what a delicious feeling that was.

Afterward, he suggested that maybe he should open a school, an academy of fellatio.

"Won't you offer any other courses?"

"Like what? Brian Van Horn's Academy of Fellatio and Hairdressing? I don't think—"

"There must be something else you could teach me," she said. "And I'm not talking about hairdressing."

Rita looked at her, took a deep breath, and took off her own nightgown. "And now you can see *my* tits, Kimmie, and watch me play with *my* cunt, while I tell you how he taught me all about rimming. Among other things."

So hot.

She had never been with a woman. It was not as though it had never occurred to her. But whatever thoughts she'd ever entertained had stopped somewhere between speculation and fantasy. She'd certainly never thought about acting on them.

Or acting them out, as Graham Weider would put it.

It would be so easy now. They were both naked, they were both touching themselves, the whole evening was about nothing but sex, and all she had to do was cross the room. *Let me give you a hand, Rita. Let me play with that for you. What a beautiful cunt, Rita. Can I touch it? Can I kiss it for you?*

And then what?

Would she have to kill her?

She considered the question later, lying alone in her own bed. She had stayed in her chair, and had confined her caresses to her own body. There had been that moment when they might have made love, and they hadn't done so, and the moment had passed. Now they were in their separate bedrooms, and all that was left to do was sleep.

But what if she'd made love to Rita? *That was lovely, Rita. My very first time with a woman, and I have to say I liked it. Excuse me a moment, will you? I have to go to the kitchen to pick up something sharp.*

Or not. How could she be sure?

When she stepped outside herself, when she allowed herself a little perspective, it wasn't hard to see why she acted as she did. The signal event of her childhood and adolescence was the long affair she'd had with her father, who'd very artfully seduced her and then, ultimately, rejected her. And she'd erased that blot from her life by erasing the man himself, and once he was dead it was as if he had never been.

Except, of course, that it wasn't. But he wasn't alive, couldn't sit smirking, remembering what he'd done to her, what he'd taught her to do to him. He remained on the list, but there was a line through his name, and whenever another man had earned a place on that list, she'd seen to it that his name had a line through it.

All but four names.

If she had sex with a woman, would hers be the fifth name? And would she feel a compelling urge, an actual need, to draw a line through that name?

No way to know. Not for sure.

She didn't want to kill Rita. She wanted to kill Graham, Christ how she wanted to kill him, and she thought of all the other men, most of their names metaphorically crossed out almost as soon as they'd been inked in. She'd wanted sex with them, and afterward she'd wanted them dead. For a while it was a matter of taking care of business, but when she thought of Steve in Phoenix, she realized that it had become something more than that. She'd reached a point where the sex act itself wasn't complete as long as her partner had a pulse. That was the true orgasm: when she struck like a cobra, and the man died.

Withheld, she was left with an itch she couldn't scratch. Even now, after God knows how many orgasms, after she'd finished herself off with the vibrator, its surface still dewy with Rita's juices, even now she found it maddening, infuriating, that she'd found a Graham Weider who'd become immune to her powers. Was he going to be on her list forever?

*Oh, for Christ's sake.*

The answer came to her in a flash. With it she felt an emotional release none of the evening's orgasms had managed to provide, and she drifted off and slept like a baby.

# THIRTEEN

"Graham? It's Kim. Please don't hang up."

A silence. Then, "All right."

"First of all, I want to apologize. I don't know what got into me yesterday."

"That's all right."

"No," she said, "it's not all right. It was completely inappropriate and wholly unwarranted. I was disrespectful to you and made a fool of myself in the process."

"I've had plenty of apologies to make," he said. "So it's not hard for me to accept yours, Kim."

"Thank you." She drew a breath. "Those apologies," she said. "Would they be in connection with those meetings you've been going to?"

"It's a 12-Step program," he said, "and yes, making amends is very much a part of the program."

"You told me the name of it, but I—"

"Sexual Compulsives Anonymous."

"Right, SCA. Funny how I can't seem to remember the name. Or maybe it's not so funny after all."

He waited, and she let the silence stretch.

Then she said, "My life's not working so well these days."

"I see."

"Not just these days. For quite a while now. What was the term you used? 'Acting out'? It seems like all I'm ever doing is acting out, or trying to, or thinking about it."

"I understand, Kim. I've been there."

"Can anyone go to these meetings? Or do you have to be a member?"

"Would you like to come to a meeting?"

"Would I like to? Probably about as much as I'd like to have root canal. But it's that or lose the tooth. Graham, it's not a question of would I like to. I think it's something I have to do."

"Hold on a minute. Okay, let's see. There's a meeting in downtown Seattle this afternoon, but I'll be busy. If you don't mind going by yourself—"

"I think I'd be more comfortable if you went with me."

"Well, let me see. How's lunch time tomorrow? There's a 12:30 meeting I sometimes go to in downtown Redmond near Marymoor Park. I could meet you there and we could walk in together."

"I'm not sure I could find it. And on a bike—"

"No, that's too far by bicycle. Maybe—"

"Graham? Suppose I come to where you work? I could meet you in the parking lot. At twelve? Or maybe a little earlier, so you can tell me a little about it before we actually walk in?"

She stayed out all day, ate dinner by herself at an Indian restaurant that served bland food dumbed down for the Western palate. She got the waiter to bring her hot sauce, and that helped, but she'd have been happier if the heat had been cooked into the food, not spooned on top of it.

It was almost eight when she got home, and she steeled herself to walk in to the smell of a home-cooked meal, and a housemate who wanted a reprise of the previous evening. But she encountered neither; there'd been no cooking since last night's dinner, and no car in the garage.

There was leftover coffee and she reheated a cup and drank it at the kitchen table while she read that month's *Vanity Fair.* She'd almost finished the coffee when she heard the garage door ascend, and she stayed where she was until she heard Rita and a man in conversation. She rose quickly, scooped up her cup and the magazine, and was in her room with the door closed before the two of them had cleared the threshold.

"Kimmie? Are you awake?"

No one, not even a devout Crystal Methodist, could have been more thoroughly awake. But did she have to admit it? If she just kept silent—

"Kimmie?"

If she kept silent, Rita would walk right in.

"I'm awake," she said. "But kind of drifty."

"He's gone. I sent him home."

*Oh? Were you with someone? I never would have guessed.*

"I suppose you heard us."

"Just barely."

"He was a guy who hit on me a couple of times. I was never interested. But after last night—well, let's just say I was in the mood."

*No kidding.*

"Kimmie, you're half asleep. We'll talk at breakfast."

Footsteps receded. Rita's door opened and closed.

And she lay in bed, waiting for daybreak.

A toasted English muffin and a cup of coffee. And Rita, wearing a belted housecoat, with her own English muffin and her own cup of coffee, and a full report.

"We fucked on the couch," she said. "He's going bald, and he could stand to lose a few pounds, but he was okay otherwise. Nice circumcised dick, medium in size. We didn't do anything you couldn't find in the *Kama Sutra,* but it was interesting enough. I mean, I came a lot."

"I know."

"That was on purpose. The noise, I mean. I knew you could hear, and the idea of you hearing made it a lot more exciting. You know what I was wishing?"

"What?"

"That you could sneak in and watch."

"Would you have liked that?"

"Are you kidding? I'd have loved it."

"It never even occurred to me."

"I didn't think it would. Or that you'd do it, even if you thought of it. You know what was going on in my head the whole time? Absolutely the whole time? How hot it would be when I told you all about it."

"Really."

"How's that for weird? I mean, it's like normal to think about fucking while you masturbate, but having fantasies of masturbating while somebody's got his dick in you?"

"But I can see how it could happen."

"So you don't think I'm weird?"

"Oh, you're plenty weird, Rita. But not in a bad way."

"I'll settle for that. And I could probably say the same about you."

"Moi?"

"You and that guy who smelled."

"Yeah, I can see where you could call me weird for that one."

"I might have done it myself," Rita said, "but I'd have wanted to kill him afterward."

*Oh, sweetie, if you only knew —*

"Oops," she said, getting to her feet. "I've got an appointment I'll be lucky to get to on time."

"You want me to drive you?"

"No, I'll be fine with the bike. But I was thinking maybe tonight—"

"We're on the same page. But I'm not gonna bother cooking. You up for it if I order a pizza?

"Sure. And I don't know when I'll be home, so don't order it until I get here."

"And this time I'll buy the wine. How do you say what we had, Nooey San George's?"

"Close enough."

"And don't worry that this is going to make us lesbians. I mean, that was a guy I was on the couch with, you know?"

"I don't know if I'm ready for this," she said. "the thing is, I still get a lot of pleasure out of it."

"Acting out?"

"Right. I realize I'm compulsive about it, and it's almost as if I don't have any choice, but, you know, it feels good."

"Of course it does," he said. "And you may not be ready to stop. It always felt good to me, too."

"It did?"

"But less so," he said, "toward the end. That's not why I stopped, I stopped because sexual compulsivity was making my life unmanageable, but the pleasure did drop off as time went on. Even at the moment of release I'd find myself thinking about the next time. And, of course, regretting everything that was regrettable about the present moment."

She told him she guessed she could relate to that.

She'd met him in the parking lot at a quarter to twelve, wearing jeans and a modest top, with a capacious shoulder bag on her arm. She'd locked her bike to the cyclone fence and joined him in the front seat of the Subaru. And now they were on their way to the meeting in Redmond, and conversation was no problem, because all she had to do was get it started and he'd carry the ball, telling her chunks of his story of sin and redemption. It would have been more interesting if he'd gone into detail, but as she already knew, not going into detail was part of the SCA program, because God forbid any of them should get any pleasure out of anything for the rest of their miserable lives.

"Here we are," he said, eventually, and waited to make a left turn into a church parking lot. There were a handful of cars all clustered at the front of the lot, and nothing but a van farther back.

She said, "Graham? Could we stop for a minute? There's something I need to say." He braked, and she said, "Maybe if you could pull up, oh, near that van? Like, away from all these cars?"

He drove to the rear of the lot, swung the Subaru around and pulled up next to the van. That vehicle's side bore the name of the church, and the injunction to get right with God.

*Now you tell me.*

She unbuckled her seat belt, slipped her right hand into her shoulder bag. He kept his own seat belt fastened, she noted with approval, so he'd be safely buckled up during the hazardous five-mile-an-hour return trip to a parking spot with his SCA buddies.

"There's this thing they do in AA," she said. "According to what I've read. Like, sometimes when they're taking a man to his first meeting, or to a rehab, they give him one final drink on the way. So he won't go into withdrawal. So what I was wondering—"

Oh, the look on his face!

"I guess that's a no, huh?"

"Kim—"

"Oh, c'mon," she said. "That was a *joke*, for God's sake! But what I really do need to do is I have to tell you why I came on so strong."

"Believe me, Kim, I understand. I've been there myself. The idea of taking no for an answer—"

"That's only part of it. See, I've got this list. There are only four names on it, and you're one of them."

"Well, I'm flattered, but as I said—"

"No, don't be flattered. What I wanted to do, I wanted to be able to cross you off the list, and in order to do that I'd have to sleep with you first."

There was a padded mailer in her bag. Her hand slipped into the open end, fastened on the handle of the knife. He was saying something but she paid no attention, concentrating instead on the move she'd make, visualizing it in her mind's eye.

"And when you turned me down," she went on, "I just couldn't stand it, and I was so upset that it kept me from seeing what should have been obvious."

"Sometimes the hardest thing to see is what's right in front of our eyes."

*Gee, Graham, I'd better go write that down.*

"What I didn't let myself realize," she said, "is that I'd already fucked you. I mean, that's how you got on the list in the first place, right? So I didn't have to fuck you again, much as I might want to. All I had to do to cross you off the list, was, well, *this*."

Just as she'd visualized it: her right hand emerging from the shoulder bag, gripping the kitchen knife, bringing it in one graceful motion into the center of his chest.

Just like that.

"You fucking idiot," she said. "You sanctimonious asshole. You could have died happy."

Did he even hear the words? Hard to say. There was no blood

to speak of, so she must have found the heart and stopped it. His eyes were wide, but the light was leaving them.

*Three.*


Now what? Her plan had worked perfectly, but it hadn't included the aftermath.

Just leave him here? But she had to go back to the Barling lot for her bike, and how was she going to get there? Call a taxi?

Take his place behind the wheel? The key was right there in the ignition, and despite what she'd told Rita, she was perfectly capable of driving anything with wheels. All she had to do was dump his body and drive his car back to where she'd left the bike. His car could return to the slot where it belonged, and she could bike off into the sunset.

Dump his body where? Just leave him in the church parking lot? They'd find him soon enough, and connect him to the SCA meeting, and who was to say he hadn't talked about her with some of his we-don't-fuck-anymore buddies? It might not lead to her, but it would guarantee headlines.

How about the church van? It was dusty, so it probably didn't get used much, and by the time anybody found a body in it there'd have been a dozen other 12-Step groups meeting there. Not a perfect idea, but—

Forget it. Fucking thing was locked up tighter than an SCA member's asshole.

If the Subaru had a trunk, that would work. Probably be a struggle getting him into it, but she could reposition the car first so that it screened her actions from observers. But the thing was a squareback, the contents of its rear compartment glaringly visible, so scratch that.

So what did that leave?

✿

Switching seats with him wasn't the hardest part. It was a little complicated, she had to maneuver him from behind the wheel into the passenger seat, but it went smoothly enough. She fastened his seatbelt and tightened it so it would keep him in position, then took his place behind the wheel and drove out of there.

Now it got tricky. Not finding her way—that was easy, as the Subaru had a GPS device, complete with a woman's voice to tell you when and where to turn, and Barling Industries was already available on his list of recent destinations, so all she had to do was select it and follow the prompts.

But there she was, driving through traffic with a dead man sitting up next to her. The premise, of course, was that his condition wouldn't be evident to a casual onlooker, and no one would see blood, because she'd adjusted his necktie to cover the wound. But he still looked dead as a doornail to her, and every time she braked for a stoplight with another car alongside, she found herself holding her breath. At any moment she'd hear sirens and there'd be people screaming and cops yanking the doors open and—

And each time the light changed and she drove away.

"*Approaching right turn,*" the voice told her at length, and this final right turn brought her into the Barling lot. "*You have arrived.*"

No shit, Sherlock.

Did the GPS doohickey have a memory? Could it tell the police where it had been?

Well, they'd have to find it first. She unhooked it from its moorings and dropped it into her handbag. Something to get rid of down the line, along with the knife.

Did the SCA people know about the GPS? Like, were they okay with him having an authoritative female voice telling him where to go and what to do? Like, couldn't he have a male voice, just to remove another possible occasion of sin?

Fucking moron.

She left him in his car, parked right where it had been when she joined him for the ride to Redmond. She took a moment to put him back behind the wheel; it would help keep him upright, and was a more natural spot for him, although it wouldn't fool anyone who took a good look.

They'd think he'd had a heart attack. Got behind the wheel, stuck the key in the ignition, and the poor devil's ticker quit on him. They'd know different soon enough, and it wouldn't take a formal autopsy to spot the knife wound in his chest, but by then she'd be long gone.

She took a moment to wipe the surfaces she might have touched. And at the last minute she remembered to go through his wallet. He had just over three hundred dollars, mostly in twenties and tens, and something made her look in the compartment behind his State of Washington driver's license, where he'd tucked away two fifties and a hundred for an emergency.

Well, this was an emergency, all right. The Nuits-Saint-Georges had left her alarmingly close to broke.

She locked the car on her way out, unlocked her bike, and left.

Now what? Back to Rita's house?

For pizza and French wine and another session in the living room? This one, she knew, would go further than the last. Their hands wouldn't be limited to their own flesh, and she could see how the evening might well end with one or both of them getting eaten out.

*It wasn't really a lesbian experience, Kimmie, because we're not lesbians.*

What would it be like, having another woman do that?

Or doing it herself?

She was getting hot thinking about it. But it wasn't going to happen, and she was going to make sure it didn't happen by skipping the pizza, skipping the wine, and skipping Rita's house altogether. If she went there, what could possibly happen afterward? Either she'd want to stay with Rita and try to make some kind of a life together, or she'd feel the need to kill her before moving on. She didn't want to kill Rita, not now, not in the least, and she couldn't stay with her in a town where she'd just murdered a man. She wanted at a minimum to be on the other side of a state line, and ideally clear across the country.

And she'd looked ahead enough to tuck what she could into her handbag. Not all she'd have liked to take, the bag was really no more than an overgrown purse, but enough to hold her until she had a chance to buy something new.

More to the point, nothing she'd left in Rita's spare bedroom could be traced back to her. Sooner or later she'd call Rita, and by then she'd have a story ready to explain her abrupt departure. But for now all she could do was disappear.

A pity she couldn't return the bike. Park it someplace, tell Rita where to find it? No, keep it simple.

She left it unlocked a block from the bus station, propped it against a lamp post and walked away from it. Someone was sure to adopt it—before her bus left, and before anyone could begin to wonder who stuck a knife into Graham Weider.

# FOURTEEN

When she first laid eyes on him, he'd looked preppy. That was in a bar in Riverdale, within walking distance of the last stop on the Bronx-bound 1 train, and she knew that much because she knew she'd walked there. She was drinking a Cosmopolitan when their eyes met. He bought her the next Cosmo, and the next thing she'd been able to remember was waking up in his bed.

He had looked a little less generic in the morning. In daylight she'd noted the vivid blue eyes, the once-broken nose, the pouting sensuous mouth. He was a Wall Street guy, she'd learned, and she could see him in that role, aiming to take his place as one of the self-styled masters of the universe.

That had been a while ago, and the years had taken their toll. Online, she'd learned that he'd come by the preppy look honestly. He'd been at Choate first, then Yale, then the B school at Columbia. Destiny had clearly meant him to wear suits from J. Press, khakis and polos from J. Crew.

Was it any wonder that he looked a little older and less prepossessing in a burnt-orange jumpsuit?

That would add years, all right. And it wasn't a simple matter of costume. Just being incarcerated—that would tend to age a man, wouldn't it?

The prison was in an upstate New York town she'd never heard of, a good deal closer to the Canadian border than to the city of New York. You had to take two buses to get there, an express to Albany and a local the rest of the way. She was one of a dozen women who migrated from the express to the local, and she figured they were all on similar errands, visiting their incarcerated mates.

An interesting word, incarcerated. As far as she could tell, it was used exclusively by persons to whom it applied—and, to be sure, by the women who loved them. The five syllables served to take the sting out; *I am presently incarcerated* didn't hit as hard as *The fuckers locked me up and swallowed the key.*

She'd noticed one woman in particular on the Albany express, a dishwater blonde with sharp facial features and a feral look to her. Not long ago she'd watched a cable documentary on crystal meth, and every woman in it looked like this one. So did half the women on any episode of *Cops.*

They'd exchanged glances, and she wasn't surprised when the blonde took the seat next to her on the local bus. "I'm Barb," she announced.

"Audrey."

"I guess we're going to the same place, huh?"

"I guess."

"I'm on this bus every week. You see a lot of the same people, and then you stop seein' some of 'em and instead you start to see different ones."

"Like life itself."

Barb had to think about that. Then she nodded. "Got that right," she said. "I don't think I seen you before."

"First visit."

"Yeah? Your man, right?"

*And I'm standing by him. Just like Tammy Wynette wants me to do.*

"Well, sort of," she said. "But I haven't seen him in years. We more or less lost track of each other. I'm not sure he'll remember me."

Barb gave her a look. "How's anybody gonna forget *you*? Only question's are you on the list. 'Cause if you're not an approved visitor, no way they gonna let you in."

"His lawyer said I'm approved, I won't have any trouble."

"Well, you're okay, then. You figure on using the truck?"

"The truck?"

"*You* know, Audrey. The *truck*." A sigh. "The fuck truck. Pardon the expression, but that's what everybody calls it. What it is, it's a trailer more'n a truck, and you get an hour in there. Like, private time."

"I don't know," she said. "See, in a way I hardly know him. He's been, uh, incarcerated for almost three years, and I didn't even find out about it until a month ago. I'm not even sure why I'm here visiting him. Would I want private time with him? Maybe, but how do I know he'd want to go in the truck with me?"

Barb gave her a look. She said, "Three years?"

"Plus a couple of months."

"Honey," Barb said, "that man'd settle for private time with a nanny goat. Will he go in the truck with you? You're kidding, right?"

But when they brought her in to see Peter Fuhrmann, it wasn't in the designated trailer, and you couldn't call it private time. After she'd passed through a scanner and been strip-searched by a matron, she wound up sitting in front of a long window. There were women on either side of her, talking to men in orange jump-suits on the other side of the window. There was an empty chair across from her, but it didn't remain empty for long. A man appeared, wearing the orange jumpsuit that seemed to be standard here, walked to the empty chair, and looked at her for a long moment before sitting down.

Would she have recognized him?

She knew him right away, saw the man she'd spent a night with in the man who sat across from her now. But she'd been expecting him. If she'd encountered him across the aisle in a subway car, or at adjacent tables in a diner, would any mental bells have rung?

No way to tell. And what did it matter? He was here now, and so was she.

He said, "Audrey Willard."

"That's right."

"Do I know you? Because the name didn't register when my lawyer mentioned it."

Well, how could it? She'd never used it before. She sort of liked Audrey, it was unusual without being weird, old-fashioned without smelling of lavender sachets. He'd have known her by another name, and she was clueless as to what that name might have been.

"I may not have given you my real name," she said.

"You look familiar, but I can't—"

"You pulled me out of a bar in Riverdale," she said, "or I pulled you, or we pulled each other. And the next thing I remembered was waking up the next morning."

"Oh, God. I owe you an apology."

"Not really," she said, "because you gave me a repeat performance that got rid of my hangover faster than any aspirin ever did."

"Jennifer."

Entirely possible, she thought. She'd been Jennifer often enough back then. It had been a sort of default alias at the time.

"I knew you looked familiar. I remember you. You gave me your number. But when I called—"

"I gave you a wrong number."

"I tried switching digits, but nothing worked."

"So I'm the one who owes you an apology," she said.

"Well—"

"Or maybe it's a wash," she said. "A wrong number, a couple of Roofies—"

"You could have died," he said.

"Like that girl."

He nodded. "Like Maureen McConnelly," he said.

She was in Ohio when she discovered what had become of Peter Fuhrmann. She sat at a computer terminal and went to work, and she'd have found him in a couple of keystrokes if she'd had any idea what to look for.

His name, for instance. Google Peter Fuhrmann and he'd pop up in a heartbeat, with a flood of articles providing extensive coverage of the case. And it got a ton of ink—a good-looking Wall Street guy, a Choatie, a Yalie, all of that preppy street cred topped off with a Columbia MBA, who wakes up one fine morning with a beautiful girl in his bed. She's a BIC, which is to say Bronx Irish Catholic, and she's all of nineteen, in her second year at Marymount Manhattan College. And she'll never graduate, nor will she ever be twenty, because, see, she's dead.

If she'd been in New York when it happened, she'd almost certainly have known about it. That's where it got a big play in the press. The story made the wire services, but it wasn't that big a story and it didn't play that well out of town, because Peter Fuhrmann never denied the charges. Yes, he'd picked up Maureen McConnelly in a Riverdale bar. Yes, he'd brought her home to his apartment— his bachelor pad, one tabloid called it. And yes, he'd poured her a drink, and helped his cause by dissolving a pill in it. The pill was Flunitrazepam, more popular under its trade name of Rohypnol. It was indeed the notorious date-rape drug, and date rape was precisely what happened to Maureen.

One enterprising reporter turned up a couple of young men who characterized feeding Roofies to Maureen as overkill. Reading between the lines, she got the message that you didn't have to drug Maureen to get in her pants, didn't have to get her drunk, didn't have to swear undying love. All you had to do was take out your dick and wave it at her.

Well, she thought, why not? The girl's dead, so let's all tell each other what a whore she was.

But she didn't spend too much time thinking about that part of the story, because there were other more important elements to consider. The drug rendered Maureen not altogether comatose but unfocused and acquiescent, a willing if not particularly active participant in what followed. One of its effects would have been retrograde amnesia, so Maureen very likely wouldn't have remembered what happened to her, but she never got the chance to find out. Peter Fuhrmann had his way with her, and during a lull in the proceedings he paid enough attention to his silent partner to realize that she was no longer breathing.

If he'd been the least bit resourceful, she thought, he'd have got her back into her clothes, slung her over his shoulder, and left her under a bush in Van Cortlandt Park. Instead, after an unsuccessful stab at CPR and mouth-to-mouth resuscitation, he'd picked up the phone and called the police.

Because it was obvious to him what had happened. He'd dosed the poor girl with a powerful drug, and it had stopped her heart and killed her.

"You called 911 right away," she said. "You didn't even call your lawyer first."

"I called a lawyer later on, from the police station. I knew I'd need assistance with the plea bargaining."

"You confessed."

"I did it," he said. "How was I going to say I didn't? It was completely unintentional, I'd never heard of anybody having a bad reaction to Roofies. Maybe a headache and a hangover the next day, but you'd get that from the alcohol, wouldn't you?"

"Normally," she said, "it would just keep a girl from resisting. Or remembering."

"If I could go back in time," he said with feeling. "And wipe it out, the way the drug wipes it from a person's memory. But you never can, can you?"

Because he was quick to confess, because he was prepared to enter a plea, the state didn't have to knock itself out preparing a case. The post-mortem examination went looking for Flunitrazepam, and that's what they found. They had no reason to look further, and death was accordingly attributed to cardiac and respiratory failure caused by the drug.

When she read about it, sitting in an Internet café in Ohio, she looked at a photograph of Maureen. She pictured the girl walking home with Peter, pictured her holding a glass of vodka. Pictured her dead.

*I did that,* she thought. *I killed you.*

Because, if they'd thought to look, they'd have found more than Roofies in Maureen's system. She couldn't even remember what she'd used, but she'd emptied the contents of a glassine envelope into a bottle of vodka before leaving Peter's apartment. She'd hoped it would kill him, but had considered the possibility that someone else might be the first to sample the vodka. A woman, a male friend, even a tippling cleaning woman, raiding the liquor cabinet for a mid-afternoon bracer.

What did it matter, really? She'd liked the idea of leaving behind something that would kill someone, without knowing—or caring, really—who she killed, or when. A couple of times she ran scenarios in her mind, imagining what might happen, and it was exciting enough, but she'd never felt the need to find out what really did happen.

And time passed, and she more or less forgot about it.

She'd been different then. Well, no, that wasn't it. She'd been the same person, she'd always been the same person, but her mission had been much less focused in those early days. She liked to pick up men and go home with them and have sex with them—though the sex in and of itself was never really the point. And she liked to end those evenings with more money than she started out, because you could almost always walk away with a few hundred dollars, and sometimes you scored big and left with a couple of thousand, and that made life easier and gave you a sense of accomplishment—but that was nothing compared to the pleasure of the kill.

No question, right from the very first time she liked to kill. It really got her motor going. The sex was a whole lot hotter when she knew she was going to kill the guy, and the money was more gratifying when she could think of it as a sort of bounty that was hers for taking her partner off the board. Sometimes she got off on the terror, when they saw it coming, and sometimes she killed them in their sleep and they were dead before they knew it, and either way it worked for her.

But there was no real purpose to it back then. It just sort of *was*.

Consciously, anyhow. Because it seemed to her now that she'd been trying to accomplish something all along, even though she had never spelled it out for herself. And then the day came when she just plain got it.

Which gave her work to do. First she had to remember them, and then she had to find them, and then, finally, she had to do what she should have done in the first place.

She had to kill them.

*

How?

There was a cab waiting when she left the prison, and the driver took her to a motel about a mile away. The office smelled of curry, so it was no great surprise when the manager turned out to be Indian, but how Sanjit Patel and his wife had wound up playing host to prison visitors in the middle of nowhere was one of life's great mysteries.

The room was clean, if a little shabby, and the shower was hot and the TV got sixty channels, so it would be no hardship to stay there while she worked out a plan. And that might take a while, because she didn't know where to start.

She was on the approved visitor list, which meant she was entitled to sit across from him with nothing between them but a thick pane of glass. She couldn't touch him, couldn't pass anything to him, and couldn't even have on her person anything that wouldn't get through a metal detector, and pass the scrutiny of the prison matron. There was no way she could get a weapon in with her, and even if she could, what possible good would it do her?

If she had a gun, and if she were proficient with it, and if she could sneak it in there, and if by some chance the glass wasn't bullet-proof, as she rather suspected it was, then she might conceivably be able to put a bullet in him. But she couldn't possibly get away with it. They'd have her in custody before he fell off his chair.

So what did that leave?

# FIFTEEN

The trailer was an Airstream, its sculpted silvery exterior badly pitted by the elements. It was small, designed to be towed behind a car, not moored permanently in a trailer park. Inside, thick dark curtains covered the windows. The maroon carpet was stained, and you could smell the toilet.

An unpainted plywood box held a mattress a foot off the floor. The sheets were not visibly soiled, and the stack of towels beside the bed were neatly folded, and apparently clean.

The fuck truck.

"You don't have to go through with this," Peter Fuhrmann said.

"But I want to."

"Really?"

Did she? Well, it was a pretty sordid space for a romantic encounter. And Peter, dressed in his orange jumpsuit and wearing his hangdog expression, didn't exactly set her pulse racing. But she was here, wasn't she? And he was one of only three names left on her list, and, well—

"Right off the bat," she said, "I can think of one thing that's definitely worse than having sex here."

"And what would that be?"

"Being here," she said, "and *not* having sex."

That at least got a smile from him. "It's no place for state dinners," he said. "I'll grant you that."

"Or intimate conversations."

"Or curling up with a good book."

"Or even a bad one. Peter? Can I ask you a question?"

"Sure."

"When was the last time you were—"

"With someone?" He avoided her eyes. "I haven't been with anyone since…"

He couldn't say the name, so she said it for him. "Since Maureen."

"Yes."

"You never—"

"No." He was silent for a moment. "I couldn't even think about it. It's as if that part of my life ended when—"

"When she died."

"Yes."

"And in prison—"

"People find outlets," he said. "Men hook up with each other. That's of no interest to me. And there are screws who can smuggle a woman in for the right price. Screws, that's what they call the guards. What *we* call the guards, I should say."

"But that's of no interest to you either, is it?"

"No. I don't even—"

"Don't what?"

"Masturbate."

"That's what I thought you were going to say. You don't?"

"No."

"And when the urge comes—"

"It doesn't."

"Oh."

"Audrey, the last time I had sex with a woman, she died."

"It wasn't the sex that killed her."

"No, it was the drug I gave her."

*No, sweetie, it was the poison I gave her.*

"And here's something I don't think I've ever said to another human being. See, there's no way to know exactly when she died. Was she already dead while I was—"

"Still fucking her."

He winced at the word, then nodded. "I'll never be able to know, and I don't even want to know, but I can't get the notion out of my mind. And I can't bear to think about it."

Actually, she thought, the whole idea was pretty hot. But that wasn't something she was prepared to share with Peter.

Instead she asked him why he'd agreed to visit the trailer with her.

"Because I didn't know how to say no," he said. "Isn't that a hell of a reason? And I thought maybe, oh—"

"Maybe you'd wind up wanting to."

"I guess."

"But you don't."

"I'm afraid I wouldn't—"

"Be able to do anything? Is that why you gave girls Roofies? A sort of Viagra by proxy? The girl takes it and you get a hard-on?"

"It may have been something like that."

"Then let's try a little role play, Peter. I'll take off all my clothes and just lie there. You can pretend I'm in a coma. Or, hey, this is even better—you can pretend I'm dead."

He stared at her.

"What's the matter, you don't think that's funny? All right, let's turn it around. You be the one in the coma."

"I don't understand."

"Take off your clothes," she said, in a tone that clearly expected obedience. "Now lie down. On your back, Peter. Eyes closed. You don't get to see me, Peter. And you can't move. You're paralyzed, you're unconscious, you've barely got a pulse. All you can do is lie there and breathe."

She got out of her own clothes, sat on the edge of the bed, reached out a hand and took hold of him.

"No, don't move. And don't open your eyes." Her grip tightened. "I'm not kidding. All you do is lie there, or I swear I'll rip it off."

She didn't know what he was doing with his mind, how he was letting it play. She didn't care. Her own fantasy was demanding all of her attention.

And it kept changing, insistent upon reinventing itself. At first it was pretty close to the reality of the situation: He was lying there, entirely in her power, unable to move because she had forbidden him to move, unable to see because her words were as blinding as a strip of duct tape over his eyes.

And then it changed, and in her mind he was physically immobilized, spread-eagled on the bed with his hands and feet in restraints, his mouth taped shut, a blindfold in place.

And in the third phase he was drugged. Unconscious, comatose, unable even to feel what she was doing with her hands and mouth.

And then—bingo!—he was dead, and that was the best of all. Oh, she'd been with plenty of dead men, but her interest in them had always ended with the sweet delight of their dying. Once they were dead, once she'd absorbed the sense of accomplishment and completion their deaths afforded her, she was ready to move on. They were off the list, out of her life even as they were out of their own, and the last thing she wanted to do was stroke their bodies, or suck their cocks.

But this dead man was different. This corpse was warm, and sentient. And so she touched and stroked the dead flesh, and the dead penis rose up in her mouth like Lazarus, and, well, she really got into it.

There was this line from an old blues song, just a fragment of a line, something about a woman who was so hot she could make a dead man come. The words echoed in her mind, *make a dead man come, make a dead man come, make a dead man come,* and he was rock-hard now, and unable to lie entirely still, unable to keep from moaning, and God she felt strong, God she felt powerful, and yes! *Yes!*

And she did indeed make this dead man come, and his orgasm triggered one of her own, not her typical long rolling climax but something very brief but furiously intense, almost masculine in nature. There was a moment when she went away, disappeared somewhere in time and space. Just an instant, and then she was back in the Airstream fuck truck, and she realized with perfect clarity that she'd accomplished something extraordinary, something more remarkable than simply raising the dead. She'd had sex with this inert being, this man who was playing dead at her command, and by so doing she had made the fantasy a reality.

He was dead. She'd fucked him to death, she'd sucked not only the life force but the very life itself out of him, and now she could cross him off her list.

*Two.*

She'd have some explaining to do. But they'd searched her enough to know she'd brought nothing into the trailer but her own self and the clothes on her back, and if his heart wasn't up to the stress of sexual activity, well, that was no fault of hers, was it? They'd let her go, they'd have to, and they'd never see her again.

"Audrey?"

Oh, fuck. The son of a bitch was alive.

Shit. *Three.*

# SIXTEEN

Conjugal visits, it turned out, were limited in both duration and frequency. You couldn't stay in the fuck truck for more than two hours—which struck her as reasonable, actually—and you couldn't go there more than once a week. On reflection, she decided that was probably reasonable, too. If prisoners got to fuck their wives any time they felt like it, they wouldn't have sufficient energy to plan future crimes, let alone organize a decent riot.

But it certainly didn't make her life any easier. She could visit him once a day if she wanted, could simply show up at the prison and get ushered into the big room where they'd sit on opposite sides of a window. But if she couldn't kill him in the fuck truck, how could she kill him in the visitors room? All she could do in there was have a conversation with him, and she'd just as soon talk to herself.

"I'll be back next week," she told him in the visitors room, a day after their visit to the Airstream trailer. "That's if you want me to."

Oh, he wanted her to.

"Then I'll come," she said. "Is there anything you need? Anything I can bring you?"

"If it's not too much trouble—"

"Just tell me."

Cigarettes, he said. If she could manage a carton of cigarettes, that would be great. What brand? Well, Marlboro would be ideal.

"I'll bring you a carton tomorrow or the next day," she said. "Just as soon as I can."

&

Two days later she presented the requested carton of Marlboros to an attendant, and he gave her a receipt for it; it would be delivered as soon as possible to one Peter Fuhrmann. She went back to her motel and wished she could pack up and leave. Did she really have to turn up the next morning? Couldn't she wait for her gift to work its magic?

She watched TV until she was able to sleep, then slept until she woke up. She turned up during visiting hours and was just slightly disappointed when they ushered her into the room with Fuhrmann on the other side of the window.

"I got the cigarettes," was the first thing he said to her. "That was really nice of you. Thanks."

"I guess you've been smoking like crazy ever since."

"Oh, I don't smoke."

Her reaction was enough to put a smile on his face. And he went on to explain that cigarettes were the preferred currency inside prison walls, that they were better than money when it came to obtaining favors. "They're too valuable to smoke," he said, "and I think if I ever had the habit I'd have to quit while I was here. It'd be like lighting up dollar bills and smoking them."

"So these packs of Marlboros just pass from hand to hand like money? Doesn't anybody ever smoke them?"

"Oh, the smokers smoke them," he said. "They're addicted, so what choice do they have? But I was never a smoker."

"And you've got an MBA," she said, "so you know how to game the system."

Which was more than she could say for herself.

Back to the motel. She packed, and found room in her suitcase for the hypodermic needle and the little vial of colorless liquid. There was still some left. She'd only used a few drops on the Marlboros.

She hadn't even opened the carton, let alone any of the packs.

There'd been no need. The hard part had been getting what she needed from a pharmacist, and she'd worked up an elaborate story which in the end she'd never needed to deliver. Because the guy behind the counter in Glens Falls practically drooled at the sight of her, so the easiest thing was to come back right around closing time and let him coax her into the back room.

He had a couch there, and she rather doubted she was the first woman he'd shared it with. But she knew she'd be the last. He went down on her first, which was promising, but before she could get anything out of it he sprang up and mounted her, and after a few thrusts he was done. That made him the fourth name on her list, but he didn't stay on it for long; there was a large all-purpose utility knife at hand, and she came up with a use the manufacturer never thought of. He was dead before he could catch his breath.

She scooped up close to three hundred dollars from the cash register, plus a pair of fifties and three hundreds in the lower compartment. That was a decent score in the age of credit cards, and she upped it with another two hundred-plus from his wallet. All very welcome, because she could certainly use the money. Cash didn't seem to last long. She was always on the verge of running out of it.

But there was a reason she'd picked Washburn Pharmacy instead of Dell Hardware or Pick'n'Pay Market, and she found what she was looking for in a locked cupboard alongside the couch where Gerald Washburn, RPh, had had the last orgasm of his young life. The lock looked formidable enough, but inches from it a key hung from a nail, and voila!

She took everything that looked interesting, including a syringe. What she didn't take she scattered, leaving the place as she imagined an impatient junkie might leave it.

On the way out, she helped herself to a carton of Marlboros. Like, why not?

✣

In the end, she decided to keep only a bare minimum of the pharmaceuticals she'd taken. She'd had the impulse to hang on to everything, because you never knew what might come in handy. But you also never knew who would go through your possessions and wonder how you'd happened to turn into a walking drugstore, and a trace of these controlled substances would lead straight to Washburn Pharmacy, and wasn't that where they found poor Washburn with a big old knife in his chest? Say, do you suppose there could be a connection?

She'd filled the syringe, worked the needle between the edges at the end of the carton, then forced it into a pack and, assuming she'd done it correctly, expelled a few drops of its contents into a cigarette. She repeated the process a couple of times, then did the same at the carton's other end.

It was hit or miss, she knew. There were two packs at each end of the carton, six more in the middle. If he started with an end pack, she might get results in a hurry, but if he started in the middle, well, how long could it take? If the man smoked a pack a day, within a week at the outside he'd be into one of the end packs, and sooner or later she'd get lucky even as his luck ran out.

Yeah, right. Who'd have guessed the bastard didn't smoke at all?

Her next visit came a full week later, and the greatest moment of anxiety was at the security check. She hadn't brought cigarettes this time, and had nothing on her person that might draw the interest of the scanner or the matron, but suppose one of her doctored Marlboros had worked its magic? Suppose an inmate had taken a deep and final drag, and someone had figured it all out?

Maybe they were looking for her, waiting for her. The possibility had dissuaded her from bringing him a second carton of cigarettes, and had nearly kept her from showing up at all. But no one looked at her twice, and if the matron's hands were almost invasive enough to earn the woman a place on her list, well, the intrusion was over quickly, and before she knew it she was in the Airstream trailer with Peter Fuhrmann.

"You're here," he said. "I was afraid you wouldn't show."

"I said I would."

"You might have had second thoughts. I mean, what are we to each other, Audrey? A few years ago we spent less than ten hours together, and you were unconscious for most of them."

"The part I was awake for wasn't so bad."

"I drugged you, and you could have died from it."

"But I seem to have survived, haven't I?"

"And thank God for that, but the point is you could have died. Another girl did."

"That's why she's not here, Peter." She cocked her head. "But I am. And they won't let us have the trailer forever, and they don't call it the Talk Truck, do they? So do we really want to spend the whole time talking?"

"Audrey," he said. "Audrey, Audrey, Audrey."

Well, it wasn't a horrible name. If he insisted upon saying it over and over, it might as well be a name she could stand.

They'd gotten past the little game of pretending he was drugged and immobilized, and their lovemaking was more spirited this time around. He'd had a week to think about what he might like to do to and with her, and he turned out to be equipped with both imagination and skill, and she didn't have to feign her response.

Oh, it might have been better. It would have heightened her pleasure considerably if there'd been a way to conclude things with his death. As she got close, she imagined him dying in a dozen different ways—shot, stabbed, throttled, hanging from a rope—and that all helped, but it wasn't the real thing.

The real thing would have to wait. Forever, apparently.

"Audrey."

She rolled onto her side, laid a hand on his chest. "I like the way you say my name."

"I didn't even know your name. You told me your name was Jennifer, and I'd pretty much forgotten you, false name and all, until you turned up here." He drew a breath. "And gave me a reason to live."

Oh?

"I hadn't planned on saying that," he said, "but I think I've got to get past keeping things to myself. I wasn't planning on killing myself, nothing like that. I've thought about it and rejected it."

*Well, think about it some more, why don't you?*

"But all I was doing was letting my life run its course. My sentence has three more years to run. My lawyer arranged for me to plead guilty to involuntary manslaughter, and I've served two years of a five year sentence. And I figured that gave me three more years to decide what I was going to do with the rest of my life, and I didn't mind postponing that decision."

"And now?"

"The day before yesterday," he said, "I filed an application for parole."

He'd been eligible since the completion of his first year. But you had to apply, and each month he'd passed up the opportunity to do so. Because all parole would do was force him to figure out what to do with his life, and that had been a decision he was unprepared to make.

Besides, he felt he deserved to serve his full sentence. He'd killed Maureen, whether or not it had been his intention, and it was only fair that he be deprived of three more years, having himself deprived her of the entire remainder of her life.

And prison wasn't so bad. He hadn't made friends inside the walls, but he hadn't made enemies, either, and he'd found it easy enough to take the days one at a time and get through them that way. They fed you three times a day, and if the meals weren't Cordon Bleu, at least they kept you alive. You could find the routine of prison life limiting and confining, or you could do as he had done and adjust to it, embracing it as something that relieved you of the burden of decision. It was, in its way, like being in the army, or working for a corporation. You did what they told you to do, and one day followed another, and you got along.

"I don't know how you feel about me," he said, "or even how I feel about you. Am I in love with you? It certainly feels like it, but I don't know that I can trust the feeling. I mean, I barely know you."

*Well, you got that right.*

"And as far as our having a future together, it seems pointless even to speculate. But what you've done, Audrey, is show me that *I* have a future, whatever form it takes. So I put in my application, and in two months I'll have a hearing, and then, well, I'll have to see how it goes. I hope I'll see you between now and then, and I hope I'll see you when I get out, but for now you've given me my life back, and I'll always be grateful to you for that. I only wish there were something I could give you in return."

She stretched out on the bed, parted her thighs. "We've got half an hour," she said. "Maybe you can think of something."

Two months until his hearing. Then, if the parole board decided in his favor, a few weeks to run the paperwork and let him out of there.

All at once it had become manageable. She'd never given a thought to parole, never imagined it might have been available to him all along.

Of course you couldn't predict what the parole board might do. Back in Hawley there'd been an inspector at Motor Vehicles who made sure nobody ever passed the road test the first time through. He'd find some way to fail you. So there was always the chance some similar tightass on the Parole Board made everyone apply more than once, just on general principles. But Peter had committed no infractions of penitentiary rules, pulled no time in solitary, and indeed had led an apparently blameless life until the single unfortunate incident that had put him behind bars. It would be hard to find a better candidate for parole, and she could only assume the odds were in his favor.

So now she had to keep her distance. As soon as he was free, she'd take him to bed in some yet-to-be-determined venue a little more private than the fuck truck. They'd celebrate his freedom, and by the time they were done she'd have her own freedom to celebrate, and one less name on her list.

Until then, she would have to do what she could to lower her profile. Every time she walked through the metal detector and into the prison, a camera recorded the visit. They wouldn't keep the tapes forever, but how long would it be before they recycled them? Probably a week, she figured, but it could be as long as a month, so if she wanted to avoid having her features on file somewhere…well, it looked as though the best way to stay out of prison was to stay out of prison.

She picked up a carton of Marlboros—undoctored, this time—and paid him a last visit to tell him through the pane of glass that he wouldn't be seeing her for a while. "I'll be in California," she said. "In fact I should have been there all along. I have an aunt in Yreka who's not in good health, and I've been splitting caretaker duties with my sister, and I'm long overdue to get out there and take my turn."

"I didn't know you had a sister."

"You probably didn't know about the aunt, either. I don't know how long I'll have to stay, and I'm not sure *where* I'll be staying."

"You can't stay with your aunt?"

"Even if I could," she said, "I wouldn't." And she riffed on what a pigpen the aunt's house was, and then went on to explain that there was someone else she had to see, not in California, because there was a conversation she had to have, and it really ought to be face to face.

"See, I've sort of been in a relationship," she said. "And, well, I don't know what the future's going to hold for us, Peter, but I'd like to make room for us to give it a chance. Do you know what I mean?"

"I didn't know you were seeing anybody."

"I know, I'm full of surprises. A sister, an aunt, and now a boyfriend. Except he's not exactly a boyfriend, and I've been ready to break it off for a while now, and this is the right time." She put her palm on the glass, and once he'd matched his palm to hers she said, "Peter, no strings. You're not under any obligation, and how can we possibly know where this is going? But I want to give it a chance, and I hope you want to, too."

"There's nothing I want more."

"I don't know when I'll be able to see you again," she said, "but I'll want to keep in touch, and of course I'll want to know what happens with your hearing, and how that goes. I suppose I could write to you, but—"

"I'll get a cell phone."

"They're allowed in here?"

He nodded. "I never bothered getting one," he said. "I never saw the point. Who would I call?"

# SEVENTEEN

"It's pronounced Why-reeka," she said, "and it's supposed to be a Shasta Indian word meaning *white mountain*, but I haven't run into any Shasta Indians who can say one way or the other."

"Isn't there a Eureka as well?"

"There is," she said, "and my own theory is that they were trying to call it that and found out there already was one, so they changed how they spelled it. I mean, they were both Gold Rush boom-towns, right? But Mark Twain had another explanation."

"Oh?"

"Something about a sign for a bakery, and it was reverse-printed on glass so it read backwards, Y-R-E-K-A, and the B was worn off. But that seems farfetched to me."

"Because the letters would be backwards," he said. "The R and the K, anyway."

"What I think happened," she said, "is Mark Twain noticed that the town's name spelled backwards was *Akery*, and he just made up the story from there. I mean, he made things up, didn't he?"

"You mean *A Connecticut Yankee in King Arthur's Court* didn't really happen? Another illusion shattered. But you're getting along all right in Yreka? Your aunt's not driving you around the bend?"

"I'm okay," she said. "And that's really great news about the board. That's a lot more important than how this place got its dumb name."

✿

Of course she wasn't in Yreka, or anywhere in California. She was in Baltimore, in a three-story house on the edge of Fell's Point, where she'd managed to rent a room. She got a part-time job clerking in a copy shop that doubled as an Internet café. One of her perks was free use of a computer during her off-hours, and she spent a lot of time free-associating her way from website to website. That was how she'd come by all that information about Yreka, which she'd passed on to Peter the next time she spoke with him.

And the following day she looked up *A Connecticut Yankee.* That led her to Bing Crosby, who starred in one of the film adaptations, and that led her somewhere else. The Internet, she thought, was like life itself. One thing kept leading to another.

There were singles bars nearby, and shops and restaurants that drew out-of-towners. But she kept a low profile and didn't wander far afield. She worked and surfed the net, she took her meals at a cafeteria around the corner from the copy shop, and she watched TV.

Now and then she used the phone.

"A halfway house," she said. "And it's in New York City? Oh, in the Bronx? Well, that could be a good thing, Peter. And that's just where you'll be living, isn't it? You can come and go as you please."

They talked about it as a way of easing the transition from imprisonment to freedom, but what she liked was the coincidence of the location. All of this had started in the Bronx, in the Riverdale section, and it was fitting that it should end there.

"I wish I could be there when you walk through the gates," she said. "But maybe it's better that you'll have a week to settle in at the halfway house first."

*

Just a few more weeks now…

She picked up her phone, keyed in the number she'd looked up earlier. Four rings, and then the machine picked up, and clear across the country in Kirkland, Washington, Rita's voice invited her to leave a message.

She broke the connection.

She found the halfway house on Laconia Avenue at 225th Street, somewhere around the border between two Bronx neighborhoods, Williamsbridge and Edenwald. It was an unprepossessing four-story building, its crumbling brick exterior imperfectly sheathed in aluminum siding. Four men sat on the front stoop, smoking cigarettes, and it wasn't hard to believe they'd done time upstate.

The three-story building to the right housed a bodega, its window filled with neon beer signs. There was an empty lot on the other side, rubble-strewn, girded with a cyclone fence. To keep the rubble in? To keep the rabble out?

Well, she supposed the place had a certain raffish charm. But she didn't figure it would be hard to coax Peter away from it.

The apartment she chose was in Riverdale, and just blocks from the one where Peter Fuhrmann had fed her a Roofie and she'd returned the favor by spiking his vodka. There was a certain symmetry that appealed to her, but she picked the neighborhood because it was easier to find a nice anonymous sublet there than in Williamsbridge or Edenwald. Riverdale was filled with Yuppies, and they were forever moving in and moving out and moving on, losing their jobs or getting better ones, breaking up with significant others, finding new lovers to move in with, and otherwise keeping the real estate market humming.

The man she sublet from was a junior executive with one of the major accounting firms, on his way to a new post in Wichita. Their deal was simple, and ideal for her purposes; it was unofficial, with no paper signed, and he'd continue to send a monthly check to the landlord while she'd send money orders to him at his new office.

Meanwhile, she gave him cash for a month's rent, and they shook hands, and that was that. By the time he started wondering where the money order was, she'd be out of the apartment, the city, and the state.

He suggested going out for a drink to seal the bargain, and it was clear that he had more than a drink in mind. He'd been checking her out since she walked in the door. And he was cute, and she wouldn't have minded, not in the least. Take him out for a drink, bring him home to what had just become her apartment, take him to bed and fuck his brains out, and then what? Kill him and look for another sublet?

"I really wish I could," she said. "But these days my life's complicated enough as it is. But some other time, huh? I mean, you never know when I might find myself in Wichita."

There was probably a shop in Riverdale that sold sex toys, the potential customer base was certainly present, but she remembered the Pleasure Chest on Seventh Avenue, and it was just a subway ride away.

She picked out a batch of items, and as she was paying for them she set one aside and asked if the store could ship it for her. She wrote out the name and address.

It would be no problem, the clerk assured her. And would she like to enclose a card?

She shook her head. "She'll know who it's from," she said.

✿

She'd been staying on the cheap in a Jersey City rooming house, but once she'd sublet the Riverdale apartment she moved right in. The furniture was generic, but everything was new and neat and clean, and it would be comfortable enough for the week or two she'd be using it.

Every few days she called Peter, and was pleased when they released him right on schedule. "I'm in the van now," he said. "It seats ten, but there's just me and the driver. He's taking me all the way to the halfway house."

"In the movies," she said, "they give you ten dollars and a cheap suit and you're on your own."

"They gave me the suit I was wearing when I got here. Got *there*, I should say, because I'm not there anymore. It doesn't fit as well as it used to."

"Still, I bet you look nicer in it than in the orange outfit."

"Jesus, I hope so. They give you a ride to the halfway house because otherwise too many guys don't make it that far."

"They lose their way?"

"In a manner of speaking. And I can understand why. All I am right now is outside the walls, maybe thirty miles down the road, and already it feels scary."

"Being free."

"Yeah."

"Well," she said, "if you miss it too much, all you have to do is find some sweet young thing and kill her. They'll take you back in a hot second."

The silence was profound. Had she gone too far?

"I'm sorry," she said. "That was supposed to be a joke, but I guess it wasn't what you wanted to hear."

"It just came out of the blue," he said. "Took me by surprise."

"I can see where it would. Forgive me?"

"Nothing to forgive, Audrey."

"Well, I intend to make it up to you," she said. "I got a place for us to be together. I know you have to spend nights at the halfway house, but that leaves a lot of hours in the day. It's a nice modern building, and the apartment's all furnished and there's even a view. Plus I went shopping."

"Oh?"

"I bought us a nice bottle of wine," she said. "Nuits-Saint-Georges. And I bought some toys for us to play with. You'll see. We'll have fun."

She gave him two days to settle in at the halfway house, then met him around the corner. He was wearing a flannel shirt and well-worn jeans, and she had the feeling he wasn't the first person to own them, that they'd been picked up at a thrift shop or handed out at the halfway house. Whatever the source, he looked good in them. They were an improvement on the orange jumpsuit, and a better choice than any suit he might have worn.

"That's some place," he said.

"Better than where you were? Or worse?"

"Well, all I had to do just now was open the door and walk out. That wasn't an option upstate, so that makes this a big improvement. But it's the same people, you know? We're none of us wearing orange jumpsuits, but outside of that we haven't changed all that much."

"Oh?"

"A lot of the guys are drinking," he said. "That's a violation of the house rules, but nobody makes you take a Breathalyzer test. Still, if you're a falling-down drunk they're gonna throw you out. And there are a few I'm pretty sure are using."

"Drugs?"

He nodded. "A neighborhood like this, how hard can it be to find somebody to cop from? And that's not just against the house rules, it's a parole violation and a quick ticket inside. You said something about a bottle of wine."

"Right."

"Well, it's fine with me if you have some, but I think I'm going to pass. I was never in that much of a rush to get out of there, you know, but then you came along, and all of a sudden I couldn't wait to breathe free air again. And drinking was never a problem for me, at least I never thought it was, but if not drinking gives me a better shot at staying out, well, I think I'll give it a try. At least as long as I'm at the residence."

"How do they feel about Coca-Cola?"

"They're fine with Coke," he said, "as long as it's not the powdered variety."

"Then screw the wine," she said. "I've got Coke in the fridge and clean sheets on the bed. And there's a gypsy cab. He's not allowed to pick up fares on the street, but I bet he will. See? What did I tell you? This is our lucky day."

The sex was sweet. They started kissing, and things proceeded from there at a dreamy pace, and there was never an opportune time to show him the sex toys. Easier to scrap that script, just as she'd abandoned her plans for the wine. It was a nice bottle, a slightly pricier version of what she'd brought to Rita's dinner table, but it could remain unopened. She wouldn't need it. And the toys could wait their turn.

Sweet kisses, sweet stroking and petting. He was quite obviously in love with her—or, perhaps more accurately, he was in

what he thought was love with what he thought was her. He'd
got it all wrong, but while it lasted she might as well go with
the flow.

And maybe, she found herself thinking, just maybe the flow she
was going with was there to bring her full circle. Maybe she had
done what she had to do, maybe she'd killed enough lovers to
wipe the last of her father's touches from her flesh. Maybe the
relentless cycle of couple and kill and couple and kill had finally
run its course.

Maybe the love he felt for her was real, and maybe it had somehow given birth to that same emotion within her. Maybe she'd
punished him enough, poisoning his playmate and sending him to
jail for her murder, saddling him not only with a prison sentence
but with a double burden of unwarranted guilt.

And maybe she was even now responding to his love, and what
stirred her now was not an itch being scratched, not the excitement of sex wedded to the anticipation of another killing, but, well,
love. Her own love for him, and her anticipation—incredibly—of
a life free from the need to bring an endless line of men to her
bed, and from it to their graves.

Maybe she could have a life, a real life, being lover and, yes,
*wife* to this man. A good man, a man who loved her, a man whom
she could love.

*Maybe*—

Her climax was surflike, waves rolling and rolling, tossing her,
drowning her, hurling her onto the shore. For a long moment she
was somewhere else entirely, lost in space and time.

And then she was in her bed, in her sublet apartment in Riverdale, with the perspiration cooling on her skin and a man lying
spent at her side.

She reached out for that last thought, a thought that cried out for violins in the background, and a visual that was all pastoral fantasy, milkmaids and shepherds, white clouds in a blue sky...

*Maybe*—

Then again, she thought, maybe not.

"I'll be back in a minute," she said. "Don't go away."

# EIGHTEEN

The thing about Coca-Cola was it had a good strong taste. You could add almost anything to it and it would still taste like Coca-Cola.

That was the good thing about it. The bad thing was that if you dropped a pill into a glass or can or bottle of Coke, it did its Old Faithful imitation and fizzed like crazy.

She knew this because of a pre-teen experiment. The word at school was that you could get high by dissolving an aspirin tablet in a can of Coke, and she'd tried, and what you got was a geyser that bubbled all the Coke out of the can. After a couple of attempts, she figured out that the carbonation had something to do with the reaction, and that all she had to do was let the Coke get flat, and *then* add the aspirin. So she did, and the tablet dissolved without generating a burst of bubbles, and she drank the resultant mixture, and, of course, nothing happened. You didn't get high. You didn't even get sick. A big nothing all around.

But, if she'd gained nothing else from the experience, she'd learned not to drop pills into carbonated beverages. Happily, her pharmaceutical score had included a couple of little bottles of chloral hydrate, and Google had led her to all anybody needed to know about that marvelous substance. It was the active ingredient in the legendary Mickey Finn, invented a century and a half ago in San Francisco. A few drops of chloral hydrate in a beer or a highball, and the next thing you knew you were part of the crew of a clipper ship in the China trade. You'd been shanghaied—that's where the word came from—and you were stuck there, at least until you got to the next port.

A few drops in a glass of Coke? Well, let's see.

"Here," she said. "Coca-Cola, with just a little lemon juice for flavoring. Come on, drink up. We'll toast our future, Peter."

Perfect.

"It could be a lot worse, Peter. Like, you wake up on the heaving deck of a ship bound for Hong Kong, and the last thing you remember is knocking back a glass of red-eye in a Barbary Coast saloon." She frowned. "But maybe this is worse. It's hard to say."

He didn't say anything, but how could he? He had a six-inch length of duct tape across his mouth. He was on his back, spread-eagled on the bed, held there by restraints from the Pleasure Chest. (*Gentle! Will leave no marks!*)

And she'd used other toys as well.

"You were sleeping so nicely," she said, "and I thought I'd just let you sleep forever, you know? Smother you in your sleep, or give you a shot of something lethal. The good thing about that is you'd never know what happened, but that's the bad thing, too, because, well, you'd never know what happened."

God, the look in his eyes. He was trying to make sense out of this, and how could he? Nor was she helping, her words wandering all over the place.

"Just to fill you in," she said, "if you'll pardon the expression, well, that's a butt plug you feel in your ass. Just to keep you from feeling lonesome for the hot nights in prison. No, no really, because I know you were too much of a tightass to let yourself go that way. It's more to set the stage, but we'll get to that.

"And the constriction at the base of your dick, well, you're wearing a cock ring. That's why you've got such a raging hard-on, even though you came like crazy less than an hour ago. The vein's constricted, but not the artery, so the blood gets in but can't get out, and your dick stays stiff as a board even though sex is the last thing you want right now."

He was trying to say something. He couldn't, of course, but a certain amount of sound came through his nose. Pathetic, really.

"Okay, cut to the chase," she said. "I couldn't let you die without knowing this part. Remember that woman you went to prison for? Maureen McSomething? You didn't kill her, dumbass. I killed her."

Wide eyes. Zero comprehension.

"You fed me a Roofie, Peter, way back when. And that wasn't supposed to happen, because I picked you up intending to fuck you and kill you, and the next thing I knew it was morning. So we had a little party, and on the way out I spiked your vodka so that the next drink you took would be your last. But I guess you weren't much of a vodka drinker, so Maureen got it instead, and since you told the cops about the Rohypnol, they didn't run a good enough tox scan to find out what else might have gotten into the little darling's system. And off you went to prison, sure you deserved whatever they gave you."

And she explained how she hadn't even known about it until he was a few years into his sentence, how she'd had to track him down, and how she'd been willing to do this because he was one of only three men she'd slept with who still had a pulse.

And she told him why it was important to her that he die, that she be able to cross his name off the list. She was pretty sure it wasn't making any sense to him, if indeed it was registering at all. Hearing her own words as she spoke them, she wasn't sure it made any sense to her, either. Why did she have to do this? What difference did it make if an ex-lover was still alive? Why should she care?

But she did care. No getting around it, she cared. Her whole life centered upon it, for better or for worse.

"So here you are," she said. "What do you figure, is it good news or bad news? You didn't kill that girl, so that's a relief, right? On the other hand, you did all that time in prison and went through all that guilt for nothing, so that's not so good, is it? But either way it doesn't matter too much, because in a few minutes you're going to be dead."

She showed him the noose.

"Autoerotic asphyxiation, sweetie. To heighten your pleasure. You'll be wearing a butt plug and a cock ring, which just might give them the idea that sex is a component here, and after you're dead I'll lose the restraints and the duct tape, and, well, what are they going to think? And if some CSI-type genius figures out that you had a woman around, for at least part of the proceedings, do you think they're gonna knock themselves out looking for her? You're a known pervert, you already drugged a girl and served time for her death, so what do they care? Poetic justice, right?"

And what would he say to that? Well, she'd never know, would she?

*Two.*


She sat at the white parson's table in the windowed kitchen and drank a cup of coffee. It was a shame, she thought, that she couldn't hang on to the apartment a little longer. But there was a dead man in the bedroom, and that meant she'd have to be moving on.

She picked up the phone, keyed in a number.

"Hello?"

"Rita?"

"Omigod, Kimmie!"

Oh, right, she was Kim, wasn't she? And now, with Peter cooling in the other room, she never had to be Audrey again.

"I sent you a present."

"I *knew* it was from you. Even if I didn't know what it *was*."

"It's a butt plug."

"Well, I know that now, silly. I had to Google it."

"How? If you didn't know—"

"I Googled 'sex toys,' and I found a site with everything illustrated, and I must have spent an hour just reading about one damn thing after another."

"Just reading?"

"Kimmie!"

Funny how easy it was, talking to Rita. Funny how she'd missed this.

"…called a flange," Rita was saying. "To keep it from, you know, getting lost in there."

"Hard to explain to the intern in the emergency room."

"God, wouldn't that be embarrassing? 'I don't know how on earth it got all the way up there, doctor.' "

"They must hear a lot of stories."

"Oh, God, you know what I read online?"


Her sudden departure was the elephant in the living room, until she had to force herself to acknowledge the beast. When the conversation hit a lull, she said, "Rita, I just had to leave. It was sudden, and I should have said goodbye, but I figured the best thing I could do was just hop on the bike and go."

"I had this vision of you on the bike, trying to get over the Rocky Mountains."

"I just left it at the bus station. I hated to abandon it but I couldn't figure out a way to get it back to you."

"I never rode it anyway. And it'd be impossible now, with a butt plug up my bottom."

"You're too much, Rita."

"That's why you left, isn't it? Not because I'm too much, but because *we* were too much. That last night, when we were—"

"Jilling."

"Yeah. It was so fucking hot, Kimmie, but then the next day it was scary."

"I know."

"I mean, it's not a lesbian thing when you're both talking about things you did with guys, right? And we never even touched each other."

"No, but—"

"But what, Kimmie?"

"Well, if we did it again, I might have wound up sitting next to you. And I might have touched you."

"I might have let you."

"The phone's safe, though, isn't it?"

"I was just thinking that myself."

"Rita?"

"What?"

"You're wet, aren't you?"

"Kimmie!"

"You have to tell me," she said, "because I'm thousands of miles away, so I can't reach over and find out for myself."

"And what about you, Miss Smarty Pants? You're a little moist yourself, aren't you?"

"Just my cunt."

"Oh God. When you say that word—"

"Have you been with anybody lately?"

"A guy. Two nights ago. It was okay, it was fun. But you know what I kept thinking afterward? That I wished I could tell you about it."

"We could probably both think of things to tell each other."

"Uh-huh."

"Rita? Why don't you draw the drapes and take your clothes off and get comfy on the couch. And I'll call you back in, like, ten minutes? And you can put me on speaker phone so you'll have both hands free."

"Oh God."

"And Rita? Wear the butt plug."


"Here's something crazy," she said. "After all the things we just did, and all I got out of it, I'm hotter than ever. And what's got me dripping is the prospect of telephone sex with a woman three thousand miles away."

She sighed. "And why am I telling you all this, Peter? You're still dead, aren't you?"

No question, she thought. You didn't have to look at him twice to know it, either. The noose that strangled him had had an effect similar to that of the cock ring, and his head was engorged with blood, his swollen face a deep purple.

And the cock ring hadn't stopped working. He was still massively erect, and she could swear he'd grown larger since she'd left him.

Jesus, it was huge. She took hold of him.

Still warm.

Hmmm.

Aloud she said, "I dunno, Peter. What do you think? It'd be a first, wouldn't it? And something for you to tell your friends about. 'Yeah, I'm dead, but I'm still getting a little pussy now and then.' "

Except, of course, he wouldn't be telling anybody anything.

"Of course there'd be a kind of poetic justice to it. I mean, Maureen McConnelly was probably dead when you fucked her. Not when you started, maybe, but by the time you got finished. God, that must have been a shock, huh? But I guess you're shock-proof now."

She sighed.

"Maybe it's too kinky. Anyway, I've got things to do. There's a lady on the other side of the country waiting for the phone to ring."

But she couldn't keep herself from reaching out and taking hold of him again. She had her cell phone in one hand and his dick in the other. It was the same color as his face. Maybe a little darker.

She said, "Waste not, want not, isn't that what they say? And when am I gonna get a chance like this again?"

She hoisted herself into position. A little lube? No, hardly necessary, she was sopping wet. Slipped right in, and it wasn't her imagination, he was really gigantic.

She closed her eyes, rocked to and fro.

Picked up the cell phone. Multitasking? Sure, why not?

Hit Redial.

"So are you wearing the butt plug?"

"Uh-huh. Are you?"

"No, but I've got something in front."

"Oh?"

"Very natural. You'd almost think it was real."

"Like with veins and all?"

"Uh-huh."

"And it's in your cunt?"

"You really like that word, don't you, Rita?"

"I love it. Tell me how it feels in your cunt."

"No, you first. Tell me about this guy you picked up."

"What do you want to hear?"

"Everything," she said. "Tell me everything."

# NINETEEN

Hedgemont, North Carolina.

There was no bus station as such. The bus stopped at a convenience store with a pair of gas pumps out front. She got off, and the bus driver climbed down after her and retrieved her suitcase from the luggage compartment.

"Bet you're glad to be gettin' home," he said.

He was a pleasant fellow, heartier than his passengers, and she saw no reason to disabuse him of the notion that Hedgemont was home to her, and that she was glad to be here. It wasn't hard to guess how he'd jumped to that conclusion. If it wasn't your home, what on earth would bring you here?

Alvin Kirkaby was here.

That was reason enough. Alvin Kirkaby, a corporal in the infantry, had shared a bed with her before his unit was transferred to Iraq. She remembered his name and rank, and not a great deal more about him. He'd been wearing his uniform when she spotted him in a bar just down the street from her apartment. She'd been living in Chelsea at the time, and the bar drew a mixed crowd, half straight and half gay, and she'd have assumed he was gay—like, a uniform in a Chelsea bar?—but when their eyes locked she knew otherwise. God knows what he'd seen in her eyes, but it had been enough to make him dump his companions and head straight over to her.

Cocksure, that was the word for him. He approached her with complete confidence, knowing she found him attractive, knowing she'd take him home with her. And he was right, of course, and his assurance was attractive in and of itself.

In more ways than one. It would make the sex better, and it would make the aftermath positively delicious. All that confidence, all that certainty, and the next thing he knew he'd be dead meat. It would mean leaving her apartment and moving on, but that was all right. She was getting tired of Chelsea.

In his uniform, he'd been generically attractive. Military haircut, face clean-shaven, broad shoulders, athletic physique. Out of it, his body turned out to be everything she could have wanted, and in bed he gave a good account of himself. He wasn't the most imaginative lover she'd been with, or the most experienced, but ardor and stamina made up for anything that might have been lacking.

Earlier, she'd had a look at his wallet when he paid for a round of drinks. Nice thick wad of bills in there. Hardly enough for a retirement fund, but it was always nice to turn a profit. Pleasure was all the better when you made it pay.

Then, while he lay beside her smoking a cigarette, he told her how he'd be shipping out the next day. To Iraq, where he'd be in combat. He'd been there once already, this would be his second tour of duty over there, and he became a little less cocksure when he talked about it.

So much for that. Once he was over there he was on his own, but she could make sure he lived long enough to go serve his country. She let him go to sleep, and woke him in time for morning sex, and after a shave and a shower she sent him off to be a soldier.

She knew all about that. "You're my little soldier," her father had told her.

So when she drew up a list, he'd been on it. Alvin Kirkaby.

Surprising, really, that she'd remembered the name, but somehow it had stayed lodged in her memory and she'd been able to dredge it up. Alvin Kirkaby. Corporal Alvin Kirkaby.

That was then.

Now he was Sgt. Alvin Kirkaby, United States Army (Ret.) He'd been promoted, and he'd been discharged, and he wasn't a soldier anymore.

And he was on her list.

She could have asked directions at the convenience store. But this was a small town, just a dot on the map, and the less contact she had with people, the better off she'd be. Earlier, at an Internet café just two blocks from Washington's Union Station, she'd asked Google Maps for directions to 24A Maple Street, and she had the printout in her purse. She didn't even need it anymore, she'd studied it enough on the train and two buses she'd been on since then, but she took it out anyway and unfolded it and looked it over. Then she picked up her suitcase and started walking.

She'd expected a house, a modest older home, with a couple of broken-down cars on the lawn and, in the driveway, a rusted-out pickup with a gun rack. What she found was a house trailer, the first of four strung in a row, 24A and B and C and D. No pickup, with or without a gun rack. No cars on the lawn, and in fact no lawn; the trailers nestled within a near-forest of scrub pine, and the fallen needles carpeted the ground.

One car, a Hyundai hatchback with a dented front fender, stood alongside the trailer.

Home Sweet Home, she thought.

She'd have phoned, but she'd been unable to find a phone listed for him, or indeed for anyone at 24A Maple Street. And maybe that was just as well, because what would she have said? *Hi, you won't remember me, but I gave you a bon voyage blow job the morning before you shipped out. I can't remember what year it was, so there may have been a few tours of duty since then for you, and a few blow jobs, too, but—*

But what, pray tell?

Better to just show up and play it by ear. She had no idea what to say in person, but she figured she'd come up with something. And he didn't have to remember her, or welcome her with open arms, or do anything, really, but let her in the front door. She could take it from there.

Wrong again.

The woman who came to the door looked as though she'd been bearing up bravely ever since the day she was born. That would have been some thirty-five years ago, and they hadn't been easy years, and she wore her long-suffering look as if it affirmed her identity.

A wife? A girlfriend? No wedding ring, and this woman didn't look like anybody's girlfriend. Too young to be Alvin's mother. Jesus, was it even the right house?

She opened her mouth to say something, not sure what she should say, but the woman stopped her by holding her forefinger to her lips.

"My brother's sleeping," she said.

Thus answering an unasked question. This was Alvin's sister, worn down by life, and now sharing a trailer in the back of beyond with her brother.

Provided this was the right address. Just because this woebegone lady had a brother didn't mean it was the man on her list.

So she whispered back, "Alvin Kirkaby?"

A nod.

"I used to know him. Years ago, I don't even know if he'd remember me, but I happened to find this address for him, and I was—"

What? In the neighborhood? The only way anyone wound up in this particular neighborhood was by getting lost and being unable to find their way home. She let the sentence trail off unfinished, and the sister nodded, as if it all made perfect sense to her.

"We can talk outside," came her whisper, and the finger she'd held to her lips was now pointing to a mismatched pair of lawn chairs huddled together beneath the pines. "I'll just be a moment."

"Hope the coffee suits you," the woman said. "It's instant."

It could have been anything, she thought. It had been souped up with powdered non-dairy creamer and a lethal quantity of sugar, and any coffee taste it might have started out with was long gone. She said it was fine.

"It's a relief to step outside," the woman said. "I don't like to leave him, you know."

"Why's that?"

"You don't know? What happened to him?"

She shook her head.

"Roadside bomb."

"Oh."

"They thought he was going to die. Shipped him home in pieces, figured he'd be gone in a week or two and they could bury what was left in Arlington. But our people are hard to kill. This place, an uncle left it to me. I was living in one room over in Charlotte, doing data entry for an HMO. Left that and moved down here where I could take care of my brother. My name's Joanne."

No idea what name she'd given Alvin, and what difference did it make? "Mine's Pam," she said.

"Pam. Why'd you come?"

"To see your brother."

"Thinking maybe y'all could have a life together? Only life he's got's gonna be in that trailer. Only life I got's taking care of him. They was sure he was gonna die but I'm making sure he lives."

"I see."

"Few months ago I'd of said he'd be getting better. Well, that can't happen. I know that now. All he can do is stay alive, and all I can do is keep him alive. So whatever you had in mind—"

"I don't know what I had in mind."

"Thing is, maybe you want to turn around and go right now. Oh, that sounded cold. I didn't mean it that way. What I'm saying is you might want to spare yourself the pain of looking at him, and he'll never know you were here. That'd be what I would do, I was you."

"I came all this way," she said.

"You want to see him."

"I do."

"Well," Joanne said, and glanced at her wristwatch. "Time I woke him, anyway. If I let him sleep too much during the day I'm just dooming him to a restless night."


Worse than she'd expected.

She thought she'd prepared herself, but the reality was worse than the images she'd conjured up on the way back to the trailer. She wouldn't have recognized him as the young corporal she'd slept with in New York. She could barely recognize him as human.

So much of him was gone. One leg ended below the knee, the other at mid-thigh. One arm was off at the shoulder. The other stopped between the elbow and the wrist.

Vivid pink scar tissue covered half his face. His eyes were a clear blue, but only one of them looked at her. The other, she realized, was glass, which struck her as a curiously futile cosmetic touch, like spray-painting a car after a head-on collision.

"This is Pam," Joanne said. "You and her knew each other in—"

"In New York," she supplied.

She met his stare, unable to tell if he recognized her. Now that she'd seen him, she wanted to push back the clock five minutes; then, when Joanne gave her an out, she could agree that slipping away was the best course for all concerned. Then retrace her steps to the convenience store, and either catch the next bus or take a shot at hitching a ride, and get the hell away from Hedgemont as quickly as she possibly could.

Because there was no work for her here. It sometimes seemed to her as if she had an important piece of herself missing, in that the rightness or wrongness of killing her lovers didn't seem to carry any weight with her. Killing was fun, there was no getting around it, and killing men she'd slept with felt appropriate, and that was as much as she had to know.

But to kill this man, this poor maimed creature, could not possibly be appropriate in any way. She'd put him on a list that existed solely in her own mind, and rather than cross him off she could hang a gold star next to his name, or a Congressional Medal of Honor.

She didn't want to kill him. Quite on the contrary, she wanted to do something for him.

But what? Cook him a meal? Joanne prepared his meals, if you could call them that, and fed them to him through an IV line.

Give him a massage? Joanne performed that function, she'd confided, because it was necessary for his circulation, but he couldn't feel it, because he couldn't feel anything below the neck. The blast that took his limbs and his eye had severed his spinal cord. So he couldn't move anything, not that he had much to move, and couldn't feel anything, either.

She should leave, she thought. Say hello, say goodbye, and get the hell out.

But somehow she couldn't.

"Paaaam."

Her name, or at least the name she'd given him. His voice was low in pitch, raspy, as if dragged abrasively through his scarred throat.

"Yes, she's right here, Bubba."

*"Paaaam."*

"I'm here, Alvin."

*"You came."* He had breath enough for a single phrase, then had to gather himself for the next one. *" 'S really you."*

"Yes."

And, haltingly, in three- and four-word bursts, he told her and his sister how much she had meant to him, how her letters had kept his morale up throughout the horror of desert warfare, how he'd longed to return to her, how he'd despaired at her ever being able to find him after his accident.

"You never said, Bubba."

*"Try forget."* A ragged breath, a gathering of verbal forces. *"She here now."*

"I'm here now," she agreed, wondering what else she was supposed to say, and hard put to guess who he thought she was, and what role she played in his personal mythology.

*"Sis…"*

And he rasped out what he wanted. Some time alone with his Pam. Joanne was hesitant, then agreed it would be a chance for her to get the grocery shopping done, and see to a few other errands she never had a chance to run. You're here all the time, he told her. You never get a minute to yourself. Take an hour, take two hours. And give him some time alone with his Pam.

It was hard to get the woman out of the trailer. She had to provide instructions for every possible contingency that might crop up during her absence. But finally Joanne was out the door, and they heard the Hyundai pull out and head off down the road.

"*She gone.*"

"Yes."

"*So who the fuck —*" a ragged breath "are *you?*"

# TWENTY

Who the fuck was she?

Well, that was easy. She told him she'd met him just once, at a bar in the West Twenties. That they'd gone back to her apartment where he'd spent the night before returning to his unit in Iraq.

He seemed to remember. Remembered the bar, thought he was in the wrong place with all the gays there, and then he got lucky after all. He remembered that. Remembered her, sort of. But her name, Pam—

"Well, I probably gave you a different name."

But her real name was Pam?

"Yes, Pamela, Pam for short. Pam Headley."

She'd come this close to saying *Hedgemont*, then remembered that was the name of the town. Changed it to Headley at the last moment.

And what was she doing there? She fumbled her way to an answer. She'd remembered his name, Googled it one day on a whim, and decided it wouldn't take her that far out of her way to stop by and see him. She hadn't known he'd been wounded, hadn't known anything, and the last thing she wanted to do was intrude. But here she was, and if there was anything she could do for him—

*"One thing."*

"What?"

Hesitation. As if he was afraid to tell her what he wanted.

Well, sure. Looking as he did, reduced to what he'd become,

the cocksure quality that had struck her years ago was nowhere to be found.

"If it's sexual," she said, "anything at all, just tell me. I won't have a problem with it. Whatever you want, just tell me."

*"Sex."*

"Whatever you'd like me to do—"

*"Can't feel anything."*

"Oh."

*"Neck down. Nothing."*

"I just thought—"

*"Sometimes it gets hard."*

"It does?"

He got the words out, one ragged phrase at a time. He had no sensation there, but sometimes he got erections, and when it happened he knew it, sensed it somehow even without sensation. If his head was in the right position he could look down and see it.

And eventually it would go soft again, because he didn't have a hand to jerk off with, and couldn't have moved it if he did, or felt anything in either his hand or his penis. He'd tried to come by mental effort, tried to increase his excitement by thinking sexual thoughts, trotting out old memories, working up new fantasies. He let his thoughts run the gamut, tender, violent, aberrant. He'd entertain the memory or the fantasy for a while, and then his erection would subside, and that would be that.

Once or twice, though, he'd come very close while he was sleeping. Almost had a wet dream a time or two. Woke up, though, before he could climax, and that was as far as it went.

Jesus, she thought.

"Is it hard now?"

*"Can't see. But no, can tell it's not."*

"May I see?"

She didn't wait for an answer. A sheet covered his lower body, and she drew it down to mid-thigh. His penis was soft, and her hand went to it automatically, held it gently.

"Can you feel anything?"

"*No.*"

"But you like that I'm holding it."

"*Yeah.*"

"And you can tell that I'm holding it, can't you? I mean, of course you can, you can see what I'm doing, but let's try something. Close your eyes, and I'll hold it and then not hold it, like off and on, and you'll know when I'm holding it and when I'm not. At least I think you will. Can we try that? Can you close your eyes?"

Eye, she thought. He only had one eye to close. Was it wrong to say what she'd said?

Well, it didn't seem to matter. And he'd closed both eyes, anyway, because that's how the eyelids seemed to work, you closed or opened them both at once, the real one and the glass one.

She played with him, fondled him. Then let go of him. Then held him again.

"You can tell, can't you?"

"*Yeah.*"

"Even if you can't feel anything, you can tell. So deep inside somewhere, you're feeling it. Your mind just doesn't know it."

"*Maybe.*"

"You have a beautiful penis. I don't want to stop touching it. It doesn't matter if it's hard or soft. It's just beautiful."

And it was, sort of. In a sense it was just a dick, and God knows she'd seen enough of them in her time, but she was connecting with it in a way that was, well, getting her hot. He couldn't feel anything, and she was getting hot. Go figure that one.

"I want it in my mouth," she told him. "I want to suck that

beautiful cock, and play with your balls, and stick my finger up your ass. I want it for me, see, and I don't give a shit whether you can feel anything or not. But you're gonna feel it, Alvin, even if the message doesn't get all the way to your brain. Your cock's gonna feel it. It's gonna get hard as a fucking rock and I'm gonna suck it and suck it and suck it and you're gonna come like crazy and I'm gonna swallow every drop. Every fucking drop, you hear me?"

"Alvin?"

His eyes opened, and the good one met hers and held it. Was it clearer now? Was there a light in it that hadn't been present earlier?

"Did you feel any of that?"

He took a moment. Then he said, *"I knew when it happened."*

"Was there pleasure?"

*"Kind of."*

"There was for me. I had an orgasm."

*"Don't have to say that."*

"It's true."

*"Yeah?"*

"I was touching myself, but I think I would have come anyway. It was all intensely hot for me. I'm glad you got Joanne to give us some time alone. I guess this is what you had in mind."

*"No."*

"Or something like it, and if there's anything else—"

*"Different."*

"Oh?"

*"You wouldn't do it."*

"Wouldn't do what? Alvin, anything you want me to do, all you have to do is ask."

His eye bored into hers. There was something there but it was hard to read.

"You're afraid to tell me what you want."

*"Yeah."*

"Because of what I'll think of you? Alvin, I won't—"

*"Don't care what you think of me."*

"Then why—"

*"Because you won't do it."*

"I can't if you won't tell me what it is."

*"Only thing I want."*

She waited. That would do it, she knew. If she just waited him out, sooner or later he'd tell her.

*"Pam…"*

Still waited.

*"Kill me."*

Words and phrases, spilling out in fits and starts:

*Can't stand it. Nothing to live for. Can't get better. Can't keep from getting worse. Dying by inches. Sis won't let me die. 'Bubba, you're all I live for.' Jesus. 'Bubba, together we'll keep you going.' Sweet Jesus. 'Bubba, keeping you alive's what keeps me alive.' Only person ever loved me and I'm starting to hate her because she won't let me fucking die.*

*Just kill me. All I want's for it to be over. Don't worry about hurting me. Can't nobody hurt me. Don't feel nothing. Except inside. Inside the pain's always there. Only one way to make it go away and that's kill me.*

*Can't ask it of you. I know that. You're good, you're gentle, you're kind. You ain't no killer. I know all that. Asking you anyway. Begging you. Nobody else to beg. Nobody comes here but Sis. Anybody ever does show up, one look and they're gone. Can't blame 'em.*

*Can't take no more of this. Can't eat, can't move, can't pay atten-tion to TV. All I got left's a heart won't quit beating and a voice in my head won't shut up. Tried to kill myself by force of will. Didn't work. Couldn't make myself come that way. Couldn't make myself die either. All my mind's good for is letting me know how miserable I am.*

*Used to think an orgasm might give me some pleasure. Was like watching it happen to somebody else. Now that's not even there to hope for. Nothing to hope for, nothing but dying.*

"Stop," she said.

After a moment he murmured something, and she had to lean close and ask him to say it again.

"*Sorry,*" he said, in his ragged whisper.

"For what?"

"*Laying it all on you. Held it all in so long, nobody to talk to. Sorry.*"

"Don't be sorry," she said. "Look, I'll do it."

"*What?*"

"What you asked. I'll kill you."

He stared at her.

"Not today," she said. "Your sister'll be back any minute. In fact I think I hear a car. I'll come back tomorrow and we can send her shopping again, and once she's out the door you can tell me if you really want to go through with it."

"*I already told you. You think I'll change my mind?*"

"You might. You told me because it was safe to tell me because you flat *knew* I wouldn't do what you wanted. Well, you were wrong about that. I'll do it. But you'll have to tell me tomorrow that it's still what you want. And that's her car, she just cut the engine. I'll get out of here in a minute, and I'll be back tomorrow, and she'll go shopping again and by the time she gets back I'll be gone forever. And, if it's still what you want, so will you."

❖

The only motel, a quarter-mile or so from the convenience store, was about what you'd expect. Hedgemont didn't get much in the way of tourist traffic, so most of the units were rented by the week to the sort of people who could only dream of working their way up to a broken-down house trailer.

She paid cash in advance for a single night and tried to remember what name she'd told Kirkaby and his sister. Pam, of course, and not Hedgemont, because that was the name of this shithole town, but it started out that way before she caught herself, and what was it? Hedges? Hedgeworth?

Headley! Pam Headley, and it was nice she remembered, but it didn't matter because the old drunk in the office didn't give her anything to sign, just took her money and slapped a key on the counter.

Half an hour later she was sitting in front of the last black-and-white TV in America and eating food from the convenience store— Fritos, Hostess cupcakes, Slim Jims. She forced herself to use the shower, dried herself with the ratty little towel they provided. Stayed up late, woke up early.

Mid-morning, she was back at the trailer.

It was hard getting rid of Joanne. She didn't have to do any more shopping, she told them. Had everything they needed. Why burn up gasoline driving around?

Alvin insisted. He wanted some time alone with Pam. She'd be leaving soon, he might never see her again, and he wanted time together, just the two of them.

The woman got a mulish look on her face. But what could she do? "Maybe I'll visit my friend Aggie," she said. "That's all the way over in Timber Creek. Say an hour there and an hour back, and she wouldn't let me leave without she gives me lunch. So four hours? That enough time for the two of you to do whatever it is you have in mind?"

Joanne grabbed her purse, got her car keys in hand, let the screen door slam behind her. Alvin was about to say something, but she made him wait until she heard the car start up and pull away. Then she asked him if he'd changed his mind.

"*No. What got me through the night was knowing it was the last one I had to get through. And you?*"

"Me?"

"*Change your mind?*"

"No. I'll do it."

"*Yeah, what I realized about you. Last night, thinking. You're steel inside.*"

She let that go.

"*Tried to spare you. Last night. Tried to swallow my tongue. Supposed to be a way to kill yourself, shuts off the air flow. Heard of it somewhere. Don't know if it's even possible, but I couldn't do it.*"

"I said I'd do it."

"*I know. There's a pillow on the sofa. No? What's wrong with that?*"

"Pinpoint hemorrhages on the eyeballs. First thing anybody'd look for, and then they'd look at Joanne."

"*Sis? Anybody who knows her'd know she wouldn't do it in a million years.*"

"So then they'd come looking for me. They wouldn't find me, but they'd come looking, and who needs it? I'm not gonna hold a pillow over your face, okay? It's not that easy if the person's conscious, anyway."

"*How do you know that?*"

"Because I've done this before, okay? And not as a fucking act of mercy, either. Didn't see that one coming, did you? Like a roadside bomb, comes from out of nowhere and takes you by surprise."

*"Jesus Christ."*

"I put a pillow over a guy's face once," she said, "and then I sat on it, and I have to say it was H-O-T. But I don't think he liked it much, and it took him a while to die. Which was fine with me, but I *like* you, and I want this to be easy, so why don't you just let me do it my way?"

God, the look in his eye.

"I have some drugs with me. Should be quick and easy, and if you feel anything you won't feel it for very long."

*"I can't swallow pills."*

"This would be an injection. There'll be a pinprick, but you won't feel that, will you?"

*"No."*

She'd prepared the syringe before she left the motel, filled it from one of the vials from the drugstore in Glens Falls. Now she retrieved it from her suitcase and showed it to him.

"All set," she said. "Anything you'd like to do first?"

*"Like what? Eat a sandwich? Take a quick jog around the block?"*

"I thought you might want to have sex again."

*"No."*

"Or, I don't know. Say a prayer?"

*"Not much for praying."*

"Me neither. You figure there's anything afterward?"

*"After you die, you mean?"*

"Maybe you'll have your body back again. You know, in another dimension. Your arms and legs, and everything healthy."

*"Not counting on it."*

"Or maybe it's a kind of existence where there aren't bodies."

*"Just souls floating around?"*

"Maybe."

*"Or maybe it's nothing,"* he said. *"Maybe it just, you know, stops."*

"Maybe. This vein looks good. Are you ready?"

*"More than ready."*

"I don't suppose I need an alcohol swab. I guess infection's not a consideration. Sorry, I'm all thumbs all of a sudden. Just as well you can't feel anything. Okay, I think I've got it in the vein. Alvin?"

*"What?"*

"Look, if there *is* something afterward, and somebody up there wants a report, would you tell them I wasn't bad all the time? That there was one time I did something good?"

Jesus, was that a tear in the corner of his eye?

She pressed the plunger, kept looking at his eye, watched the light fade from it.

*One.*

# TWENTY-ONE

One.

A bus, a plane, another bus. A Rust Belt city in east-central Ohio, immune to economic cycles because it had been in its own permanent recession ever since the end of the Second World War. A dingy SRO hotel, her drab room so small that the initials might as easily have stood for Standing Room Only as Single Room Occupancy.

And a minimum-wage job two blocks away, in a shop that sold rolling papers and recycled jeans. She wore the same basic outfit every day, loose jeans and a bulky sweater, and she didn't put on makeup or lipstick, or do anything with her hair. She kept herself as unattractive as possible short of putting on weight or breaking out in pimples, but a certain number of guys hit on her anyway. Some guys were like that; the mere possibility that you might be the possessor of a vagina was all it took to arouse their interest.

She deflected any attention that came her way, meeting their gaze with a slack-jawed, bovine stare, missing the point of their innuendo. Some of them probably thought she was retarded. One way or the other, they all lost what minimal interest she'd inspired.

After work she'd pick up half a barbecued chicken or some Chinese take-out and eat in her room; when that got old she'd stop at a diner and sit in a rear booth reading the paper while she ate. Back in her room she read library books until it was bedtime. She went to bed early and didn't get up until she had to. If this city was a place to hide, well, so was sleep.

❖

It was strange. She'd felt uplifted after she left Hedgemont, felt she'd done something good, something transcendent. She'd given Alvin Kirkaby something he longed for, and something no one else could or would have given him—the liberation of a peaceful death.

And that made her feel good, in an unfamiliar way, and she enjoyed the feeling while it lasted.

But it didn't last very long, and when it passed it gave way to a feeling of emptiness. Her life stretched out in front of her, and she saw herself going on like this forever, hooking up with men, sleeping with them, killing them, and moving on. What she had always enjoyed, what had indeed never failed to thrill her, all at once seemed unendurable.

So she worked in the daytime and read in the evenings and slept at night. And put everything on hold, waiting.

One afternoon she bought a phone. Prepaid, good for a couple of hours of calls. You could trace it back to the store where she bought it, but no further than that. They didn't make her give a name, let alone show ID.

She took it back to her room, put it in a drawer. Three nights later she picked it up and made a call.

"Kimmie!"

"Hi, Rita."

"I was wondering if I'd ever hear from you again."

"Oh, I'm harder to shake than a summer cold."

"It's so good to hear your voice. Only the thing is—"

"You've got company."

"How'd you know?"

"Is he cute? Has he got a nice cock?"

"*Kimmie…*"

"You want to call me back when you're done? I'll give you my number."

There'd been no calls, to Rita or to anyone else, since she left Hedgemont. There'd been no phone—she'd left the battery in one trash receptacle and the phone in another, and hadn't bothered to get a new phone until just the other day, when a store she'd passed every day suddenly drew her in.

And then, the new phone in her possession, she'd left it alone until tonight. She'd bought it for one reason and one reason only, to call Rita. So why did it take her three days to get around to making the call?

"So did you fuck him?"

"Kimmie! Suppose it was somebody else calling?"

"Not much chance of that. Nobody else has the number. Anyway, I know the answer. Either you fucked him or there was something really good on TV, because I was just about ready to give up on you and go to sleep."

"What, at nine-thirty? Oh, you must be in one of those weird eastern time zones."

"Central. It's eleven-thirty here."

Talking, back and forth. She found herself talking a little about her job, about the place where she was staying. And realized how she'd missed this contact, this connection.

"Such an exciting life," Rita was saying. "A new job, a new address…"

"Feeding a Xerox machine. Picking up General Tso's chicken on my way home. I don't know if my heart can stand the excitement."

"I guess you don't want to hear how I spent the evening."

"By the fireside, knitting sweaters for our troops in Siberia."

"We have troops in Siberia?"

"Not yet. Well? Let's hear it."

"Let's see, you called me when, two hours ago?"

"More like two and a half."

"How time flies. Well, in those two and a half hours I slept with over a hundred and fifty men."

"Huh?"

"One hundred and fifty-two, to be precise. You don't have any idea what I'm talking about, do you?"

"Not a clue."

"He was a Mormon, Kimmie."

"The guy."

"Yeah."

"So he had what, five or ten wives? How does that put you in bed with a hundred and fifty guys?"

"A hundred fifty-two."

"Whatever."

"And he's not polygamous. He's not even married. He's engaged to be married, but the wedding's not until sometime next year."

"I'll clear my calendar. I still don't get it."

"Okay, I'll explain. There were two of them, and they came to my door and rang the bell."

"Him and his fiancée?"

"No, she's back in Utah. Him and another guy. What happened, I was online a month or two ago, I can't even remember, and I guess I checked something about wanting information on the Mormon faith. I thought they were going to send me a book."

"And instead they sent you two guys? And you fucked them both? That still leaves a hundred fifty unaccounted for."

"I only fucked one of them. They were there to hand-deliver a copy of the Book of Mormon and some other literature, and, you know, to convert me. And one of them was really drippy-looking, like he'd have been a nerd but his IQ wasn't high enough."

"But you liked the other one."

"Kellen, his name was. Tall, blond, big shoulders, small waist."

"Your basic hunk."

"And, you know, we connected. I managed to get him away from his buddy—"

"The failed nerd."

"—and we set it up that he'd ditch Dopey and come back. And he did, and things were moving along nicely, and then you called."

"Sorry about the timing."

"It was no problem. I got off the phone, and then, well—"

"You got off."

"You bet. And no, I didn't wear the butt plug. I thought I might have my own personal Mormon butt plug, but that was out because of his fiancée back in Provo. See, ass-fucking is one of the things he's saving for marriage. But the man couldn't get enough of my pussy. Listen to me, will you? I don't know why I'm talking like this."

"Don't stop now."

"Are you wet, Kimmie? Are you touching yourself?"

"Uh-huh."

"Well, don't stop. Because it was really hot…"

"Rita, you're something else."

"Did you come good, Kimmie?"

"You know I did."

"Me too. When he was doing me, and I was really into it and everything, I couldn't stop thinking how I'd call you back and tell you all about it. And once we were done I couldn't wait to get rid of him so I could call you. I don't care if we're lesbians."

"You'd probably have a tough time convincing Kellen you're a lesbian. Speaking of Kellen—"

"I know, I still didn't tell you how he got to be a hundred and fifty-two people."

"Right."

"He was baptized."

"Well, so was I, not that I can claim to remember it. And it didn't make me sprout a hundred clones. I'm still only one person."

"One very special person. If I'm a lesbian, I'm just a lesbian for you, you know. If you were here right now—"

"We'd go down on each other."

"Yes, we would."

"And do a lot of other things."

"Most of which I've been thinking about."

Deep breath. "Can we get back to Kellen, Rita?"

"He was baptized a hundred and fifty-two times."

"He was? Why, for God's sake?"

"Exactly."

"Huh?"

"For God's sake, and for the sake of a hundred and fifty-one poor souls who went through life *without* being baptized. It's a Mormon thing, Kimmie. It's called proxy baptism. You know how they've got this big genealogical research project in Salt Lake City? How they're trying to get the names of everybody who ever lived?"

"I guess I read something about that."

"Well, their goal is to baptize all the people who lived and died without going through that sacrament. And participating in the process is one form of missionary work. Instead of turning up on people's doorsteps—"

"And fucking them senseless."

"—you go through a ceremony designed to get the unbaptized dead into Heaven."

"Salvation for the unsaved."

"That's the idea. New hope for the dead."

"I never heard of that before," she said. "It's deeply weird."

"Well, so was Kellen. He wouldn't go down on me."

"He wouldn't? The moron. *I* would."

"Would you?"

"Uh-huh."

"Oh, tell me. Tell me what you'd do."

In the morning she showered and put on her sweater and jeans and walked to work. On her break she sat down at one of the back-office computers and Googled her way to *Mormon proxy baptism*. It was pretty much as Rita had reported, and there was no question about it, the whole business was deeply weird.

On the other hand, who was she to hang that label on anything anybody did? She was crisscrossing the country, trying to regrow her psychic hymen by killing every man who ever had sex with her, and she was involved in a wildly exciting lesbian affair with a woman she'd never laid a hand on. How was that for weird?

Two nights later she couldn't sleep. She'd sat in her room reading until she couldn't keep her eyes open, and then she got undressed and slipped under the blanket and hovered for half an hour on the edge of consciousness. She almost went under, and then she surfaced, and she sat up in bed, knowing it wasn't going to happen.

There was one man left, one blot on her record, and no way on earth to track him down. You could find anything and anybody with Google, but you had to have at least a vague idea what you were searching for, and all she had was a first name and the vaguest possible recollection of a face, undefined in her mind but for a gap between his two top incisors.

And she knew where she'd picked him up, in a Race Street bar in Philadelphia, but all that told her was that he was from some place other than Philadelphia, because he took her to his hotel room, and he wouldn't be staying in a hotel if he lived there, would he? And he'd told her his name was Sid, and maybe it was and maybe it wasn't, and where did that leave her? The one man who'd fucked her and lived to tell the tale was not from Philadelphia, and his name was or wasn't Sid. And, just to narrow it down still further, he had a gap between his teeth.

*Wonderful. Google that, see where it gets you.*

She got out of bed, put on the clothes she'd worn earlier. Was it too late to call Rita? No, not with the time difference. She picked up the phone, put it down again. It was, she decided, not too late to call but too early. Maybe in a few days, maybe in a week, but not yet.

She didn't know what she was going to do about Rita. Well, how could she? She didn't know what she was going to do about her whole goddamn life.

She couldn't keep on doing this forever, could she? Shedding one name and taking on another, leaving one town and moving on to another, sleeping with men and leaving them lifeless? How long could you do that?

She'd rarely stopped to take long views, living in the moment, but something had happened to her in Hedgemont. She couldn't define it or figure it out, but it had changed her by more than the simple subtraction of a name from her list. She'd left North Carolina feeling somehow ennobled, and ever since then she'd seen herself and her life not in extreme close-up but as if from a distance.

Like she was seeing a bigger picture, sort of.

She added a hoodie for warmth and walked down a flight of stairs and out of the hotel. The city shut down early, and the streets were empty, with no traffic to speak of. The bars were closed. There was sure to be an all-night café somewhere, but she wasn't hungry, didn't want coffee, didn't want company. She just felt like walking for a while and letting her thoughts run free.

Could she possibly have a life? A life, say, where she stayed in one place, and had the same name all the time? A life she might even share with another human being?

Like, for example, Rita?

It seemed ridiculous even to imagine it. She'd never had sex with another woman, never wanted to, never really gave it a thought. Then she and Rita spent one unplanned night, having a weird sort of phoneless phone sex, and the next day she was out of there like a bat out of hell. And since then they'd had real phone sex, which is to say they did it over the phone, telling each other stories, and most recently talking about what they'd do to each other if they ever found themselves under the same roof again.

Would she even want to?

Would it be repulsive to kiss another woman on the mouth? Or on the breasts? Would it turn her on to go down on another woman? Or would it turn her stomach?

She'd done just about everything there was to do with men, and she always enjoyed it. The fact that some people regarded an act as perverted or unnatural never bothered her. For God's sake, hadn't she killed a guy, crossed him off her list, and then fucked him one last time? If she could get off doing that, why draw the line at eating pussy?

No, that wasn't the problem. The sex would be all right. It might be quieter and less exciting if it was girl on girl, but it might just as easily be better.

The question was what came afterward.

With men, there was no question. The bed a man shared with her was his deathbed. As soon as she could arrange it, she whisked him out of the world and wiped him off the slate.

And with women? Would she feel the same compulsion, the same genuine need to take her partner's life?

Maybe. Maybe not. She could see the logic in either answer.

It was her father's sexual abuse that sent her down the path she'd been walking all her life. He'd been her first lover, and she'd killed him for it, and all the men since then had been her lovers on the way to becoming her victims. If she slept with a woman, that wouldn't be her father all over again, would it? Women were different. Women were soft where men were hard, yielding where men were obdurate. Women had never abused her.

And yet…

The first person she ever killed was her mother.

That was something she didn't think about too often. For some reason it was easy to forget, even as her mother had been an essentially forgettable person. And it was easy, too, to regard her mother's death as a means to an end. By killing her mother, she set the stage for the murder/suicide the police would discover.

Still, it was hard to pass off matricide as an afterthought. And, no question, she blamed her mother for the abuse. Either the woman deliberately overlooked it or she was willfully obtuse, refusing to see what was right in front of her eyes. She probably welcomed it, because it saved her from the unpleasant duty of satisfying her husband.

Well, she had a lot of ways to look at it. But it was hard to get past the fact that she'd killed the woman, and would she feel a need to kill other women?

She didn't want that to happen to Rita.

For God's sake, she had *fun* with Rita. She enjoyed *being* with Rita. And it wasn't just girls being pals, girls dashing off to the bathroom together to talk about which boys were cute and which weren't.

No, it was sexual. It was sharing sex histories—Jesus, getting her gay hairdresser to teach her how to give a blow job! And it was phone sex without a phone, and then phone sex with a phone, and lots of mutual assurances that there was nothing genuinely lesbian about what they were doing, until they'd passed that point and recognized that it didn't matter whether their actions made them lesbians. *If you were here I'd touch you. If you were here I'd go down on you. Wish you were here...*

All she had to do was get on a plane to Seattle. A nice dinner for two in a comfortable suburban house. Rita would cook, she'd bring the wine. Nuits-Saint-Georges, because it had certainly done the job before.

And then what?

What was required, she realized, was an experiment. She had to go to bed with a woman and see what happened. Not what happened in bed, although it would be good to know if the acts repelled or delighted her, but what happened afterward. If she could walk away from her female partner without harming her, and if the woman's continued existence didn't drive her crazy, then maybe she and Rita had a chance.

If not, she'd stay the hell away from the whole state of Washington. Because she didn't want anything bad to happen to Rita. Because, well, she seemed to care about Rita.

Maybe even loved her. Whatever the hell that was, and it wasn't something to think about, not now. If ever.

First things first. Was there even a lesbian bar in this perfect shithole of a town?

There almost had to be, and it couldn't be too hard to find. But

it would be closed at this hour, and in any case she wasn't in shape
to go cruising. Not in this outfit, not with her hair such a mess, not
when she sorely needed a shower. It wouldn't be hard to pass as a
lesbian, dressed and groomed as she was, but it might be tricky to
find somebody who'd want to go home with her.

A different outfit, she thought. And her hair fixed in a more
becoming fashion, and maybe just a touch of lipstick.

She had to get out of this town. But when?


"Little late to be out walking."

She'd been aware of the car alongside her but hadn't paid attention until the driver lowered the window and spoke. She turned
her head, took in the dark late-model sedan, the driver's face hard
to make out. And just then the dome light came on, as if a look at
him would be reassuring.

And it was, sort of. Forties, jacket and tie, eyeglasses, balding,
hair still dark. A little jowly, a little pudgy. A businessman, maybe
a corporate guy. A solid citizen, for sure.

"Neighborhood's coming back," he went on. "Still, I have to say
it's got a ways to go. Young woman like yourself shouldn't be
walking around at this hour."

"I couldn't sleep," she said.

"Neither could I. Full moon, gets me every time." He leaned
across the seat, opened the door in invitation.

She had to get out of this town. There might be a lesbian bar
here, but there'd be a lesbian bar in another city, and she could go
there and get a fresh start. But it was so easy to give in to inertia,
to wear the same schlumpy clothes to the same time-killer job, to
bring home take-out food to her squalid little room, to put the
world on hold while the days turned into weeks.

All she had to do was get in the car and that would change. The back pocket of her jeans held a folding knife, and its four-inch blade was long enough to reach his heart. By the time his body worked its way down to room temperature, she'd be on a bus out of here.

She'd leave because she'd have to leave. That made him her ticket out.

So what was she waiting for?

*Not a good idea,* a little voice warned her. *Say something, or don't say anything, but turn around and go back to the hotel. Whatever you do, don't get in the car.*

She got into the car.

# TWENTY-TWO

"Seat belt," he said.

He was looking straight ahead, hadn't glanced at her since he pulled away from the curb. So he'd noticed earlier that she hadn't fastened her seat belt, but waited until the car was rolling before saying anything.

Because she might have changed her mind and opened the door, but it had locked automatically when the gears engaged. She noted the set of his jaw, the sheen of perspiration on his forehead.

*Whatever you do, don't get in the car.*

Yeah, well. I heard you loud and clear, little voice. I just didn't pay attention.

He said it again, wrapping the words in a smile. "Seat belt. There's a state law, I could get a ticket."

"You're not wearing yours."

His face registered surprise. "Had to unhook it to open the door for you," he said. And he fastened his own belt, and she could almost hear his thought: *Won't take me any time to unhook it again. And you're not going anywhere, little girl.*

Any reason to stall? None she could think of. It would just put him on guard, and that was the last thing she wanted. He outweighed her by eighty or a hundred pounds, and there looked to be muscle under that corporate façade. Surprise was the only edge she had.

She fastened her seat belt.

✼

He hadn't asked where she lived, where she was headed, where she wanted to go. Hadn't asked her name, hadn't told her his.

Because she knew she'd stopped being a person in his eyes the minute she got in the car. Not that she'd been a person before that. She'd been a quarry, to be tracked and played, and he'd played her well enough because here she was, in his car, and now all he had to do was make use of her. And that was easier if she was depersonalized.

So she wasn't a person anymore. Once her bottom was planted in the passenger seat, once her seat belt was fastened, she no longer existed as a human being. She was whatever he'd leave when he was done raping and torturing her. She was dead meat. She was body parts.

"Where are we going?"

She didn't think he was going to answer. She was trying to decide whether to repeat the question, whether to let a touch of panic come into her voice, when he said, "There's a place I think you'll like."

"Oh?"

"Near the lake."

Was there a lake nearby? She hadn't paid any attention to the local geography, but she supposed there was always a lake in the area, unless you were out in the middle of the desert.

"I hope it's not too far."

"Why? You got a train to catch?"

"I was just thinking that I'd like to suck your dick. You know, while you're driving? But I can't as long as I'm wearing my seat belt."

Well, he hadn't expected that. She was watching his face, and saw his expression change. She couldn't read it, not looking at him in profile, but something registered.

"Whore."

It was remarkable how much contempt he could get into a single syllable. He hated her, just plain hated her. But she responded as if oblivious to all that.

"I know," she said. "I'm just terrible. I'm a bad little girl and I just can't help myself."

He was breathing a little faster. And was it her imagination or had his grip tightened on the steering wheel?

"It's probably the full moon," she went on. "I get restless and all I can think about is sucking cock."

"You're a fucking whore."

"I know," she said. "Look, let me suck it now, while you're driving. Okay? And then when we get to where we're going, you can punish me for being bad." She uncoupled her seat belt. "Would you do that? Would you give me a spanking for being so bad? And maybe you could think of other things to do, so I'll really learn my lesson."

She swung around, brought her face to his crotch. Unbuttoned his pants, lowered his zipper. No underwear. A suit and a necktie, but no underwear, and no great commitment to personal hygiene, either. His uncircumcised penis, soft and small, did not smell like anything you'd want to put in your mouth, or even be in the same room with.

But if there'd been any question in her mind, this answered it. He'd been out hunting, and he meant to kill her.

She took hold of him with her left hand, reached around with her right hand for the knife in her hip pocket. Her mouth took him in even as her fingers fumbled with the knife, finally got it out of the pocket. She palmed it, held it out of sight, and he didn't seem to have noticed.

Now if she could only get it open. There were knives you could open readily with one hand, switchblades and gravity knives, but this was your basic Dollar Store jackknife, with fake mother-of-pearl grips and a single four-inch blade. She tried to open it with one hand, couldn't.

Maybe the blow job would be distraction enough. But he didn't seem to be responding. He was breathing more rapidly, but he wasn't getting hard. Well, that almost figured; he was a sadist, a killer, and he'd only get an erection if he was in control and she was in pain.

Just as she had that thought, she felt his hand on her throat.

His right hand, because he was still driving the car, still had his left hand on the steering wheel. His fingers settled on the back of her neck, his thumb at the base of her throat.

His grip tightened.

Don't panic, she told herself. You can't strangle a person with one hand. It's hard enough with both hands.

But was that necessarily true? He was strong, he had big hands, and he was exerting a lot of pressure. Jesus, what a way to die, with a truly disgusting dick in your mouth and one huge hand throttling the life out of you.

And he was saying something. Hard to make out at first because he was muttering, but he was saying the same thing over and over and eventually she got it. *"You filthy cunt you're gonna die you filthy cunt you're gonna die you filthy cunt…"*

She used both hands, fought to get a grip on the knife blade, fought for breath. He was cutting off her air and it made her head swim and turned her hands clumsy. Then she got the knife open.

She bit down on his cock as hard as she could. His grip softened. She gasped for air and sank the knife blade into his balls.

✻

The car was all over the road. He'd let go of the wheel and made fists of both hands, raining blows on the back of her head. She kept stabbing with the knife—his balls, his belly—and when the pain was enough to stop his fists, she reached out blindly and found the key in the ignition, turned it, shut off the engine.

The car was veering off the road, and he grabbed the wheel to right it, but with the engine off the steering was locked. The car powered through a wire farm fence, bounced crazily over uneven ground, and by the time it stopped moving she had managed to get the knife in his chest.

She had to get out. Had to catch her breath, had to unlock the doors, had to get out of the car and find her way back to her hotel.

But she'd been holding the darkness at bay ever since his hand fastened around her throat, and it had taken all her strength. Now she sighed and let go, and a tide of black rolled in and swept her under.

# TWENTY-THREE

She didn't know how long she was out. The darkness carried her
away, and at some point another wave brought her back. She
opened her eyes to darkness, listened to silence, and wondered
for a moment if she was dead. But dead people didn't feel pain,
and she had pain in her head and neck and shoulders, and she sat
up and confirmed that she was alive.

And he was dead. She remembered stabbing him in the groin, then
in the chest, but she'd evidently stabbed him more times than she'd
realized, and the whole front of him was a lake of blood from multiple
wounds in the chest and abdomen. Her hands were bloody, and her
face, and her hair. Blood everywhere, and it smelled, everything
smelled. She had to get out of there but she couldn't because the
doors were locked and she was trapped with his rotting corpse and—

She breathed against the panic, stuffed it down, willed herself
to rise above it. She figured out how to work the locks, opened the
door on the passenger side, stepped out into the middle of a field.
The car had continued some fifty yards after it left the road, and
whether she'd been unconscious for three minutes or as many
hours, no one had yet taken any notice of it.

She put a hand on the car for balance, drew in deep breaths.
She listened intently but couldn't hear anything. No traffic, no
human sounds. The sky was dark overhead. He'd said something
about a full moon, but if the moon was indeed full it was no match
for the clouds. No moon, no stars, and she was stuck in the middle
of nowhere, and soaked in blood in the bargain.

*All right. You're alive and he's dead, which wasn't the way he planned it. You can get out of this. One step at a time and you can get out of this just fine.*

The first thing she got out of was the bloody sweatshirt. She had a plain T-shirt underneath, and there was likely to be blood on it, but it wasn't soaked and sticky the way the outer garment was. She found a clean portion of the sweatshirt and used it to wipe her hands and face, then tossed it aside. It would be crime scene evidence, but of what? The blood on it was his. As for her own DNA and fingerprints, she couldn't worry about that, not now.

She returned to the car, found the button to open the trunk. There was a suitcase, locked, but there was also a tire iron, and she picked it up and smacked the locks until they popped open. She did some more cleanup with one of his T-shirts, then drew out a white button-down shirt still in its wrapper from the laundry. It was much too big for her, but with the sleeves rolled up and the tails overhanging her jeans, it didn't look too ridiculous.

She went through the suitcase, not sure what she was looking for, and had just about decided she was wasting precious time when she found the little drawstring pouch. She weighed it in her hands. Pennies? Gold coins?

She opened it, and poured its contents into the open suitcase. Rings, a bracelet, a wristwatch, some earrings. Souvenirs.

Well, why should she be surprised? It was hardly news that the son of a bitch had done this before.

His name was Rodney Casselhart, and he was a long way from home. He was in Ohio, driving a car with Pennsylvania plates, and he had an Iowa driver's license in his wallet, and other ID that showed an address in Michigan.

She hadn't wanted to search him, but forced herself, and his wallet was in the first place she looked, his left front pants pocket, with $245 in it.

Not enough. Driving all around the country, picking up women and killing them? That would take cash. He had a couple of cards, Visa and MasterCard, both in his name, but he wouldn't want to use them unless he had to.

God, did she really have to do this?

She decided she did, and in his right hip pocket she found a roll of hundreds secured with a thick rubber band. She didn't waste time counting, just transferred the roll to her own pocket.

Now what?

Just leave everything, she thought.

And the knife? Just leave it in his chest?

They wouldn't need the knife to know he'd been stabbed. You really couldn't miss the wounds. And the knife in her possession would tie her to him. She could boil the thing for an hour and not get all his blood out of it.

But suppose she needed it?

Oh, please. You're wasting time. Just go.

She was a few yards from the road when she heard a car approaching, the first traffic she'd heard since she came to. A ride, she thought, and then she thought No, don't be an idiot. She hunkered down where she was, and the car turned out to be a truck, running its high beams, rolling on down the road.

And it was going away from the town, not toward it. She had her bearings now, remembered that they'd spun left when they went off the road, so the town was to her right. She couldn't guess how far it was, or if there were any turns along the way, but that was the direction she had to take. Because she had to get back to her room, there were things she couldn't just walk away from.

She waited until the truck's taillights were out of sight. Then she started walking.

She'd been walking ten or fifteen minutes when she heard a vehicle behind her. She stepped off the road before the headlights could find her, concealed herself in the darkness. This time it was a car, a squareback sedan, with a man driving and a woman seated beside him. She watched them sweep on by and wished she'd been where they could see her. They'd have given her a ride, and they'd certainly have been safe.

But if they noticed the blood—

She probably could have explained it to their satisfaction. Still, she was probably better off walking. How much farther could it be?

She must have heard the motorcycle well before it registered on her. She'd gotten into the rhythm of walking, and her mind found things to think about. She was thinking how Rita had slept with something like a hundred and fifty men just by fucking that whacko Mormon.

Suppose it had been her? Would she have been killing a hundred and fifty men when she took Kellen out of the game?

Then she became aware of the engine noise, even as the pavement brightened in front of her from the bike's high beams. Too late, she thought, and stepped off onto the shoulder, and turned toward the sound, even as it changed pitch. Whoever he was, he was slowing down. If it was a cop—oh, Jesus, if it was a cop she was screwed.

No point in trying to run. She stood there, waiting, and he braked to a stop. Her eyes registered that he wasn't a cop, but she was only relieved for an instant.

A big man, clad entirely in black leather. Black leather pants, a black leather jacket with a lot of metal studs and zippers. Black leather gloves. Mirrored biker goggles covered his eyes, and a full dark beard obscured the rest of his face.

She'd have been better off with a cop. She wished she'd kept the knife, then knew it wouldn't do her any good. This man would snap the blade between his fingers, then fuck her and kill her and eat her. He'd crack her bones for the marrow, floss his teeth with her hair.

"Rough night?"

His voice was low in pitch. Well, no surprise there. She couldn't see his eyes, but she could feel them taking in the blood, the general disarray.

"Kind of," she said. "I got a ride with a guy and the car got wrecked."

"I saw where somebody went off the road about two miles back. That you?"

She nodded.

"You looking to get help?"

She shook her head. "He's dead."

"Died in the wreck. I got a phone, if you want to call it in."

"No."

"Okay."

Oh, what the hell. "He was going to kill me," she said. "Rape me and kill me. I wouldn't have been the first, either. I went through his bag afterward to find out who he was. There were these rings and bracelets and stuff. You know, women's personal items."

"Souvenirs."

"Yeah."

"Guy had a hobby. You don't want to report it?"

"No." He just stood there, waiting for more, so she said, "Going off the road didn't kill him. It didn't even knock him out. I had a knife. I—"

"Stabbed him."

"It was self-defense, but—"

"You don't want to have to lay that all out for the law."

"No."

"I can dig it. You live around here?"

She pointed in the direction she'd been walking, the direction he'd been heading himself. "I have a hotel room. I need to get my stuff. But once I do—"

"You want to get out of Dodge." He patted the seat behind him. "Hop on."

She didn't pass out during the ride, or fall asleep, but it was almost as if she did. The bike sent the rest of the world away. All she heard was its engine, all she felt was the rush of the wind. She had her eyes closed, her arms around his broad back, her face pressed against the black jacket. She breathed in its old leather smell. Her mind took a break, and the next thing she knew the bike had stopped across the street from her hotel.

She said, "Can you wait? I'll be like two minutes, I just have to grab one or two things."

"Okay."

"Or…"

"What?"

"Well, if you could wait, like, ten minutes, I could clean up and change my clothes. But if you're in a hurry—"

"You ought to do that," he said. "No rush. I'll be here."

✿

She stripped, showered, washed her hair. Dressed in clean clothes, spread out Rodney Casselhart's white button-down shirt on the bed, piled the clothes she'd been wearing on top of it, and folded it to make a bundle, tying the sleeves to secure it. Everything she could use, like her drugs and cash, or that might point them to her, like her cell phone, went in her shoulder bag.

She left the rest, along with her suitcase, locked the room behind her, and walked past the hotel desk with the bag over her shoulder and the bundled clothes under one arm. The clerk barely registered her presence, and her rent was paid for another five days, and by the time they realized she was gone they'd be past connecting her to the car in the field a few miles up the road, or the dead man behind the wheel.

She wasn't sure he'd be waiting, but there he was, her knight in black leather armor, standing beside his bike. He reached for the bundle of clothes.

"Everything I was wearing," she said. "And that was his shirt, I got it from his suitcase."

"I'll get rid of it for you."

He stowed the bundle in a saddlebag. She said, "I'm glad you stayed."

"I said I would."

"Yeah, well. I don't know what I'd have done if you didn't."

"You'd have thought of something. Where are you headed?"

Her thoughts hadn't gone that far. "Just…some other city. Which way are you going?"

"South and west. Cincinnati for starters, but you probably want to get clear out of Ohio."

"Probably, but if you could get me that far…"

"I could cut west now," he said, "but that'd be Indiana, and I got reason not to go there."

"Oh."

"So I'll run you through Cinci and into Kentucky. Let you off in Lexington or Lou'ville. That be all right?"

"Sure."

He patted the seat behind him.

She said, "I really appreciate this. You're going to a lot of trouble for me."

"Not that much trouble."

"Well, the thing is, if there's anything I can do—"

"You could kick in ten or twenty bucks for gas. But if you're short on dough, don't worry about it."

"No, that's easy. And if there's anything else—"

"You pay for gas and breakfast's on me. But not until we're on the other side of the Ohio River. There's a good place in Covington. Can you hold out until then?"

"Sure. But what I meant—"

He turned to look at her, his eyes invisible behind the glasses.

"Just if there was, you know, anything *else* you wanted. It'd be okay."

"Oh," he said.

"I just—"

"Thing is," he said, "I'm not really into girls these days."

"Oh."

"Girls, women. Or guys either. I'm just, you know, keeping it real simple these days."

"Me too," she said. "Real simple."

She paid for their breakfast in Covington—eggs and grits and link sausage, and coffee that had stayed too long on the hot plate. She gave him twenty dollars for gas, and he took it only after she'd assured him that she was okay for cash. When he dropped her at a Louisville hotel, she still hadn't told him her name, or learned his.

She dismounted, then remembered the dirty clothes in the saddlebag. He waved a hand dismissively, said he'd toss them once he'd crossed another state line. She wanted to say something, but all she could think of was "Thank you."

"We're cool," he said, and reached out a gloved hand to touch her lightly on the shoulder. Her eyes stayed on him until he and his bike were around the corner and out of sight.

She took a room and paid cash in advance for four days, which was as much time as she figured she needed to spend in Louisville. Two hours later she was back at the hotel with new clothes and a suitcase. She took a long shower and put on some of the clothes she'd just bought, and decided to throw out the ones she'd arrived in.

By now, she thought, he'd probably crossed another state line.

Would she ever see him again? Jesus, would she even recognize him if she did? She didn't know what he looked like. Except for his nose she hadn't seen any portion of him that wasn't covered by goggles or leather or beard.

She could smell his leather jacket. She could feel the touch of his gloved hand on her shoulder.

She couldn't keep from having fantasies about him. They were full of the physical presence of him, and yet they weren't specifically sexual. She envisioned the two of them on the bike, crisscrossing the nation together, stopping for gas, stopping for food, then moving on. They barely spoke, even as they'd barely spoken during their time together. You couldn't talk over the roar of the engine, and the rest of the time there was no need for talk—as there'd been no need for it earlier.

He'd looked so scary. But the look that she'd feared at first glance had turned out to be a comfort. There was an individual beneath the leather, behind the mirrored lenses. There was a person with a history and an outlook and a world of likes and dislikes. But she didn't get to see any of that, didn't need to know any of it. There was safety, somehow, in all that impersonality.

*I'm just keeping it real simple these days.*

An older brother, she thought. A male cousin. Or, oh, a guardian angel, if you believed in that sort of thing.

She stayed in the Louisville hotel for the four nights she'd paid for. Took long walks, went to the movies, watched TV in her room. Ate three meals a day at the Denny's on the next block. Took two showers a day, sometimes three.

By the time she left—a cab to the airport, a plane to Memphis— she had let go of the memories. They were still there, but they'd lost their edge. The man who would have killed her, the man who got her out of there, were both now just a part of the past.

# TWENTY-FOUR

Rita said, "Memphis! Did you see Elvis yet?"

"I was in a restaurant," she said. "Just a diner, really. And there was an Elvis at one end of the counter and another one in a booth. Those were the only two I've seen and I saw them both at once."

"Elvis impersonators."

"Well, duh, yeah. I mean, if it was just one, I suppose it might have been the King himself, but with two of them—"

"What I meant was have you been to Graceland."

"Oh. No, not yet."

"That would have been my first stop. Kimmie, every time you call you've got a new phone."

"Well, they're disposable," she said. "So I tend to dispose of them."

"Kimmie, you kill me." *Oh, don't say that.* "You know, I thought I saw you the other afternoon. In Seattle, in Pike Place Market?"

"It wasn't me, Rita."

"Oh, don't I know that? I took a good look, and she didn't really look like you at all."

"She was a lot prettier."

"Silly! But you know what I went and did?"

"Picked her up and took her home."

"Kimmie!"

"And ate her pussy."

"Kimmie, you're *terrible!*"

"Am I?"

"You know you are. But what's really bad—"

"You thought about it."

"Yes! I went home and jilled about it."

"And is that what you're doing now?"

"Not exactly."

"Oh?"

"But I'm sort of in the mood."

"Oh, are you?"

"Uh-huh."

"Well…"

And a little later:

"So I was out walking one night, and this guy gave me a ride on his motorcycle. I never saw his face. He was all in leather, and he had a beard, and he was wearing these mirrored goggles. And I rode a couple of hundred miles on the back of his motorcycle."

"You're making this up, right? It's okay if you are, because I like it just fine, but I was wondering—"

"No, this is real, Rita. Anyway, nothing happened."

"Nothing happened? What's that supposed to mean?"

"There was no sex."

"Why not? I mean, even if you were having your period—"

"Neither of us wanted it."

"How come?"

"I don't know. We just didn't. So I'm sitting behind him on the big Harley, and we're zooming through the night, and there's nothing in the world but the vibration of the bike and the smell of his beat-up leather jacket, and—"

"And you came in your pants."

"No."

"You didn't? *I* almost did, just from hearing about it. How come you didn't?"

"I don't know. I suppose I could have."

"What stopped you?"

"I just…let it go. Have you ever been, like, out on a cold day, and you're not dressed for it, and the wind's like a knife?"

"And that's like being on a bike and smelling leather?"

"No, let me finish. When that happens, out in the cold, there's a thing I'll do sometimes. I let the cold just blow right through me, and I visualize it passing through without affecting me. Have you ever tried that?"

"No."

"Well, it sort of works. It's a mental thing, I guess, but it sort of works."

"And that's what you did? You let this biker guy blow through you?"

"The feeling I had," she said. "I just sort of let it pass on through. It stopped being sexual, and then it just went away."

"Wow."

"I know, it's hard to explain."

"That woman I saw? In the Pike Place Market?"

"Still thinking about her?"

"I mean, I never could have approached her. It's one thing to think of it and something else to act on it."

"I know."

"I keep thinking I want to try it with a woman. I'm like, Well, if Kim were here, yadda yadda yadda. But you're not here, and what am I gonna do, walk into a gay bar?"

"You could."

"I know I could. There's one I keep driving past. I don't even slow down, but I keep finding excuses to drive past it. Kimmie, tell me the truth, okay? Have you ever been with a woman?"

"No."

"And here we are, a couple of phone sex buddies, and we don't even know what we're talking about. Except we sort of do, don't we?"

The place she found was just off Beale Street. The windows were blacked out, and an unobtrusive sign told the establishment's name: The Daiquiri Dock. There was nothing to suggest that it might be a lesbian bar, but she evidently sensed something, and lingered in a doorway across the street. And, sure enough, the door opened and a pair of visibly gay women left arm in arm. She stayed where she was, and another woman turned up and walked into the bar, and two more followed shortly thereafter.

She could have a glass of white wine. Get a sense of things, then go back to her room alone.

And that's what happened, except that it was two glasses of red wine, not one glass of white. She bought one, and a woman who said her name was Sandy insisted on buying her the second. Sandy wasn't very attractive, there was a stolid quality to her that she found unappealing, and anyway Sandy lost interest and went off to study the jukebox selections. A couple of other women glanced her way, but she kept her face unexpressive and let her body language suggest that she just wanted a quiet drink.

Back in her hotel room, she began loading her clothes into her suitcase. She wasn't quite ready for this, but she was getting there. She'd get a good night's sleep, leave town in the morning. And in the next city, or the one after that, there'd be a lesbian bar and she'd be ready.

# TWENTY-FIVE

St. Louis, on a quiet street near Carr Square, within sight of the famous Arch. Another city, another lesbian bar, and when she'd scouted it out the previous evening she hadn't even allowed herself to cross the threshold. Instead she'd spent the better part of an hour in the diner diagonally across the street, nursing a cup of coffee, watching through the fly-specked window as women passed in and out of Eve's Rib.

Now and then, a man. Not a mannish woman, there were plenty of those, but occasionally a man entering or leaving, sometimes accompanied by a woman, sometimes alone. One of these—alone, shoulders slumped, hands in pockets—reminded her for a split second of Sid.

Sid from Philadelphia, who of course was not from Philadelphia, and was probably not named Sid. Sid the Cipher, Sid the Unfindable, the one remaining name on her list of Things to Undo. Sid who, just by existing, kept her from—what?

Living her life.

But this wasn't Sid. It was just a man who looked disappointed, as if he'd expected to find the secret of the universe in a dykery, and—

Oh, for Christ's sake. *That's* why they called the place in Memphis *The Daiquiri Dock*, even in the utter absence of a Caribbean motif. Daiquiri = Dykery. It had taken her a week and a few hundred miles to get the joke.

She shook her head, finished her coffee. Then she'd returned to her hotel room.

Tonight she was back, and dressed and groomed for the place, more femme than butch, but certainly no housewife, no sorority girl, no cheerleader. Just a woman looking to meet a woman.

Missy, she thought. Tonight her name would be Missy.

And tonight she didn't hesitate. She went inside, made her way to the bar.

*While his eyes grew accustomed to the darkness, the man led the woman to a booth with a good view of the bar. He sat down opposite her and breathed deeply, watching the women around him. And they were all women; he hadn't seen another man since he crossed the threshold.*

*He said, "God, I love this place."*

*"You love what we find here."*

*"And the place itself. This bar, and others like it. I like the atmosphere, Jesus, I like the way it smells."*

*"You like dyke bars because you like girls," the woman said. "That's the smell you like. You like the way they smell, and their softness, and how they yield, how they give in. How they submit."*

*"Well," he said.*

*The bar was called Eve's Rib, and you had to be looking for it to find it, tucked away on a side street on the edge of the warehouse district. It catered to lesbians, but men were not unwelcome, so long as they didn't make unwelcome advances to the women customers. There was a sad-looking older gentleman he'd seen there once or twice, always by himself, always wearing a suit and tie, always with a glass in his hand. But the fellow wasn't here this evening, and he himself seemed to be the only man.*

*His name was Brady. That was his last name, but it was all anyone ever called him. He'd never cared for his first name, which was Winston, and had thought of changing it from Winston Brady* to Brady Winston. Or perhaps to Brady Brady. With B for a middle initial. B for Brady, naturally.

He was tall, and he'd maintained the same weight effortlessly in the twenty years since college. He didn't care that much about food, sometimes missed a meal. He didn't run or go to a gym or do martial arts, but he somehow got enough exercise to maintain good muscle tone. The only thing he could be said to work at was his suntan, a deep bronze tone courtesy of the beach in the summer and a tanning salon in the winter. He was handsome, with strong facial features and high cheekbones, and he knew it, and knew the tan added to it.

His hair was dark, with just a touch of gray at the temples. He hoped it would stay like that, but knew it wouldn't. A touch of gray was all right, it was even an asset, but he didn't feel ready for a full head of gray hair. Maybe he'd dye it, if it came to that. But in any event he'd preserve the gray at the temples, because he liked the effect.

On the jukebox, an Anne Murray record ended and a K. D. Lang record followed in turn. A waitress came to their booth, took their drink order. She was neither tall nor short, a little thick in the waist but not objectionably so. She came back with two glasses of Chardonnay, and Brady watched her walk off.

"I wouldn't mind," he told the woman.

"Hands off the help."

"Oh, I know. It was an observation, not a suggestion."

"Anyway, she's Girls Only. It sticks out all over her."

"Not the only thing that sticks out."

"She wouldn't like it," the woman said, "and you'd try to make her like it, but it wouldn't work."

"So? It could still be interesting. But it's idle speculation, because, as you so kindly pointed out, it's a case of hands off the help."

*"Exactly."*

*"All the same," he said, "I wouldn't mind."*

She was sitting alone at the bar. She had ordered an Orange Blossom, straight up, without being all that certain what it was, but she'd heard the name and liked the sound of it. And wasn't it something a sweet young thing named Missy would order? This one showed up in a stemmed glass, like a Martini, and it was orange, which figured, and garnished with an orange slice. She took a small sip and identified two of the ingredients, gin and orange juice, but there was an undertone of something else, some cordial, that she couldn't place. Triple Sec? Cointreau?

She kept her eyes facing forward but surveyed as much of the room as she could out of the corners of her eyes. She felt someone looking at her, actually felt the gaze, and she turned her head just enough to catch an oblique glimpse of them. A man and a woman, and she was a beauty while he was movie-star handsome. And they were looking at her, and wasn't that interesting?

But someone else was looking at her, and not from a distance. And walking toward her, no, not simply walking, striding toward her, with an aura of butch self-confidence overlaid upon a core of nervous anxiety.

"What's that you're drinking?"

"An Orange Blossom."

"Good?"

"It's all right."

"Well, drink up and I'll buy you another."

A deep voice, probably deeper than the one God had given her. She'd read about a film star—a gay man, actually, although he kept it a secret until AIDS got him. He'd started out with a high-pitched voice, and did something about it; every day he went to a local subway stop, and when the express train roared by he screamed at the top of his lungs. After a few months his voice dropped a full octave, and he went to Hollywood and started playing romantic leads.

Did this one know the subway trick? Or was she just forcing her voice into its lower register?

Then again, what did she care? It was nice to be admired, but she wasn't interested. If she was going to try being with a woman, what did she want with one who was trying to be a man?

*The woman set down her glass of Chardonnay. "Hell," she said.*
 "Oh?"
 *"That one would be ideal," she said, "but that swaggering bull-dyke got there first."*
 *"Have a look to their right, why don't you."*
 *"How did I miss her? But isn't that —"*
 *"Susan."*
 *"No, but that's close. Suzanne."*
 *"Suzanne it is. We called her Suze, as I recall."*
 *Which rhymes with cooze, she thought.*
 *"Which rhymes with cooze," he said, predictably enough. "She was delicious. And she really didn't want to play, not at first."*
 *"She wanted to play with me. She didn't get unhappy until you joined the party."*
 *"And then she got very unhappy."*
 *"Yes. Fear and anger in equal parts. I have to say it added a little something."*
 *"But she got over it. In fact by the time we were done with her I was afraid she was going to propose marriage."*
 *"She did show some enthusiasm, didn't she?"*
 *Her own name was Angelica, or at least that was the latest vari-*

ation on the theme. Her parents had named her Angela, which early on got shortened to Ange and Angie. And then she resumed being Angela again, until for a while she morphed into Angelique, but that never felt entirely natural. She'd barely considered Angelica, until one night that was her response when someone asked her name, and she'd been Angelica ever since.

She was beautiful, and she knew it, but there was a portion of her psyche that would never entirely believe it. You could be better, it had said, always and forever, and it had led her to lighten her hair the slightest bit and warm its tone to a rich honey blonde. You could be better, it told her, through four minor plastic surgeries, smoothing the imperceptible bump on the bridge of her nose, lifting her full breasts a few degrees, erasing a crease here and a wrinkle there. "Gilding the lily," her São Paulo surgeon said on her most recent visit, but she knew what she wanted, and he did the work.

"Suze the Cooze," Brady said. "What an eager little thing she turned out to be, and inventive in the bargain. I'll tell you, I wouldn't mind a return engagement. And I don't think it would be all that hard to persuade her."

"No."

"No? You certainly had a good time, at least the way I remember it."

"Another time," she said. "Tonight I want someone new."

"You want the conquest."

"I do," she said. "I want the yielding, the submission. And then I want the fear, the shock and awe, when she discovers she's getting more than she thought. And then that delicious moment when she yields all over again."

"To me, you mean."

"Yes."

"I love that part," he admitted. "And if she doesn't yield, well, in certain ways that can be even nicer."

*"It's delicious either way," she said. "That's what I want."*

*"Well, I want what you want, my dear. And she'd be perfect, so it's a shame your little dark-haired friend is taken."*

*"But I don't think she is," she said. "Watch."*

"Thank you," she said. "But no."

"Hey, I just got here, you know? My name's Bobbie."

No response.

"You're not gonna tell me your name?"

"I'm not interested."

"Hey," Bobbie said. "I'm just being friendly, you know?"

"I'm still not interested."

"Man, that's cold. All I said was my name and I'd like to buy you a drink. I wasn't suggesting we take a place together and go pick out drapes."

"You're not my type," she said. "So why should we waste each other's time?"

"I'll bet you've never been with anybody like me. Am I right?" She didn't answer, and the woman took that for assent. "You don't know what you're missing, sweetie."

"And I won't find out," she said, putting a little steel in her voice. "Not tonight, at any rate, so why don't you go find someone who's looking for what you've got on offer?"

"Women," Bobbie said, heavily, and sighed. And got up from her seat.

*"My turn," Angelica said.*

*Brady watched her go. His eyes clung to her bottom as she crossed the room, and he didn't have to check to know that his were not the only eyes on her. She was beautiful, and they were gorgeous together, he and she, and they hunted as a team, spotting their prey, cutting her off from the herd, running her down together, and sharing in the feast.*

*Always a delight. And sometimes it seemed to him that the best part of all was afterward, when it was just the two of them together, and no matter how much energy they'd already spent, they always seemed to have enough left for one final embrace.*

*When she was standing beside the girl, he watched their body language. She was wary, the little darling, but not resistant as she'd been with the butch. Definitely interested, he decided, and his decision was confirmed when Angelica seated herself beside the girl and beckoned to the bartender.*

*Often in their hunting it was he who made the first contact. "I'd like you to meet my wife," he'd say. "I think the two of you would like each other." And the woman's face would fall, because she thought she'd been making a romantic connection and the man was already taken, and thought she and his wife would make good friends. But then she'd learn just what sort of friendship they had in mind, these two beautiful and charming people, and the next thing she knew —*

*But it was different in a venue like Eve's Rib. Then it was up to Angelica to make the move, and to decide what came next. If the woman was bisexual, as so many seemed to be these days, and imbued with at least a minimal sense of adventure, Angelica would beckon him forward, and they'd all three go off together. If, on the other hand, the woman was a genuine lesbian, Angelica would raise an index finger to send him a message. Then Brady would slip away, only to turn up later as a lovely surprise.*

*This girl wouldn't want a man. It would be up to him to make her change her mind. Or to have her anyway. Whether she wanted it or not.*

❖

"I don't think I've seen you here before."

"My first time," she said.

"I'm Angelica."

"That's a beautiful name," she said. Without thinking about it, she'd let her voice come out higher in pitch than usual, and soft and breathy. "Mine's a long way from beautiful."

"Oh?"

"It's Missy."

"Why, that's a sweet name!"

"My parents named me Melissa, but all anyone's ever called me is Missy. I guess it fits me."

Had she ever called herself Missy before? Not as far as she could remember, or Melissa, either. She'd picked Missy out of the air when she walked into Eve's Rib, and now it struck her that she'd made the perfect choice. It was properly soft and girlish, submissive Missy, and that ought to be catnip for this one.

"A few minutes ago," Angelica said, "I thought you might need rescuing."

"Why would I—oh, that woman. Bobbie."

"I couldn't help noticing that you weren't interested, and that she rather emphatically was."

"She's not my type."

"No, I wouldn't think so. You'd want someone secure in her identity as a woman."

"Yes."

"But strong," Angelica said. "Someone a few years older than yourself, I should think. Someone who'd be prepared to lead, and allow you to follow."

Angelica turned to look at her, and she hesitated, but only for an instant. Then she met Angelica's eyes and returned her gaze, holding nothing back, letting herself drink the woman in through her eyes.

For a long moment they sat on their stools, gazing silently into one another's eyes. Then she drew a quick breath, and said, "Wow," and took another breath, and said, "I'm not sure what just happened, but—"

"You and I," Angelica said, "just happened."

"Wow."

Angelica put an arm around her, cupped her shoulder gently but firmly. "You're a beautiful girl," she said.

"You're the one who's beautiful. I'm just—"

"Stop it. You're extraordinarily attractive, and I'm going to make it my personal business to make you realize how stunning you are. Missy?"

"Yes?"

"You and I," Angelica said, "are going to have a perfectly wonderful time." And Angelica's index finger tapped three times on her bare shoulder.

# TWENTY-SIX

*Brady was spinning a fantasy when Angelica put her arm around the girl, but it didn't keep him from spotting his cue. The index finger, tapping three times.*

*He got to his feet, put a twenty on the tabletop, weighed it down with his wine glass. He'd scarcely touched his Chardonnay, and Angelica had taken no more than a sip of hers. Twenty dollars for two sips of so-so California wine, and worth every penny, because his woman had just connected with a sweet young thing who was going to make them both very happy.*

*He slipped out the door, found Angelica's Honda squareback in the lot, and drove off in it, leaving his own Lexus for her. It was a much more luxurious car, and would make more of an impression on his wife's new friend. While it hardly mattered what car got him back to their house.*

*They always took two cars. On the rare occasion when their connection was effected as a couple, they'd leave the Honda and come back for it in the morning.*

*Before the signal, tap tap tap on the bare shoulder, he'd imagined what might have been. Suppose, just suppose, that Angelica had headed not for the sweet little ingénue but for the swaggering butch. That one, with her short hair and her broad gym-muscled shoulders, would have thought she'd missed the brass ring only to get a solid gold one dropped in her lap. Angelica, supermodel-beautiful Angelica, picking her out and hitting on her? Butch would have thought she'd died and gone to heaven.*

*He didn't know about heaven. But she'd have to die.*

*Because the only way he'd be able to have her was by force, and he couldn't delude himself that he could make her learn to like it. It would have to be rape, and while that wasn't altogether unappealing, it made for complications at the end. They couldn't just drop her off on a street corner and expect her to be so ashamed of herself that all she wanted to do was forget the whole thing. If she didn't go straight to the cops and the newspapers, then she'd come back with a couple of friends and a gun.*

*He couldn't let that happen. So he'd have to kill her.*

*And he knew just how he'd do it. He'd read descriptions of the method, and he'd seen it demonstrated more than once in action films. You used your hands, you took the chin in one hand and gripped the back of the head with the other, and you twisted abruptly, forcing the chin up and to the left, yanking the head down and to the right, and if you did it properly you were rewarded with the sound of the neck snapping.*

*If it didn't work the first time, well, she wouldn't be going anywhere. You could keep trying until you got it right.*

*His hands tightened on the steering wheel. It was funny, he thought. Angelica had just connected successfully with the most attractive woman in the place—well, next to herself, anyway. The most ideal prospect for the evening, certainly, and she'd be bringing the girl home, and a wonderful time was virtually guaranteed—for the two of them, certainly, and very likely for the girl as well.*

*And here he was wishing she'd picked up the bull dyke instead. Whose face was handsome enough, perhaps, and who'd have a nice healthy body, but who was by no means his type, or Angelica's either. Oh, he'd enjoy forcing her. He'd get pleasure from the sex. But the only thing that made the butch so irresistibly appealing was the fact that she'd have a broken neck by the time the evening was over.*

*Something, perhaps, for him to think about.*

*Once she'd signaled to Brady, all Angelica wanted to do was corral the girl and herd her out of there. But she forced herself to give him time to get home and get settled in, forced herself to listen, or at least pretend to listen, to some tedious story Missy was telling about a childhood pet. Forced herself to take a taste of the girl's Orange Blossom and speculate as to what the mystery ingredient might be, along with the gin and orange juice. Missy thought it might be Grand Marnier, but wasn't too clear on what Grand Marnier tasted like all by itself.*

*That sounded like a cue, and Angelica offered to buy her one, but Missy said she didn't want any more to drink, and that one Orange Blossom was plenty. "Because, you know," she said, "it dulls the senses. It picks you up at first, but then it sort of numbs you."*

*"And you don't want to be numb?"*

*The girl did whatever it was she did with her eyes. And her lips were just the least bit parted. "No," she said. "No, I don't want to be numb."*

*"Would you like to come home with me, Missy?"*

*"I shouldn't."*

*"Oh, I think you should."*

*"I'm a little afraid, to tell you the truth."*

*"Afraid? Afraid of what?"*

*"I don't know."*

*"You're not afraid of me, are you?"*

*"Maybe I'm afraid of myself. And of you, in a way."*

*"Oh?"*

*The girl looked away, as if the words would be easier to say without eye contact. "I always hold back a little," she said. "With you I think I might not."*

*"You might let go."*

*"Yes."*

*"And find out who you really are."*

*"Yes."*

*"And would that be so bad?" She didn't wait for an answer, but stood up and took Missy in tow, holding her upper arm with a grip that was gentle but firm. And led her, wordlessly, out of the bar.*

The car was a Lexus, which suggested that Angelica was not living on food stamps. That was all to the good, but only confirmed what the woman's dress and manner had already established.

And none of that mattered much, not to her, not now.

Angelica triggered the remote to unlock the doors, then held the passenger door open for her. Well, wasn't that courtly? It was rare enough for a man to hold the door for you. Who would have guessed a woman would do it?

She started to get in, then stopped and straightened up. Angelica asked her if something was wrong. For answer, she turned toward Angelica, thinking *Come on, what are you waiting for?*

And Angelica kissed her. *Oh, sweet,* she thought, and held back at first, then yielded to the embrace and let herself melt utterly into it.

The kiss lasted a while, and when it ended she drew a breath and held onto the car roof as if for support. She was acting, but only in part, because the kiss had turned her on something fierce. She liked the way Angelica's mouth tasted, liked the way she smelled, liked the way their bodies felt together.

She'd thought she would like it, but how could you know for sure until you actually tried it? What was that song, something about *I kissed a girl and I liked it?* Well, there you go. She did and she did. And now she knew.

She said, "You could do anything you want to me. You could do me right here, in the parking lot. And you could make me do anything, anything at all."

*Even as he triggered the remote to open the garage door, Brady had a moment of fear that he recognized as irrational—that the door would lift to reveal the Lexus, that Angelica and her new playmate would have beaten him home. That was impossible, he'd left while they were still getting acquainted, had driven straight home while they'd almost certainly dallied long enough for the first lingering kisses. And, if he knew his wife, a little preliminary fondling to set the stage and raise the temperature.*

*He, on the other hand, had driven directly home, and knew the garage would be empty, and of course it was. He tucked the Honda into its spot on the right, lowered the garage door, and let himself into the house.*

*A drink? No, whatever for? He used the downstairs lavatory because one really didn't want the nuisance of a full bladder in medias res, poured himself a glass of Evian water because one didn't want a dry mouth, either, and mounted the stairs to the master bedroom.*

*And that, he reflected, was a singularly appropriate name for it. The bedroom of the Master, and of the Mistress. And, on nights like this, of their…what? Companion? Slave?*

*Victim?*

*He checked the bedroom. Angelica had already done so before they left the house, setting the stage, but he fussed over it anyway, lowering the already softened lighting the slightest bit, then changing his mind and returning it to pretty much the level she had chosen.*

*Busywork, he thought. He went over to the bed, already turned down in invitation, and ran his hand over the linen. Percale sheets, high thread count, properly silky and luxurious. An abundance of pillows, to cushion the head or elevate the hindquarters, as circumstances required.*

*He checked the drawers in the little bedside chests. Toys in one, ties in another. He pictured the girl, imagined her naked, face downward, spread-eagled, wrists and ankles tied to the brass handholds he'd mounted on the corners of the bed frame. A pillow under her, presenting him with her little-girl bottom, offering him a choice of sheaths for his weapon.*

*And there'd be plenty of time to try them both.*

*Was that the Lexus? Even if it was, he had plenty of time. But there was no need to dawdle. He stopped on the way out, adjusting the position of the three-panel Japanese screen, and deciding, as he'd decided with the lighting, that it had been just right to begin with.*

*More busywork, and it only served to show the stake he had in what lay ahead. So it was a good sign, wasn't it? As often as they'd entertained themselves in this fashion, you might have thought he'd be more casual about the whole enterprise. Even blasé.*

*There was a small room just next to the master bedroom, a third bedroom, really, but he used it as a den. He settled himself in there now, and closed the door.*

*By the time he heard the Lexus, heard it stop at the driveway, heard the garage door as it ascended, he had taken off all his clothes, hanging his slacks and jacket in the den closet, tucking his socks into his shoes, placing his folded shirt and underwear on an arm of the easy chair.*

*He sat in the chair, and unconsciously he touched himself, more for reassurance than anything else. Could something have gone wrong? Had Angelica come home alone? That was always a possi-bility. Sometimes one of them changed her mind. A woman's pre-rogative, after all. To change one's mind.*

*No. He heard voices, the two of them in conversation. He couldn't make out what they were saying, but it was enough to know they were both there together.*

*So the girl had not changed her mind. And now it was no longer her prerogative. She was theirs.*

When they turned on Ordway Avenue, she said she didn't know they had apartments here. Angelica told her she lived not in an apartment but in a free-standing house. "A townhouse," she said. "That's what they call it. It's part of a development, and the associ-ation takes care of all the exterior maintenance, the lawn-mowing and landscaping and all that. But in every other respect it's a private home."

"And you live there all by yourself?"

"I'm married, Missy."

"Oh."

"He's the perfect husband," she said, "in that he makes a lot of money and doesn't care how I spend it. And best of all, he travels a good deal of the time."

"Is he away now?"

"He's out of town," Angelica said, "and I'm out *on* the town. That's how it works."

"Does he know—"

"How the mouse plays when the cat's away? It's hard to say what he knows and what he chooses not to know. One time he said, very pointedly, that he wouldn't like it if I was with another man. And he put the emphasis on man, which left me feeling that he had his suspicions, and that he didn't mind if I found a playmate now and then."

"And when he's home—"

"I keep him very happy."

"I see."

"Do you, Missy? And when he's away, I keep *myself* very happy. I drove him to the airport this morning, and he called this afternoon to let me know he was safe and sound in Kansas City. From there he goes to Omaha, and then I forget where in South Dakota. And so on, and he won't be back for ten days."

After a moment she said, "And when he comes home you'll sleep with him."

"Indeed I will. You disapprove?"

"No, I just wondered. I mean, do you enjoy it?"

"I like girls more, Missy. But that doesn't mean I don't like boys."

"Oh."

"And you?"

She paused, as if considering the question. "Just girls," she said at length.

"You're so sweet," Angelica said, and put a hand on her thigh. "You wouldn't believe the fun we're going to have."

Angelica's hand stayed on her thigh until she braked the car in front of a well-proportioned two-story house, a center-hall Spanish Colonial with a tiled roof and an attached garage. The hand moved to the visor, and Angelica worked the remote and raised the garage door, then parked alongside a smaller Honda.

She said, "His car?"

"Mine, actually. But when he's out of town I get to drive his Lexus."

"You get to do just about everything, huh?"

"Everything good," Angelica said.

They both got out of the Lexus, and the garage door descended as they approached the door leading to the kitchen. She was a few steps behind, resting her hand on the Honda's hood while Angelica turned the key in the lock.

*Click!*

*What the hell was Angelica doing? Giving the little darling a guided tour of the downstairs? And, while she was at it, nailing her on the couch?*

*Waiting like this was sweet torture. But at length Brady heard their feet on the carpeted stairs, heard them walk down the hall and turn at the bedroom. And now he could make out their voices:*

*The girl: What a big bed.*

*Angelica: In case you want to hide from me.*

*The girl: And then you'd have to search for me.*

*Angelica: I found you at the bar, didn't I? I think I'll be able to find you in the bed, Missy.*

*Ah, so her name was Missy. And she had a little-girl voice, to go with her little-girl name.*

*Missy: This is nice. Is it Japanese?*

*The screen. They always noticed the screen. And more often than not looked behind it, perhaps unconsciously needing to reassure themselves that there was no one lurking there. Because there could be a man there, a savage creature with a shark's grin and a massive erection, an unwelcome intruder in a girl–girl scene, but no, the screen was purely decorative, and there was no one for it to conceal.*

*Angelica: My husband saw it in a shop in San Francisco. He bought it and had them ship it here, and the first I knew about it was when the UPS truck turned up.*

*Missy: It's beautiful.*

*Angelica: He has an eye for beautiful things.*
*Missy: Well, that's obvious, isn't it?*
*Angelica: And so do I. Come here, you beautiful thing.*

If you were going to try going to bed with a woman, she thought, it might as well be a beautiful one. Angelica was that and more, and it wasn't surprising that she proved to be a gifted lover. She had been certain of that from the first touch, the hand on her shoulder, and had been certain of her own response from the first kiss in the parking lot.

And in certain respects it was easier to be with a woman. She always felt the slightest bit shy the first time she undressed in the presence of a man. It was a sort of reflexive timidity, and it never lasted long, but it was always there. Tonight though, when she was about to do something she had never done before, and thus had every reason to be apprehensive, the act of disrobing had no attendant shyness.

Because she'd been comfortable undressing in front of women ever since she'd been a little girl, changing in and out of gym clothes at school, getting into a bathing suit at the beach. Angelica looked her over while she undressed, but other women checked you out all the time; if they weren't interested in you sexually, then they were sizing you up as potential competition.

Whatever it was, she was entirely at ease. And if she had any anxiety about joining Angelica in bed, any concern that she wouldn't know what to do, that was gone in no time at all.

Angelica made it easy for her by taking the lead, which was no real surprise. Their roles in this performance were a given, with herself as the bottom and Angelica as the top. "Just close your eyes," Angelica said, in case there was any doubt, "and lie back, and let me love you."

Easy enough to comply. Easy enough to give herself up to Angelica's hands and Angelica's mouth, and, really, what could there possibly be to object to in any of that? There wasn't a thing Angelica did to her that hadn't been done by men, and if some of those men had been awkward or clumsy or in a hurry, not a few had known what they were doing and done it with skill.

Angelica, a woman herself and the experienced lover of women, knew what to do and how to do it, and picked up cues from her responses. And Angelica was in no hurry for her to arrive at her destination. Instead she kept taking her to the brink, keeping her right on the edge, then easing back and letting her cool down just a little before she started in all over again.

There was an element of torture to it, because she reached a point where she really wanted to come, and yet it was all so exquisite that she didn't want it to end. It was a little unsettling to have a lover who was so utterly in control of her responses, and at the same time it was quite wonderful.

Oh, and there was something she hadn't been expecting. Angelica's spit-lubed finger, finding its way unerringly into her bottom. And moving in an insistent rhythm, but not the same rhythm Angelica was employing elsewhere. Jesus, the woman was playing her like an African drum. With a tap tap here and a rat-tat-a-tat there, and, omigod, oh, *yes*...

*Don't stop*, she thought. *Please don't stop.*

Jesus, did she speak the words aloud?

It didn't matter. She wasn't going to stop this time, she was going to come, yes, and she kicked her feet and thrust with her hips and cried out, because why not, men liked it when you made a little noise, so why shouldn't a woman like it, and what difference did it make who liked what, because she could no more hold back her cries than she could hold back her orgasm.

*Yes!*

＊

*Was there anything more beautiful than two women making love?*

*If so, he couldn't imagine what it might be. He was not, in ordinary circumstances, a voyeur. He could neither imagine himself as a Peeping Tom, lurking at bedroom windows in the hope of a glimpse of the forbidden, or as a spectator at orgies, watching others having sex. Watching a man with a woman, or a man with a man, held no appeal for him.*

*But two women, that was somehow different. And when one of the women was his woman, his Angelica, the appeal was irresistible.*

*And this one, this Missy, this doe-eyed ingénue, complemented her perfectly. He couldn't imagine a more ideal partner for his magnificent wife.*

*He'd given them a few minutes in bed before leaving his den and taking up his position behind the Japanese screen. He was barefoot and the floor carpeted, so no one could hear his footsteps, and the screen was so situated that his brief passage from the doorway was invisible to anyone in the bed. Even so, he'd walked lightly and quickly, and held his breath until he was where he wanted to be. Then he put his eyes to the tiny viewing slits, and saw the two of them, and he'd been watching them ever since.*

*He never tired of watching Angelica bring a partner to climax. She loved to tease, and he sometimes suspected that he was no less the object of her teasing than the woman upon whom she was performing. He fancied that he could feel what Missy was feeling, that her excitement was his excitement, and when she came he felt a tremor of the spirit, a sort of psychic equivalent of orgasm.*

*And now it was Missy's turn.*

# TWENTY-SEVEN

And now it was her turn.

As she lay quietly beside Angelica, giving herself over to the afterglow, she was struck by the sudden undeniable awareness that she was being observed. She could feel him there, behind the Japanese screen, could feel his eyes on her. She had the urge to look over there, even to wink at him, but she suppressed it. She was, after all, sweet young Missy, who could not possibly suspect Angelica's well-heeled traveling man was even in the house, let alone in the room with them.

So she couldn't acknowledge his presence. But she could damn well give him something to watch.

She rolled over on her side, kissed Angelica's mouth, put a hand on Angelica's breast, caressed it, then ran her hand over the flat stomach and down. Angelica was smooth as silk, she must have had it waxed, and was that a lesbian thing? Did they all do that, and was she herself less desirable for having hair there? If so, she thought, the woman had done an Oscar-worthy job of concealing her distaste.

Still, it was something to think about. Touching it—and she couldn't seem to stop touching it, not that Angelica gave any sign of wanting her to stop—touching it was quite irresistible.

She'd wondered if she would know what to do when her turn came, but could see now that she knew everything she needed to know. She knew what she liked done to herself, for starters, and she had just learned what Angelica liked to do, and could thus be presumed to like done in return.

And her fingers were eliciting the desired response. She found things to do with them, and got the woman off that way, because teasing was Angelica's trick, and she sensed that she would not want to be teased in return. And then, while Angelica was still in the throes of orgasm, she put her mouth to work.

She'd thought that she might not like doing it, but she did. And, from what she could tell, it turned out she was pretty good at it.

Angelica certainly seemed to be having a good time. She could only hope it was fun for the guy behind the screen.

*Brady, perversely, was thinking of something else.*

*His eyes were glued to the action before him, and he was paying close attention to what they saw. But his mind had slipped almost a year into the past; while he watched one thing, he remembered something quite different.*

*The boy.*

*His name was Darwin, and he was their first — and thus far only — male playmate. It had been Angelica's idea, and she'd made the suggestion several times before he agreed to it.*

*"For variety," she'd said. "To test your limits, stretch yourself a little. And so that you can experience what I have every time, utterly dominating someone like yourself."*

*He protested that he wasn't gay, wasn't bisexual, didn't find himself attracted to men. "Curiosity," she'd said. "You've had your cock sucked; what's it like to suck one? You've fucked women; what's it like to fuck a man? Or get fucked by one?"*

*"I wouldn't let a man inside me."*

*"Why not? You like it when I do you with a strap-on. Don't tell me you haven't got the urge to try the real thing."*

*In the end he agreed to it. "To keep you happy," he'd told her, but that's not all it was. He'd dismissed the questions she'd raised, shrugged them off and waved them away, but they came back. They were, truth to tell, things he'd wondered himself.*

*But not in St. Louis, not anywhere in Missouri. Instead they flew halfway across the country where they checked into a good hotel under false names. They had dinner in their room, and he barely touched his.*

*If he was this nervous, he told himself, then he really did need to go through with this.*

*There was a gay bar just blocks from the hotel. He walked to it and sat in a corner nursing a gin and tonic. Men approached him, and his manner was amiable but distant.*

*"Pick a cute one," she'd said, but none of them struck him as cute. They were men, they didn't appeal to him. But in the end he chose a sort of male ingénue, a willowy young man whose big brown eyes were his most remarkable feature. Their lashes were long, and enhanced by mascara.*

*Brady bought him a drink, a Stinger, and the youth said he could really use it, because his rent was past due and he didn't know how he'd be able to pay it. Brady said he might be able to help, and Darwin said that would be just wonderful.*

*Back at the hotel, Darwin was not happy to discover that he had two people to play with, and that one of them was a woman. It took a few drinks to loosen him up, and Brady learned the answers to a couple of the questions Angelica had raised. The acts were interesting, though not ones he'd feel a need to repeat, and the satisfaction of imposing his will on the boy was similar to what he felt with the women Angelica picked up.*

*But Darwin cringed at Angelica's embrace, and was unable to maintain an erection with her. And when they tried to get him to go down on her he burst into tears. It was not the ending they might have hoped for, and they stuck him in the shower to sober up, then gave him several hundred dollars and sent him off into the night. He left, whimpering, and that was the end of that.*

*Now, though, Brady realized the evening should have ended differently. With Darwin's face forced between Angelica's legs, while Brady was lodged deep inside him. And then, at just the right moment, one hand on the boy's chin and the other gripping that long hair. And a quick yank, and the neck snapping.*

*It would have been so simple, and so satisfying. By the time anyone found the body, they'd have been halfway home, and no one would have a clue who'd snuffed out the young man with the slim hips and huge eyes.*

*And that young man wouldn't get to tell his friends about the disgusting couple he'd been with, and how Mr. Macho Man had sucked him off.*

*Brady, watching the two women now, thought of what might have been. He wished he could turn back the clock and the calendar and make that singular evening come out right.*

*He looked at Missy, who was every bit as doe-eyed as Darwin. And he felt an unaccustomed tingling in his hands.*

Angelica lay on her back with her eyes closed and felt Missy's hand settle on her belly and make its way to her loins. How tentative that hand had been earlier, and how sure of itself it had become!

"It's so perfect," Missy said.

"You do seem fond of it."

"So smooth and bare. Like a little girl's, but not like a little girl's at all, you know? I can't keep my hands off it."

"The first time I had it done, I couldn't keep my own hands off it. And as for my husband —"

"He likes it?"

"I knew he would. It was a surprise. And it made him very happy."

"Well, it came as a surprise to me. And I have to say it made me very happy, too." A pause. "Maybe I should have mine done."

"If you decide to," she said, "there's really only one place in town to go. I'll write it down for you later. And if you tell her I sent you, you may get a little extra." Missy seemed baffled. "Catherine's an artist," she explained, "and a great fan of her own work. If she likes you, you'll get a muffing along with the waxing. I always do, and that's the part Brady never hears about."

But of course he did, and was always after her to recruit Catherine for a party. But then where would she go for a waxing? One had to be practical.

"But that's for later," she told Missy. "Get over here and kiss me."

Should she have the girl one more time? She loved to keep Brady waiting, but not forever. And she really didn't want to wait any longer herself. She wanted to see the look on Missy's face when Brady appeared, and when she realized what was coming, and that there was nothing at all she could do about it.

Deftly she slipped free of Missy's embrace. She opened a drawer in the nightstand, took out a handful of silk scarves. Missy caught sight of them, puzzled, and Angelica moved her hand and let the silk trail over the girl's body.

She said, "Missy, darling, can we try something?"

"What?"

"It's my favorite little game. I want to tie you up."

"Oh."

"I know you'll love it." As she talked, she reached for Missy's wrist, and was taken aback when the girl pulled her hand away.

"*Just let me show you,*" *she began again, and reached out, only to have Missy once again draw away.*

"*I'm sure it'll be wonderful,*" *Missy said, and there was something different about her voice. It seemed stronger.* "*And we'll try it in a little while. But before we do that I'd like to tell you about my own favorite fantasy.*"

"*Oh?*"

"*It's something I've always wanted to do,*" *Missy said,* "*but I've never had the chance. Can I tell you? You won't laugh when you hear it, will you?*"

"*Of course not.*"

"*I have this fantasy of being with a couple. A man and a woman, and all three of us in bed together. The ideal woman—well, you're the woman of my dreams, no question. And the man would be tall and dark, and very distinguished-looking, with just a touch of gray at the temples. Like the man you were sitting with tonight before you came over to the bar.*"

*Was this really happening?*

"*That was his car in the garage, wasn't it? The engine was still warm. He left before we did and was here when we got home, and he's behind the screen right now, isn't he?*"

"*Who are you, Missy? Really?*"

"*Me? I'm just a girl who's never had such a hot evening in her whole life, and I have the feeling it's just getting started. What's your husband's name?*"

"*It's Brady.*"

"*Brady and Angelica. Perfect. And little Missy, the luckiest girl who ever lived. Brady? Come out from behind the screen, why don't you? Wouldn't you like to get over here and fuck me?*"

# TWENTY-EIGHT

So many ways to do it. Combinations and permutations, no end of them.

Curiously, sex had never been that important to her. For all the men she'd gone to bed with, the sex was never what it was really about. She enjoyed it and she was good at it, she liked giving pleasure and liked taking it. Her partners always had orgasms, and she liked it when they did. And she generally had one herself, and she liked that, too, because what was there not to like?

But it wasn't about sex.

In the beginning, with her father, it had been about making him happy, and making sure that he kept on loving her, that he was proud of her. And yes, she liked it, liked when he moaned with pleasure, liked the way his lovemaking made her feel.

Until she let him down by beginning to grow up. At which point he decided they couldn't make love anymore. Which disappointed her greatly, but not because she'd miss the sex. That, she knew even then, was something she would always be able to get.

But he didn't want her anymore. That was crushing, knowing that. She hadn't known what to do, but then she came to know, and she did it, and since then everything had been pretty much all right.

And she'd found that it was as she'd figured, that sex was never hard for her to come by. And God knows she got her share of it, but the fact remained that it wasn't about sex.

But it was really wonderful to try all the things that were available to you when you had three performers instead of merely two. A third mouth, a fifth and sixth hand, another set of genitalia—the possibilities increased exponentially, and when you added in the toys Angelica kept on hand, paraphernalia for the genitalia, as it were, well, there was no limit to what you could do.

Now, though, there was a welcome lull in the action, and she lay between the man and the woman, breathing in their scent and the aroma of their mutual passion, with her face nuzzled between Angelica's breasts and one of her arms extended, one of her hands lightly gripping Brady.

And she said, "Did I mention that I was an orphan? I don't think I did, and I know for sure I didn't say anything about how it happened. See, what it was, I lived with my parents, no brothers or sisters, and I was in high school and I spent this one night at a girlfriend's house. Not a girlfriend in the Eve's Rib sense, just my best friend in school, and I called home to say I was sleeping over and there was no answer, and I got a funny feeling. And in the morning I went home and they were both dead, my mother and my father, and what happened, he shot her and then he shot himself. So it was very sudden, how I got to be an orphan."

And, while they were taking that in, she said, "Listen, there's something I'd like to do, if it wouldn't freak you out. I mean, it's not physical or anything. It's just inside my mind, really, but do you think it would be okay if I called the two of you Mommy and Daddy?"

*Brady lay on his back, his eyes closed. It occurred to him that anyone observing him would think he was relaxed and at peace. He was neither, and he knew what would have to happen in order for him to relax, to be at peace.*

*He heard the girl say she'd be back in a few minutes, felt the* mattress adjust itself as she got up from it. Heard her footsteps as she left the room, then as she descended the stairs.

He sat up, opened his eyes.

"She took her purse," Angelica said.

"She's not leaving?"

"Not unless she plans to run naked through the streets. She left her clothes."

She started to say something else, but he put a hand on her flank to silence her. "There's something you have to know," he said, "because I don't want it to take you by surprise. But it's something I need to do."

"Oh?"

"I'm going to do her," he said. "I have to."

"For Christ's sake, Brady, you've been doing her six ways from Sunday for a couple of hours now."

"I've been fucking her," he said, "and I'm going to fuck her some more, but when I'm done with that I'm going to do her."

She looked at him. "You know, you're just gonna to have to spell it out for me, honey. Say what you mean."

If he came out and said it he'd be one big step closer to the act. Did he want that?

He drew a breath and said, "I'm going to kill her."

"Jesus Christ."

"I have to."

"Some Daddy you're turning out to be."

"You don't have to be in the room when it happens. I'll give you advance warning."

"Considerate of you. You know what I was thinking? That you were ready to adopt her and try living as a trio. I don't know that I'd like that."

"No."

"It might be fun for a while, but then it wouldn't. But what you said, you're serious, aren't you? How are you going to do it?"

"With my hands." Saying the words, spelling it out, bringing the act another little bit closer to reality. "I'll take hold of her," he said, "and break her neck."

"You can do that?"

"There's a technique," he said, and put his hands out in front of him and mimed the movement. "You twist hard," he said, "and the neck snaps."

"You've never—"

"Of course not. But I've thought about it. It's been playing in my mind for a long time now."

"A fantasy."

"Yes."

"And you want to make it real."

"I need to. Listen, she'll be back any minute and—"

"We'll hear her on the stairs. When is this going to happen?"

"When we're done playing."

"That may be a while."

"We've got the rest of the night. And I'll give you warning, so that you can leave the room."

"Are you kidding? I want to be here."

"Really?"

"If it's gonna happen," she said, "I damn well want to be here when it does. I want to see you do it, I want to watch her face when she knows what's happening, I want to watch her big eyes when the life goes out of them."

"Jesus, Angelica."

"God, feel how wet I am just thinking about it. And I swear it's never been my fantasy, but I have to tell you it is now. But not too soon, all right? Because all of a sudden there are a lot of things I *want to do with her. I want to teach her something new."*

*"You think there's anything she doesn't already know?"*

*"Well, let's see if anybody's ever taught her that fist is a verb."*

*"She may not like that."*

*"So? You're going to break her fucking neck, so what difference does it make what she likes and doesn't like? And once she's dead I want to lie on top of her while you fuck me."*

*"God, you're something."*

*"And so are you. Thank God we found each other. And I can't wait to—shhh, she's on the stairs."*

# TWENTY-NINE

Something had changed.

She sensed it the moment she entered the bedroom. She could feel it in the air, as unmistakably as she'd felt Brady's presence behind the Japanese screen. No one had entered or left. They were both there, Brady and Angelica, both of them in bed, both of them naked. They were just as she'd left them, but something was different.

Whatever it was, she had the feeling that it would be a mistake to wait.

She'd put on a gingham apron, and she was carrying a round tray she'd found downstairs, a flat disk of polished walnut with an inch-high rim to keep drinks from sliding off. The tray held two glasses, small crystal tumblers each filled halfway with orange juice.

"Sorry I took so long," she said, and curtseyed elaborately, then giggled. "Does the apron make me look like a French maid?"

"It makes you look hot," Angelica said. "What have you got there?"

"Something you'll both like."

"I don't want a drink," Brady said. "I don't think we need them."

"It's just orange juice," she said, "from the fridge. Plus a miracle ingredient."

"Oh?"

"It's this herbal tonic somebody turned me on to. It's pretty amazing. I mean, it's all natural and organic, and it's actually good for you, but what it does right away is give you energy like you wouldn't believe."

"Energy?"

"For sex," she said. "I put some in my Orange Blossom at the bar, that's why I made sure I finished it. And that's why I got so hot so fast, and was as bold as I was. I had some more just now, while I was downstairs. And I divided the rest of it in two, and as soon as you both drink it, the night's going to be even more amazing than it's already been."

"What does it do?"

"It sort of makes everything moreso," she said, "plus it gives you energy so you can just keep doing stuff. Just drink it, I promise you you'll be glad you did. You'll thank me for it, you'll want to know where you can get more. And it can't hurt you, it's genuinely good for you, so please drink it, okay? For me?"

*The first sense to awaken was touch. Angelica's eyes were closed, her limbs heavy, and she was being touched. Her thighs were spread and a hand had reached under her and one finger was moving slowly, ever so slowly, up and down. She felt herself begin to respond, and then, tantalizingly, the finger stopped. And then it started again, and stopped, and started.*

*Her hips began to move in response. And, as the finger did its work, the rest of her senses began to come awake.*

*She was lying face down. There was something beneath her, not smooth and even like a mattress, and it took her a moment to realize that it was in fact a person. She was lying on top of another human being.*

*It was not until she tried to move her arms and legs that she discovered she was unable to do so. Her arms and legs were fastened in place. The person under her was spread-eagled on the bed, and* her wrists and ankles were somehow fastened to his wrists and ankles.

His, because she knew that it was Brady upon whom she was lying. Brady lying on his back and herself lying on her stomach, on top of him, and fastened there. And someone—it could only be Missy—was fingering her.

But why had she lost consciousness? Had the sex been so intense that she blacked out?

She remembered Brady's remarkable announcement, and her own astonishing reaction to it. One moment they'd agreed that Missy would never leave their house alive, and the next moment she herself was lying on top of her husband, unable to move. How had that happened?

Missy: "What's the last thing you remember?"

"Orange juice."

Her own words surprised her. But even as she spoke them she remembered—Missy had brought two glasses of orange juice. She and Brady had each taken a glass, but she didn't remember actually drinking anything.

But she must have, and there must have been something in the orange juice. Not the energizing substance they'd been promised—she remembered the promise now, remembered the skimpy apron that revealed more than it concealed. Not something to let them make love for hours but something to put them to sleep.

A drug. She'd been drugged.

Only to wake up to a finger wave from the girl who'd drugged her. But Missy had withdrawn her hand now, and it rested lightly on Angelica's hip.

Should she open her eyes?

If she kept them closed, it might all remain a little unreal. If she opened them—

She opened them.

Her face was resting on Brady's, their cheeks together like a pair of romantic ballroom dancers. She moved so that she could see his face. His eyes were open, and she looked into them, barely able to focus at such close range, and their sightless stare confirmed what she must have known all along.

She gasped.

"I'm afraid so," Missy said. "He never really felt it, if that's any consolation. You were both out cold, and I got the icepick from my purse and took care of him right away. Slipped it between his ribs and right into his heart, and he gave this little twitch, and just like that I could feel the life go out of him and into me. Then I took out the icepick, and I didn't even have to wipe it off because it came out clean as a whistle. No blood on it and none where it went in. I could show you, and you'd have trouble finding the spot. You could find it, but you'd really have to look for it."

"Why?"

"Because dead bodies don't bleed. The heart stops so there's no circulation, and when the wound's tiny there's no room for anything to leak out. But that's not what you meant, is it? You meant why kill him."

There was a pause. Then Missy said, "Well, see, it's what I do. With, uh, men. Not always with an icepick, although I did use this one once before. I don't remember how it got into my purse, but I guess I must have bought it somewhere along the way, or just took it from someplace. But I was hitching, and I got a ride from Uncle Ben. Calling him that makes him sound African-American, like the brand of rice, but his name was Ben and he was real avuncular, so there you go. He was nice, and I was hoping he wouldn't want to do anything, but no, he wanted to stop at a motel, and I wasn't going to say no to him. And then he wanted to fuck me, and

*I wasn't going to say no to that, either, so we went to bed, and he drank most of a pint of whiskey and got all teary and emotional about his dead wife, and I finally blew him and he passed out. And I thought, well, I could just leave him like that, but rules are rules, and where would we be without them? And anyway I'd been wondering how it would be with the icepick. And it turned out to be pretty much the same as it was just now, with Brady."*

*And I must have liked it,* she thought, *or I wouldn't have kept the icepick.*

"What's funny," she said, "is I went to that bar tonight because I figured it was my shot at having sex without killing anybody. There's not a man alive who can tell his friends what I'm like in bed, or even warm himself with the memory. Well, there's one, the only one I haven't been able to find. I tracked down all the others. But, see, I thought I'd be all right with a woman. Only I didn't know if I'd like it. See, you're my first."

"I don't believe you."

"Well, I guess that's a compliment, huh? But it's true. There's a woman I've been thinking about a lot, and we've become very close. And there was one night when we sat across from each other in her living room and had phoneless telephone sex, telling stories and watching each other masturbate. And I want to go to bed with her, but not if I'm gonna kill her afterward, you know?"

"I don't—"

"Shut up, let me finish. Her name is Rita and she's beautiful and she's really hot. She got her hairdresser to teach her how to suck cock, can you believe it? And a few weeks ago she went to bed with a hundred and fifty-two men rolled into one, and—oh, *wow!*"

"What?"

"Never mind. I just thought of something, but never mind. Anyway, where was I? Back at Eve's Rib, I guess. See, I knew all along about Brady, I saw you with him in the bar, and I was pretty sure he was part of the deal. And the minute you told me about your out-of-town husband I knew it for certain, and then the hood of the car was warm, so by the time you and I were in bed I knew he'd be joining us, which meant I'd wind up using the icepick."

Idly, she stroked Angelica's bottom, listened to the woman's measured breathing. There was a question on the way, she could feel it, but still it came as a surprise.

"What's it like?"

"What's what like?"

"Killing somebody."

"Wow," she said. "Nobody ever asked me that before, but then how could they? *What's it like?* I don't come from doing it or any-thing like that. But it's, oh, satisfying. I mean, the sex is always okay, even if it's nothing much, but no matter how good it is or how many times I get off, it's never over. Not until the life goes out of him and into me. Not literally, I mean I'm not sucking up anybody's soul, but it feels like it's a zero-sum game, and I get stronger every time I do it."

Another long silence. Then, "Please don't kill me."

"Silly. I only kill guys."

"Could you take the tape off? It's uncomfortable, lying like this."

"Not just yet," she said. "You have to tell me about the money."

"Money?"

"I got what was in your purse, and I found his pants in the other room and emptied his wallet. See, I'm traveling all the time, and I constantly wind up having to buy new clothes because I some-times leave places in a hurry. And I don't have a job. So this is how

I support myself, and I know you've got money in the house. So you'll tell me where it is, and then I'll cut you loose."

Angelica was silent. Thinking, she figured. She extended her forefinger, poked Angelica's back. "Otherwise," she said, "I'll do this—" she poked harder "—with the icepick. In the kidney, which is supposed to be very painful. So you'll wind up telling me anyway, and at that point I'll have no choice, and I'll kill you. But I don't want to, because I've never killed a woman, so—"

"God, I don't care about the money! You're welcome to all of it. I was just trying to think where it is."

She gave her a minute.

"The top drawer of my dresser. The high chest is his, the wide low one is mine, and the top left-hand drawer—"

"Three hundred dollars," Missy said. "I already found it, I wanted to see if you'd tell me about it. Now the second half of the test. Pass this part and you won't have the icepick to worry about, and that's a promise. There's more money here somewhere, money your husband would want to keep handy. Now where do you suppose that might be?"

There was a locked drawer in the kneehole desk downstairs in the living room. He'd never let Angelica see what was inside it, but if he had money stashed anywhere, that was where she thought it might be.

Angelica didn't know where he kept the key, and she didn't waste time looking for it. She figured a desk drawer wasn't exactly Fort Knox, and a hammer and a screwdriver got her into it in hardly any time at all.

The drawer held a revolver and a box of shells, along with various legal documents; she left all of that untouched and went straight for the cash. There was a stack of it, all hundreds, and she took her time and counted it. It came to $3,800, a huge score, enough to keep her going for a long time.

Back upstairs she said, "Can you believe he kept his gun in a locked drawer? Real handy if somebody breaks in. But you were right, that's where he kept his cash."

Angelica was saying something about jewelry, but she didn't want to hear it. She had the money and that was all she wanted. And she didn't want to hear anything else the woman might say, didn't want her begging to be let loose. She'd prepared a square patch of duct tape earlier, when she'd bonded the woman to her husband, wrist to wrist and ankle to ankle, and now she slapped the gag over Angelica's mouth, cutting her off in mid-sentence.

"Sorry," she said, "but I want to talk now, and I don't want you interrupting. I lied to you before. Well, lots of times, but when I told you and Brady about being an orphan. Which I am, but I lied about how I got that way. See, that's what the cops thought happened, and how they explained it to me, but what they didn't know is I shot my mother, and then I called my father at the office and told him to come home, and when he did I shot him, too. And *then* I went to my girlfriend's house, and got myself invited to spend the night, and went home in the morning and discovered the bodies and called the cops, di dah di dah di dah. So it's not really true that I never killed a woman."

She went to the nightstand, took out a silk scarf.

"And I'll keep my promise," she said, "and not do you with the icepick, but how could I let you live? Not because we had sex, but because, duh, you know what I am and what I do."

Angelica was struggling, trying to free herself. No way that was going to happen. Missy slipped the scarf around her neck.

"This is Hermés, isn't it? Very nice. It's what you were going to use to tie me up, right?" She took a breath, tried to focus on what she wanted to say. "You're really beautiful," she told Angelica, "and I had a wonderful time with you, both before and after Brady joined the party. And I wish I could get the name of your waxing person, but I'll be leaving town as soon as I'm done here, so I wouldn't have time anyway. But I'll find somebody else, somewhere, and get it done, so I guess I'll have plenty of occasions to remember you."

She told herself, *Do it, for God's sake. Don't draw it out.*

"This ought to work," she said. "It's supposed to be pretty easy to strangle somebody this way. But you'll have to bear with me. I've never done this before."

# THIRTY

"Kimmie, a threesome!"

"I was just looking to go home with a girl," she said, "but she was there with her husband, and he was kind of cute."

"You've got to tell me everything."

Well, not exactly everything. She gave Rita the *Reader's Digest* version, abbreviated and toned down. Even so, with Rita's questions and exclamations, she used up a chunk of the new cell phone's prepaid minutes.

"It added something," she said of the husband's presence. "But at the same time it took something away."

" 'Cause it wasn't just the two of you."

"Right."

"Kimmie, I really wish you were here."

"Me too."

"I won't even ask where you are."

"Actually, I'm out west again. Not as far west as you are, though."

"Oh?"

"A place I've never been before. Provo, Utah?"

"I've never been there either. When I was a kid we took a family trip to a national park, and I think it may have been in Utah. Arches?"

"I never heard of it."

"It was pretty neat. There were these great natural rock formations, sandstone eroded by the wind, and there was this one huge freestanding stone arch and you could stand under it and get your picture taken. And it fell down."

"While you were standing under it?"

"No, silly! I was there fifteen or twenty years ago, and just last year it fell down. It was on the TV news."

"Oh."

"I'm pretty sure it's in Utah. Hang on. Thank you, Google. It's in Utah, and the nearest town is Moab, and I remember now because that's where we stayed. In a motel with fake wood paneling on the walls. Now why do I remember that?"

"Maybe the wood grain looked like a cunt."

"Kimmie, you are just *terrible*!"

"I know."

"Where did you say? Provo? Hang on. Okay, you're a hundred and ninety-one miles away if you take Route Six. Oh, you know what? That's where he's from."

"That's where who's from?"

"That crazy Mormon. What was his name? Not Kelly. Damn, why can't I—Kellen!"

"The one who wouldn't go down on you?"

"Yeah, the pig. Saving his tongue for his fiancée. Asshole."

"Probably saving his asshole for Brigham Young."

"Ha! You know what? You should look him up."

"You think?"

"Sure, why not? He was pretty hot, except for what he wouldn't do."

"Well—"

"And wouldn't you want the experience of screwing a hundred and fifty guys at once?"

A hundred fifty-two, she thought. And said, "What are you— oh, right, you told me. Proxy baptism?"

"That's it."

"But you wouldn't mind, Rita?"

"Me? Why should I mind? I'm not the one who's engaged to him."

"Well, still. I mean, you saw him first."

"And when am I gonna see him again, and why would I even want to? I don't have to go all the way to Utah to find a guy who won't go down on me. As a matter of fact…"

"What?"

"Well, I have to admit I kind of like the idea of us having him in common. It'd be a new kind of threesome, the kind with an interval."

"Kellen," she said. "It'd help if I knew his last name. Still, how many Kellens can there be? Unless it's the Mormon equivalent of Jason."

"He told me his last name. But I can't possibly—Kimball!"

"You can't possibly Kimball?"

"That's it, it just popped into my mind. Kellen Kimball. Just think what your name would be if you married him."

"Yeah, right. I probably won't look for him, and nothing's likely to happen even if I do."

"But if it does," Rita said, "I want to hear all about it."

He remembered Rita. Vividly, it would seem, because the recollection brought a blush to his pink cheeks.

"Outside of Seattle," he said. "I can't recall just where."

"Kirkland."

"That'd be it, Kirkland. A friend and I, we saw her as part of our missionary work. She'd expressed some interest in LDS, so we paid her a home visit to discuss it with her."

"LDS."

"Latter-Day Saints. What you probably call the Mormon religion, the official title is the Church of Jesus Christ of Latter-Day Saints."

She'd found out where he lived, which hadn't proved terribly difficult. There was a whole column of Kimballs in the phone book, but only one Kellen. The phone book provided his address, and finding one's way around Provo was ridiculously simple, because the streets were in a numbered grid, and if you could count you could get anywhere you wanted to go. His apartment was on East 300 North Street, just around the corner from Dragon's Keep, a store on University Avenue that sold games and comic books. There were items on display, sword and sorcery paraphernalia, that wouldn't have looked out of place in the Pleasure Chest. The clientele, however, was vastly different—nerds and geeks instead of pervs and players.

It was where he'd suggested they meet, and the staff there greeted him by name, which suggested that he had a rich life reading comic books and playing Dungeons & Dragons on those lonely nights when he couldn't find somebody not to go down on.

For all that, he was a tall, good-looking young man, with the fresh-faced handsomeness of a male model in the Lands' End catalogue. One cheek was lightly pitted with old acne scars, and that was a plus; it kept him from being too pretty.

She knew at first glance that he would certainly do. But it wasn't his good looks that had led her to Provo, Utah, nor was it the chance to go where Rita had already gone. That was appealing, no question about it, but she had something more important in mind.

"LDS," she said. "At first I thought you were a dyslexic talking about LSD. You know, acid? But that didn't make sense, because Mormons don't use drugs. Or do they?"

"I take aspirin for headaches, and anything my doctor prescribes for medicinal purposes. But in the sense of mood-altering drugs, no, that's something we don't do."

"Well, I'm with you on that one," she said. "Kellen—is it okay to call you Kellen?"

"Well, sure. That's my name. And you're Marsha?"

"But everybody calls me Marcy."

"Then that's what I'll call you, Marcy."

Laughter erupted from one of the tables to their right, where three nerdy-looking young men were clustered around a game board. When it died down she said, "Kellen, there's something I need to ask you about. Could we go someplace a little quieter? And maybe get a drink or a cup of coffee?"

"Which would you prefer?"

She shrugged. "Whichever you feel like."

"Well," he said, "I'm afraid they're both out of bounds for me."

"Oh," she said, light dawning. "Mormons don't drink alcohol."

"Or coffee."

"I didn't know about coffee. Well, could we get a Coke? Or a cup of tea?"

He was grinning now. "Stimulants," he said.

"So they're a no-no?"

"I'm afraid so. But that doesn't mean you can't have whatever you want, and I can keep you company."

"If we were both Mormons," she said, "where would you take me and what would we have?"

"Well, there's a juice bar that's quiet and comfortable. And only a couple of blocks from here."

"Then let's go there."

"But you'd be pretty much limited to fruit juice."

"That's fine," she said. "In fact that sounds pretty good right about now."

❖

"There's something Rita told me about you," she said, and damned if he didn't blush the least bit. The place he'd taken her was a little more brightly lit than your average bar, and she could see the color rise to his cheeks.

"Besides that," she said.

"Besides—"

"Look, let's clear the air, okay? I know you went to bed with Rita, and incidentally she said you were a wonderful lover. And I can't say I'm surprised, because you're certainly an attractive man. And yes, I know you're engaged, and that's not the point, either. I don't mean to embarrass you, bringing all that up out of the blue, but otherwise it's just going to hang in the air between us, and I don't think that's what either of us wants."

"You're very direct."

"But don't you agree?"

"Well, yes," he said, and picked up his glass of lemonade like an alcoholic reaching for his Harvey Wallbanger. "Yes, best to clear the air."

Right. "What Rita told me about, and what really stuck in my mind, is the experience you had with proxy baptism. See, I never even heard of that before, and I've been thinking about it ever since. I did some research online, and, well, I keep thinking about it."

"I suppose you'd like to find out about getting your own ancestors baptized. Well, that's not hard to arrange, and—"

"No."

"No?"

"It's a little more complicated than that," she said. "See, I had this boyfriend, and we were really deeply in love."

"Oh?"

"We were meant to be together forever, I know we were. But he was married to somebody else."

"Oh."

"He filed for divorce, and the legal proceedings were underway. And he and I weren't living together, but we had, you know, a full relationship. And then—"

"Yes?"

"He died."

"I'm so sorry."

She reached across the table, put her hand on top of his. "It was very sudden," she said, "and completely unexpected. We were making love, and what we were doing—I don't know, maybe I shouldn't go into detail. Would I be embarrassing you?"

"It's all right."

"Well, I think they call it the Reverse Cowgirl position. He was lying on his back, like, and I was sitting astride him, but facing toward his feet. That was always a very effective position for us, because his dick hit my G-spot perfectly that way, and—is it okay to talk like this to a Mormon?"

He nodded.

"Well, that made it super good, and I could regulate the depth and everything, and he could just lie there and enjoy it. Plus I could use one hand for balance and use the other on my clit, just to, you know, help things along. Like."

"I see."

"So it was really great, and I had this super orgasm with bells and whistles, one of those long rolling things that just goes on forever, and when it finally stopped I said something, I don't know what, telling him I loved him, that kind of thing, and he didn't say anything. And the one thing I *don't* like about the Reverse Cowgirl is you don't get to see his face, and I didn't even know if he came or not, or much of anything. And he wasn't moving or making any sound, so I swung around to get a look at him, and, well, he was dead."

"How awful."

"They said he had a congenital heart condition, that it had just been there all his life and remained asymptomatic all that time, so nobody ever knew about it. And then it popped up and killed him. It could have happened while he was playing basketball or hurrying to catch a bus, or it could have happened in the middle of a night's sleep. It was going to happen sooner or later, and the time it picked was right when I was squirming around on his dick in the throes of an amazing orgasm."

She touched his hand again. "Anyway," she said, "that's what I thought of when I learned about proxy baptism."

"You want him baptized, so that he's guaranteed eternal life in Christ everlasting."

"No."

"No?"

"He was baptized as an infant. I don't remember which denomination his parents were, and I know he'd lost his faith over the years, especially when his marriage went sour, but he was definitely baptized. Now maybe a Mormon proxy baptism would still do him some good, I don't know about that, but if you want to put his name on the list, well, I'd have no objection to that. But it's not what I came to Provo for."

"Then—"

"We were meant to be together," she said, "and I knew that from the moment I met him. And I still know it. I've been with other men since then, because I'm a healthy woman with healthy appetites." Her hand brushed his. "You probably sensed that much."

"Well, the way you were talking about the Backwards Cowboy."

"Reverse Cowgirl. But that's an interesting idea—someday we'll have to work out just what the Backwards Cowboy might entail."

A perfect blush this time, a really deep reddening of those pink cheeks.

"But here's what I'm getting at," she went on. "We would have been married. We were supposed to be married, and it's what we would have done the minute his divorce became finalized. And then we'd be together forever." She took a deep breath. "So what I want," she said, "is a proxy marriage. I want you to stand in for him, as his proxy, and we'll be married."

He had a whole batch of objections. There was no such thing as proxy marriage in the LDS church, and she wasn't a Mormon, and the person she wanted to marry hadn't been a Mormon, so how could they go through an LDS sacrament, let alone by proxy?

"I know all that," she said. "It wouldn't have to have anything to do with the church, or with any church. Or with the government, either, and there wouldn't need to be any clergy involved."

"I'm not sure I understand."

"It would be a private exchange of vows," she said. "Without witnesses. Just the two of us, just you and I, except you'd more or less become him during the ceremony, using his name and standing in for him. As his proxy—that's what it would come down to."

"And this ceremony—"

She reached into her purse. "Actually," she said, "I've written it out. See what you think."

He unfolded the sheet of paper, read it through. " 'I, Sidney Teibel'—that was his name?"

"Yes, but it's not TEE-bel. It's TIE-bel, rhymes with bible."

She'd made up the surname. Read it somewhere, couldn't even remember where, and had no idea how its original owner may have pronounced it. So why was she correcting Kellen's pronunciation?

" 'I, Sidney Teibel, do hereby take you, Marsha Anne Whitlock, to be my wife in the eyes of God and man…' "

The vows were lengthy ones, and on the flowery side. She realized as she heard Kellen read them out that she might have gotten the least bit carried away.

"Ever since I met you on Race Street in Philadelphia, there has been no one in my heart but you. Your lips, your breasts, your thighs, your private parts…"

She'd composed their vows a few days before she got to Provo, at a computer terminal in an Internet café, and that third cup of coffee had put her one caffeinated toke over the line.

That wouldn't have happened if she'd been an observant Mormon. Maybe they were on to something, keeping their distance from coffee. But when their alarm clocks went off, how did they keep their eyes open?

"…to have and to hold, to love and to cherish, to have earth-shaking sex with…"

They were in Kellen's apartment. Over their glasses of lemonade, she'd said they would need someplace quiet and private for their exchange of vows, and he'd only hesitated for a moment before suggesting his apartment. She found this reassuring, along with the way his eyes kept dropping to her breasts.

"…as long as we both shall live."

Her turn now. She took a breath, lowered her eyes to the piece of paper with her vows all printed out. "I, Marsha Anne Whitlock…"

Good thing she looked at the script. She'd almost said Whitcomb instead of Whitlock. A hell of a thing if she got her own name wrong in the recitation of her marriage vows.

"…to have and to hold, to love and to cherish, to suck and to swallow, to admit and to welcome into all the openings of my body…"

Fucking coffee. That third cup was murder.

She'd brought the rings, matching unadorned wedding bands, gold-plated rather than solid gold, and probably a good bet to turn their fingers green if they wore them for any length of time. But they'd do for now, and he'd placed one on her ring finger, and she'd done the same for him. And now, their vows concluded, it would have been time for someone to tell him that he could kiss the bride, but in the absence of clergy he'd have to figure that out for himself.

And damned if he didn't manage to do just that. He took a step toward her, and she picked up her cue and moved at once into the circle of his arms, and raised her mouth to his.

Lips that had never touched liquor—or tobacco or coffee or Coca-Cola, or, God help us, pussy—now touched hers, and the depth of her own response surprised her. Without any conscious thought she opened to his kiss, and put a little tongue into it, and when his hand cupped her bottom and drew her in closer, she let a moan escape her lips even as she pressed her loins into his.

"Oh, Sidney," she said. "Sid, my darling. My beloved husband."

He looked uncertain what to say, so she spared him the need to say anything. "We have to consummate our marriage, my darling." And when it looked as though he might hesitate, she said, "You're Sidney now, you're his proxy, you're my husband in the sight of God. So it's not only right for us to go to bed. It's essential."

He nodded, swallowed, said he'd be back in a minute. He went into the bathroom, and she used his absence to get something from her purse. She tucked it between the mattress and the frame, where she could reach it easily.

Then she shed her clothes. A white wedding gown would have been nice, but she'd exchanged vows in the skirt and sweater she'd worn to meet him at Dragon's Keep, and she took them off now, took off everything, and when he emerged from the bathroom with a towel wrapped discreetly around his middle she met him wearing nothing but a smile.

His eyes widened at the sight of her, and his mouth fell open. And did the towel suddenly protrude a little in front, or was that her imagination?

Well, that was a question she could answer readily enough. She went to him, unhooked the towel, let it fall to the floor. He was tumescent but not fully erect, and she was pleased to note that his penis was large and nicely shaped. And circumcised, which was always a plus, but she'd known it would be. Mormons circumcised their male infants, it said so all over the Internet. They didn't throw a party to celebrate it, the way the Jews did, but they got the job done.

"Oh, Sid," she said, sinking to her knees before him. "I know how much you like this." And she took his dick in her mouth.

He liked it, all right. He liked it so much that she thought he was going to consummate their marriage on the spot, and she herself was into it, and had to force herself to draw away before he could finish.

"Oh, Sid, my darling," she said, getting to her feet, holding him by his dick. "Now, my love, I want you to do what you love to do so much."

She led him to the bed, arranged herself upon it, and managed to indicate by gestures what she wanted him to do.

It wasn't what he had in mind.

"I can't," he said. "Not until I'm married."

"But you *are* married, silly. What do you think we just did?"

He shook his head, held up a hand as if to ward off Satan. "I'm engaged to be married," he said, "and when my fiancée and I are man and wife in the eyes of the Church, then I will, uh, perform oral sex on her. But I've never done that with her, or with anyone else. I can't, I won't, I—"

"That's why you wouldn't go down on Rita."

He gaped.

"Yeah, she told me. 'This gorgeous guy, he's got a beautiful dick, plus he's a really great kisser, but he wouldn't kiss me where it counts.' But you wanted to, didn't you?"

"If circumstances had been different—"

"They are. Look, it's fine for Kellen Kimball to save the tip of his tongue for the girl he going to marry. But that's got nothing to do with you right now, because you're not Kellen Kimball anymore. Right now you're Sidney Teibel, and you're married to me, so you get to have your cake and eat me, too."

"But—"

She touched herself, dipped her fingers into her wetness, then held her hand to his face. "Can you smell how hot I am for you?"

What was he going to do, hold his breath? He hesitated, then took hold of her wrist, brought her moist fingers to his nose, inhaled her essence.

"That's me," she told him. "That's me, that's my love for you, Sidney. You breathe me in and part of me becomes a part of you. Open your mouth."

His lips parted. And it was his hand on her wrist that brought her fingers into his mouth. His lips closed around her fingertips, and he sucked on her fingers like a greedy infant.

"Oh, Sidney," she said, and arranged herself again on the bed, making room for him to kneel at her feet.

"Oh, yes," she said. "Take your time, Sidney. Eat me good. Make me crazy."

What he lacked in acquired skill he made up for in enthusiasm. He took hold of her buttocks in his hands and he glued his mouth to her crotch, and he went at her as if for sustenance. If he could have maintained an elementary tempo she'd have gone off in minutes, but he had the natural lack of rhythm of a white boy from Utah, and she kept getting thrown off stride.

Maybe she couldn't get off, but she could tell he wasn't more than a few strokes away, just from thrusting against the bedsheet while he worked away at her. Her hand fastened on the knife she'd wedged beneath the mattress. It was a folding stiletto, and she'd tucked it away already opened and ready for use, and she looked down at the back of his head and rehearsed the movement in her mind: lean forward, the arm swinging in a great half-circle, the blade descending…

No.

This wasn't a game, for God's sake. The marriage had to be consummated.

She put the knife out of sight, sat up, tugged at his upper arms. "Now!" she cried. "Sid, Sid, I want you inside me. Now!"

He flung himself forward—on her, in her, and she locked her thighs around his hips and met his feverish pelvic thrusts with thrusts of her own. His mouth sought hers and she tasted her own juices. He was right on the brink, and she figured she'd fake an orgasm of her own, timing it to coincide with his, but her body surprised her with a genuine orgasm before she could create a bogus one.

"Oh, Sidney," she said, as he lay panting on top of her. "Oh, my darling husband. Oh, what could be better than this?"

And almost without effort, and certainly without a second thought, she slipped the knife right between his ribs and into his heart.

# THIRTY-ONE

*Zero.*

The first thing she did was take a shower. He had one of those infinitely adjustable shower heads, and she fixed it so that hot water sprayed down on her with great force. His shampoo and conditioner were one of those overpriced signature brands they sold in hair salons, and she used them lavishly, because what good would they do anyone after she left?

*Zero.*

Nobody left on her list, because while there might be only a single body in the bedroom, slowly working its way from 98.6° to, say, 72° on the Fahrenheit scale, Kellen Kimball wasn't the only man who'd just died. He'd also been Sid, the man she met on Race Street, the man who took her to bed in Philadelphia and never paid the price.

Until now. Now he was dead, and she'd killed him.

Oh, not literally. She wasn't delusional, she knew what she'd done and to whom she'd done it. But she also knew that Kellen Kimball was a Mormon, that he'd participated in proxy baptisms, and if a proxy baptism could get some dead guy into heaven, why couldn't a proxy marriage get Sid off her list? Yes, she'd killed Kellen—but the same thrust of the knife had killed Sid as well. And if there was a real living and breathing Sid out there, well, so what? Because in her own little world he was a dead man.

She got out of the shower, finally, and used two of his towels to dry herself. There'd been a third towel, the one he'd wrapped himself in, the one that had hidden his hard-on-in-progress when he returned to her. His sport shirt and chinos were folded on top of the lidded toilet, along with his socks and underpants, and she carried them to the bedroom and arranged them on the chair next to the bed.

She thought there ought to be another article of clothing, and she found it on a hook behind the bathroom door, a single white cotton affair with some marks on it that might have been Nordic runes, or perhaps Masonic symbols. This, she knew from her Internet research, was his Mormon garment, to be worn beneath his clothes at all times, for reasons the Internet had been unable to explain all that coherently.

Should she put it on him? It was constructed like a jumpsuit, except without arms or legs. Sort of like a clumsy and loose-fitting leotard. No cinch to get a live person into it, and sure to be trickier still with a dead one.

Never mind. He seemed a safe candidate for Mormon heaven, whatever sort of place that might prove to be, and she didn't figure he needed to be wearing his garment to get in.

She went through his wallet. His cash came to less than a hundred dollars, but she took it all the same. If there was any more money hidden in his apartment, she certainly couldn't find it.

She took the knife. She'd bought it in Provo, in a sporting goods store, and the clerk might remember the sale. Not that it mattered—plenty of people had seen her with Kellen, in Dragon's Keep and the juice bar and on the streets of Provo, and they could describe her to the cops, and what good would that do them? A pretty young woman in a skirt and blouse. So?

Still, she held the knife under running water for a few minutes, then closed it and stowed it in her purse. She added the ring from her finger and went back for the one she'd placed on Kellen's. The rings and the knife could all go in a storm drain, or could as easily be abandoned in some public place where they'd be quickly scooped up and carried off by new owners.

She left, and locked the door after herself. With any luck at all, she'd be long gone before anyone unlocked that door, or broke it down.

*Zero.*

# THIRTY-TWO

"The Sumatra Blue Batak Tarbarita Peaberry," the man said. "Could you describe that for me?"

*It's coffee*, she thought. *From Sumatra. What more do you need to know?*

"Well, it's a sort of medium roast," she said. "And it has a good deal of body. I would say that it's assertive without being overbearing."

He nodded encouragement. He had a high forehead and an academic presence, the latter reinforced by his clothing—an olive-brown corduroy jacket with leather elbow patches, owlish glasses with heavy tortoiseshell frames, clean jeans, chukka boots. A strip of lighter skin on the appropriate finger showed he'd once worn a wedding ring. But the lighter skin was starting to blend in, so he'd stopped wearing it a while ago.

"As for the taste," she went on, "that's always hard for me to describe."

"It's so subjective. And yet I've a feeling you'll get it right."

Getting ready to hit on her. Well, she'd seen that coming.

"Hmmm. Well, how can I put it? I'd say it's autumnal."

"Autumnal."

"And…dare I say plangent?"

She caught a glimpse of Will, the shop's co-owner, rolling his eyes.

"Brilliant," her customer said. "Let me have a pound, then. Who am I to pass up a beverage that's at once plangent and autumnal? And that'll be whole bean, please. It's the sheer aroma of freshly ground beans that gets my heart started in the morning, even before I get the coffee brewing."

As she was ringing up the sale he asked her name, and she provided one. He said he'd remember it, and that his was Alden.

When the door closed behind the man, Will said, "Cordelia, eh? When did your name become Cordelia?"

Will was tall and thin; his lover and business partner, Billy, was short, with the muscularity of a relentless weightlifter. They'd both gone by Bill when they met, but found it confusing, so one became Will and the other Billy.

Will—and Billy, for that matter—knew her as Lindsay. And she might have given that name to Alden, but there was an instant when she couldn't think of it. *Not Lynne, not Linda, now what the hell was it?* And the result was Cordelia.

"I don't know," she said. "For some reason I didn't want to give him my name. And what came out was Cordelia."

"Better than Regan or Goneril, I suppose. This way you're the good daughter."

She didn't know what he was talking about, but she often didn't. Better than gonorrhea? What was that supposed to mean?

"Anyway," she said, "I figured it had a nice autumnal sound to it."

"Oh, that it does. Not to mention plangent. Where the hell did you come up with that one, sweetie?"

She shrugged, but she knew exactly where she'd gotten it from. A few years ago, a very brief stint in a seafood restaurant in Rehoboth Beach, Delaware. A customer had never had orange roughy before, and asked what it was like. *A firm, white-fleshed fish*, she'd told him, which was something you could say about almost everything but salmon and squid. *And as for the taste, well, dare I say plangent?* The line, she remembered, had gone over well enough. If it worked for a fish she'd never eaten, why wouldn't it do for a beverage she'd never tasted?

"Plangent. Do you even know the meaning of the word?"

"It's hard to define."

"Oh, really? Try plaintive. Think of a sort of lingering sadness."

"So? He'll be having a cup of coffee on the porch, with his feet up on the railing, and he'll find himself thinking about the woman he used to be married to, and wondering why he married her in the first place, and why the marriage failed, and why all his relationships seem to fail. But he won't be heartbroken, because he's got tenure at Willamette, and everybody says he looks good in corduroy, and he grinds his own coffee beans every morning, so it's a good life, even if it is a sad one."

He stared at her. "You did all that on the spur of the moment," he said, "just to cover the fact that you'd been caught using a word you couldn't define. There's a short story of Saki's that you remind me of. 'Romance at short notice was her specialty.' That's the last line, and doesn't it just fit you to a tee? Aren't you the plangent queen of romance at short notice? Now don't go rolling your eyes, sweetie. That's my trick. I'll tell you this, Cordelia, or Lindsay, or whoever you are this afternoon. You're the tiniest bit scary."

"Don't worry," she told him. "You're safe."

She was in Salem, the capital of Oregon, working afternoons at the Bean Bag, and living in a rooming house near the Willamette University campus. When she left Provo she'd planned on heading back east, but the first bus available took her north to Salt Lake City, and from there she continued north and west to Boise, and she'd kept gradually drifting north and west, and here she was in

Salem, and Google Maps had already informed her that she was less than two hundred fifty miles from Kirkland, Washington.

Not hard to see a pattern here.

When her shift ended she picked up a small pizza and a fruit-flavored iced tea on her way home. She ate in her room, took a shower, and wrapped up in a towel. She picked up her phone, then decided she wanted to be dressed for this conversation. She put on clean underwear, jeans, a loose-fitting top, and was on her way to the mirror when she told herself she was being ridiculous. She sat down in the room's one chair and made the call.

"Kimmie, two calls in what, three days?"

"I guess. Listen, if you don't feel like talking—"

"You're kidding, right? There's never been a time when I haven't felt like talking to you."

It was the same for her. But she wasn't ready to say it.

There were things, though, that you had to say whether you were ready or not. If you waited until you were ready they would never get said.

She said, "Rita, there's a conversation we need to have."

"Should I put on a nightgown? And get my toys ready?"

"Not this time."

"Kimmie, this sounds serious."

"Sort of, yeah. See, there's things you don't know about me. I was never a graduate student, I didn't have a thesis to write."

"Well, duh."

"You figured that much, huh?"

"Kimmie, every time I hear from you you're someplace else and you've got a new phone number. It's pretty obvious you've got a whole life that I don't know anything about."

"And that doesn't bother you?"

"It makes me wonder. And, you know, I can't help having my own fantasies."

"Oh?"

"Which I'm sure are miles from the truth."

"For instance?"

"This is just crazy guessing, but—"

"Go ahead, Rita."

"Well, what I decided is you're sort of a spy. Like with some super-secret government agency? And you travel around on assignments, and when I don't hear from you for a really long period of time, that's because you're out of the country."

"Wow."

"I told you it was crazy. And then I thought—now this is even crazier, and maybe I shouldn't say it."

"No, say it."

"Well, I thought whatever it is that she does, you know, it's for our government, so it's okay. And next I thought, well, suppose it's *not* our government. Suppose it's some other government, suppose Kimmie's on the other side. Though it's sometimes hard to know what the different sides are, anyway."

"I guess."

"But what I realized was I don't care. What side you're on, I mean. I don't *care* if you're really an alien and you're working for the flying saucer people. It doesn't matter. You're still my Kimmie, and I get tingly when I pick up the phone and it's you, and I'd rather jill off to one of your stories than fuck Brad Pitt while I'm blowing George Clooney."

"Although that does sound like fun."

"Yeah, it sort of does, doesn't it?"

"I don't work for the government, Rita. Not ours or anybody

else's, either. I work in a pretentious coffee shop in Salem."

"Where they burn the witches?"

"That was in Massachusetts, wasn't it? Somewhere in New England, anyway. I'm in the one in Oregon, and all we burn is the French Roast coffee."

"You're in Oregon?"

"Uh-huh."

"That's not so far, is it?"

"It'd take a while on a bicycle," she said. "Rita, it's not far, not really, and anyway I wouldn't have to take a bike. I know how to drive. But first there are things I have to tell you, and the only way this is going to work is if you just listen and don't interrupt. And then when I'm through you can ask anything you want, or say anything you want. Or just tell me you don't want to have anything to do with me, and hang up, and I'll have to live with that."

"My God, Kimmie."

"So here goes."

Long pause. "Kimmie?"

"Yeah, I'm here. I'm just having a little trouble getting started."

It was very difficult to get started, and not much easier once she did. She couldn't say anything without worrying about the way it would be received. But she forced herself to keep going, and there was a point where she stopped being concerned by Rita's reaction.

She'd asked Rita not to interrupt, and she didn't, not even with an occasional sharp intake of breath. She found herself entertaining the notion that Rita wasn't listening at all, that she'd put down the phone and left the room, that her own carrier had dropped the call.

None of that mattered. She was speaking of things she had never confided to anyone, and it was as if all those words had been dammed up somewhere within her, and the effect of releasing them was surprisingly powerful.

All those years of being the good little soldier, and you couldn't say they'd ended when she killed her parents. That just gave her another secret to keep.

She'd shared bits and pieces with some of the men she'd been with, just before or after she killed them. And she'd told a bit of her story to Angelica while she got the woman to tell her where the money was stashed, and while she slipped the Hermés scarf around her neck.

Maybe those brief confidences had been an attempt to break the dam, to let it all out and relieve the pressure. But this was vastly different, and somewhere along the way she slipped into an altered state, as if she were a trance medium channeling her own thoughts.

When she stopped, when the words ran out, she couldn't have guessed how much time had passed. Nor would she have been able to say what incidents she'd recounted and what ones remained unreported. All she knew, really, was that she was done, that she'd said all she needed to say.

She was waiting for a response from Rita, but Rita was silent herself. She knew she was still on the line, though. Her breathing, while shallow, was audible.

When it was clear Rita wasn't going to speak, she said, "That's it. You can talk now. Or not, if you don't want to."

"I wasn't sure you were done."

"Oh, I'm done."

"I never would have guessed any of that, Kimmie. Except—"

"What?"

"Well, you know. Thinking you were a secret agent. I wondered if you ever had to kill anybody."

"And what did you decide?"

"That you probably had to, and that you were probably good at it."

"Because I'm a heartless bitch."

"Because you're the strongest human being I've ever met in my life."

"I guess you don't get out much."

"I mean it, Kimmie. Should I be calling you that? That can't be the name you started out with."

"I like it."

"Really?"

"I like it when you say it."

"What's so funny?"

"Oh, I was just thinking. I like when you say Kimmie almost as much as you like it when I say cunt."

"Kimmie, you're awful!"

"I've killed more men than I can remember and saying a yummy word like cunt makes me awful?"

"It is a yummy word, isn't it?"

"Delicious."

"If you were here—"

"If I were there what?"

"If you were here, I'd grab you like a bowling ball with two fingers up your ass and my thumb up your cunt, and I'd suck on your clitty until your bones melt."

"You didn't just come up with that, Rita."

"No, it's one of a few hundred things I think about all the time. *All. The. Time.*"

"But now that you know what I am—"

"You're my Kimmie, that's all I need to know. I love you."

"Oh God."

"I do, I do. I love you and I'm in love with you. And I don't have to be jealous of any of the guys you've been with because they're all dead. Not that I was ever jealous anyway, because what do I care what you do with men? What has any of that got to do with us?"

"Nothing. I love you, too."

"I know you do."

"You want to know something awful about me? I *love* that you killed them. Kellen Kimball, I liked the idea that you were going to fuck him, that we'd have him in common."

"You said it would be a threesome with an interval."

"And I thought he was a pretty nice guy, even if he wouldn't go down on me. Did he go down on you?"

"He didn't want to."

"But he did, didn't he?"

"Well, see, he *did* want to, really. He wanted to do you, too, but he had this fidelity issue. Once I got him to see that he was my proxy bridegroom Sidney, not some lucky girl's fiancé, well, he got into the spirit of things."

"That is so great. And he's dead, and you killed him."

"Yeah."

"I guess I'm crazy, because on the one hand I liked him a little, and at the same time I'm really glad you killed him. That's weird, isn't it?"

"I think so," she said. "But I'm not sure I'm the best person to say what's weird and what isn't."

And, a little later:

"I know you can drive, but I bet you don't have a car. What I could do, I could drive down and pick you up."

"I'll take the train."

"Are you sure? I swear I don't mind driving."

"Amtrak takes a little over five hours and costs all of sixty-five dollars. I'll get to watch the scenery, and I won't have to worry about keeping my hands off the driver."

"You already checked this out."

"Yes."

"You were planning on coming."

"Or leaving you alone forever, depending on what you wanted."

"Well, you know what I want."

"It sounds like we both want the same thing."

"Oh, God."

"Tomorrow," she said. "There are a couple of things I have to do. Pack my stuff, tell my boss to find someone else to sell plangent coffee."

"Plangent?"

"Long story. There's a train at two in the afternoon, gets to Seattle at a quarter after seven."

"I'll be there."

"I could take a cab."

"Yeah, right. Or maybe my bike's still there where you left it. You never know."

"It still bothers me about the bike. Just abandoning it like that."

"Well, get over it," Rita said. "I'll be there when your train gets in. And Kimmie? I love you."

Her morning appointment took longer than she'd thought. She'd packed first and stopped en route at the Bean Bag to pick up her pay and tell Will she was leaving, then found her way to the salon. She'd found their ad in the local alternative newspaper, and the operator wore spike heels and a lot of leather; if she wasn't a dominatrix, she needed a new agent.

She had one more stop to make after the Leather Girl finished with her, but it didn't take long. When she left her suitcase was heavier, but not too heavy, and she wound up catching her train with ten minutes to spare. She grabbed a window seat, plopped her bag onto the aisle seat beside her, and hoped no one would make her move it. A lot of people got on in Portland, but they all walked past her bag and found seats somewhere else, and the seat beside hers remained empty all the way to Seattle.

For five hours her mind kept offering up objections, telling her that she was crazy, that she and Rita were partners in a *folie à deux*. There was a rock album with that name, and it meant a shared delusion, and wasn't that what was going on? A few hours together months and months ago, a whole bunch of deliberately erotic telephone conversations, and only one in which she'd actually let this great love of her life get a glimmer of who she really was.

She remembered a joke she'd overheard in the Daiquiri Dock:

*Q: What does a lesbian bring on a second date?*

*A: A U-Haul.*

She laid a hand on the bag next to her. Not a U-Haul, but it held everything she owned in the world, so it amounted to pretty much the same thing.

Half an hour north of Portland she started wishing she'd put her bag in the overhead rack. Someone might be sitting next to her now, some jabbering biddy with pictures of her drooling grandchildren, some gormless college boy who'd ask her a million questions, then dart off to abuse himself in the restroom. One way or another she'd be stuck with a companion who'd bore her to tears—and wouldn't that be better than having to listen to her own wretched mind?

No way it was going to work out. Like, what were the odds?

Slim and slimmer, she thought. There was a fair chance they wouldn't even go to bed, because Rita could turn out to be far more adventurous over the phone than she was prepared to be in person. And even if they did, and even if it was great, then what?

In a day or a week or not much more than that, she'd be getting on another train. Or a bus, or an airplane, but whatever it was it'd have the state of Washington in the rear-view mirror, and that's where it would stay for the rest of her life.

And then, of course, there'd be no more phone calls. For so long now she'd lived for those calls, coming alive during those moments on the phone in a way she never did the rest of the time. Not when she was fucking, not when she was killing, and certainly not when she was marking time.

Sitting on the edge of her bed in some ill-furnished room. Talking, listening.

God, she thought, remembering. Riverdale, talking on the phone while she rode off to orgasm on the still-rigid penis of the late Peter Fuhrmann. It was incredibly hot, and it damn well had to be or it would have been disgusting. Yet what she'd focused on throughout was not so much the dick inside her as the woman on the other end of the phone.

Along with the phone calls, she'd be giving up the fantasy. Because that had sustained her even before she and Rita had begun speculating about the possibility of sharing sexual moments face to face. The idea that the two of them could, well, be a couple, that they could actually love each other, that together they could create, well, a life.

*Hey, we tried, sweetie. And we'll stay in touch, okay? You know, on the phone. And who knows, maybe we'll get together again in person sometime. You never know, do you?*

Except sometimes you knew. It would either work or it wouldn't, and if it didn't then it didn't matter what lies they told each other, because they would both know it was over.

And then what? Where would she go, and what would she do, and why should she even bother?

She glared at her suitcase. *Say something,* she told it. *Are you just going to fucking sit there in silence?*

"Let me give you a hand with that."

It wasn't the suitcase that broke the silence, but the tall young man across the aisle. She'd noticed him once or twice since he'd boarded in Portland, and had noticed him noticing her. Briefly, she'd allowed herself to speculate on what might have happened if she weren't on her way to Rita, but the fantasy never got anyplace because her mind had quickly gone back to spinning its wheels, telling her everything that was sure to go wrong in Kirkland.

Now they were slowing as they entered the Seattle station, and he'd taken hold of her suitcase before she could tell him thanks but no thanks.

"I can manage it," she said. "Really I can."

He smiled, showing good teeth. "Of course you can," he said, "but why should you? This way you can allow me to feel manly and useful, and save your strength for the hug you're going to give your husband."

Interesting. He knew she wasn't married, could not have failed to note the absence of a ring on her finger.

Well, she could hold up her end of the conversation. "No husband," she said.

"Your boyfriend, then."

She smiled, shook her head.

Well, why not? Rita wouldn't be there, she would have come to her senses, and there'd be nobody at all to meet her, and where was it written that she had to be alone with her disappointment? He was a good-looking fellow, clean cut and well turned out, and he'd take her out for a decent dinner, and that was a good idea all by itself, because all she'd had to eat all day was the croissant with her morning coffee.

And then she could fuck him, and once she'd done that she could figure out a way to kill him, and then she'd have no choice but to get out of Seattle in a hurry. And she'd give it a few days and then call Rita from Omaha or Dayton or Lynchburg, and—

"Kimmie!"

And there was Rita.

Jesus, how had she forgotten how beautiful the woman was? Just stunning, and positively glowing, and with the most wonderful light shining in her eyes.

She took a step toward her, and before she knew it she was running. And then they were in each other's arms.

Had she ever kissed anyone like this? Putting every atom of her being into the kiss, drawing all she could of the other person back into herself? Had she? Ever?

"Kimmie, I think that's your suitcase."

"How did it—"

"Unless it's a bomb, but that guy didn't look like your typical terrorist. He was actually kind of cute."

"Kind of."

"I guess at first he thought we were sisters, or best friends, you know? And then when we really got into it he got the message, and his expression changed. I guess he was disappointed."

"I guess. Where'd he go?"

"He put the suitcase down," Rita said, "and then I guess he went away, but by that time I was too busy kissing you to pay attention. I never kissed a woman like that."

"I never kissed *anybody* like that."

"No, neither did I. I always liked kissing guys, but it's a completely different thing, isn't it? God, you're beautiful."

"This is nothing. Wait till you see me naked."

"Kimmie!"


"How did you find a parking spot so close?"

"The city reserved it for me," Rita said, "by putting a fire hydrant there. I figured I'd get a ticket, and I figured I didn't care, but I guess the meter maid was busy giving somebody a blow job. Kimmie, I never talked like this before I met you."

"I'm a terrible influence."

"You are. I loved the way our tits pressed together when we kissed."

"You may be disappointed, Ree. Mine are on the small side."

"Ree."

"Is it okay to call you that? Or do you hate it?"

"No, I like it. And speaking of tits—"

"That's right. We were speaking of tits."

"I saw yours, remember? When we had phoneless sex."

"Oh, right."

"And I thought they were adorable. Mine are these big pillow tits. Maybe you won't like them."

"Yeah, I'm disgusted just thinking about them."

"Really?"

"They're much too large. Maybe I can whittle away at them with my tongue."

"We're gonna have fun, aren't we, Kimmie?"

"Oh, yes."

"I'll do anything you want. You know that, don't you?"

"Same for me."

"God, this traffic! But there's something nice about having to wait, you know?"

"I was thinking the same thing."

"You know what I did? I cooked dinner, isn't that nuts? It's a casserole, it's in the oven keeping warm."

"I figured you would. I brought the wine."

"Really? Is it that kind I can't pronounce?"

"Nuits-Saint-Georges. No, but it's like that. Another hearty red burgundy, according to the wine store guy in Salem, and I decided to take his word for it. This one's a Pommard."

"Poh-mahr."

"Right."

"I don't know, Kimmie. I'm not sure how comfortable I feel with a wine I can actually pronounce."

"There's a D on the end, but it's silent."

"Well, that's something. I feel better already."

A cloth and candles on the table. Good food, good wine. As hungry as she was, all she wanted was to be in bed with Ree. But it was nice to postpone it for a little while. The anticipation was as savory as the meal, as tantalizing as the wine.

*Dare I say plangent?*

"Kimmie? You want to know a secret? I'm wearing the butt plug."

"Really?"

"I've been wearing it all day. Sometimes I'll do that. I like how it feels. The fullness, you know? And the idea that nobody knows. Of course there are times when I have to take it out."

"No kidding."

"And you gave it to me. That adds to it."

"I brought you another present."

"You did?"

"Well, sort of. I picked it up this morning, before I went to the wine store."

"A sex toy?"

"No, I don't even know if they sell sex toys in Salem. Well, they must, but I didn't really go looking for them. And this isn't a thing. It's more of a surprise. But it's for you. Ree, you look completely lost."

"Well, what do you expect? You're talking in riddles. Am I supposed to guess? Give me a hint."

"I went to Brazil for it."

"You went to *Brazil?*"

"In a manner of speaking. I got a Brazilian." She got to her feet. "Come on," she said. "I'll show you."

Lying on her back, with Ree's head on her shoulder. The bedroom in shadows, with a table lamp in the hallway the only source of light. Ree's taste in her mouth, Ree's scent and her own scent permeating the room.

This was how it was supposed to be.

"Yes, Kimmie. It's exactly the way it's supposed to be."

"Did I say it out loud? I thought I was just thinking it."

"Maybe that's all you did and I picked the thought out of the air."

"Can you do that?"

"I never could before, but everything's different, so who knows what I can do?"

"Isn't that the truth? That bowling ball trick—"

"A guy did that to me once. Just one finger, plus the thumb. I thought two fingers would be better."

"Definitely."

"Did it hurt?"

"The two fingers? No, it felt nice."

"The Brazilian, silly. What did they use, hot wax?

"Yeah, but it wasn't so bad. And I thought it would be worth it. Do you like me without any pubic hair? It's not unnatural, is it? Or just plain dopey?"

"It's beautiful."

"Or all little-girly? All pedophilia-creepy?"

"Daddy's little soldier."

"I swear I never even thought of that. Is it like that?"

"Kimmie, I love it. There's no hair, everything's all sweet and smooth and silky, I can just kiss and lick everything. I'm a whole forest down there. You must have been disgusted."

"Yeah, right. I had to force myself to get anywhere near you."

"But wouldn't you want me to get it done?"

"For your sake, Ree. Everything's more intense."

"Really? I don't know if I can stand that. But I *have* to get it done. God, yours is so smooth, I can't keep my hands off it. Give me a kiss. You know what's remarkable? Your mouth tastes like a pussy."

"Here's a coincidence—so does yours."

"Kimmie, this is all so *easy*! I had no idea."

"Me neither."

"I think there's some more wine left. You want some?"

"Not particularly."

"Some Poh-mahr. It was nice, but I had enough. The only thing I haven't had enough of is you."

"Ah, baby. Let's see what we can do about that."


And, a little later:

"Kimmie? I guess we're lesbians, huh?"

"I suppose so."

"But we're still us, right?"

"Well, we don't have to learn the secret handshake. Or deepen our voices."

"Do we have to wear those plaid shirts from L. L. Bean?"

"No way. We don't have to get a cat, either."

"That's a relief."

"Or adopt a Chinese baby."

"Kimmie? You'll move in, won't you?"

"If you can stand it."

"You can have your old room back. But we'll sleep here. Unless we try your room occasionally as a change of pace."

"To ward off boredom."

"You think we'll get bored?"

"No."

"Me neither. I want us to do everything."

"We will. And Ree? There's no reason you can't have a guy anytime you want."

"Really? You wouldn't be jealous?"

"Why should I? I'm not jealous of the ones you've been with. You're not jealous of my lovers, are you?"

"Kimmie, they're all dead."

"That's a point."

"But if they weren't? No, I wouldn't be jealous."

"Because it doesn't subtract from what we've got."

"No, it adds to it. Right now I don't want anything but you and me in bed, but that doesn't mean I don't want us to tell each other stories. And sooner or later we might want to have new stories to tell each other."

"Right."

"And I've always liked fucking guys, Kimmie."

"Me too."

"And now I'm thinking about doing some new guy and then telling you about it, and I don't know what's getting me hotter, the idea of doing him or the idea of telling you."

"Over the phone?"

"Silly. Lying in bed, and feeling your breasts against mine, and looking into your eyes—"

"Like you're doing right now."

"Like I'm doing right now. And telling you all about it."

"I suppose you realize that you're sopping wet."

"Like I'm the only one? And I am definitely getting a Brazilian."

"But not right this minute."

"No. Right this minute I'm busy."

She spent the next several days settling in, and by Friday she had a working set of ID in the name of Kimberly Austin. She liked Austin for a last name, but she wasn't crazy about the Kimberly part. Names had never mattered much to her when she'd used each one for such a short time, but maybe that was going to change, maybe she'd take a shot at being the same person with the same name for, well, as long as she could.

No problem. Kimberly could turn into Kim, and she'd pump up her new identity with a library card and some generic student ID cards as Kim Austin, and by the time she picked up a Washington State driver's license, she'd be able to shrink Kimberly to Kim once and for all. And then maybe get a lawyer to have her name changed by court order? If she did that, she'd be able to get a passport. Not that she had any urge to leave the country, but suppose Ree wanted to see Paris?

*Omigod, Kimmie, here we are in the country where they invented eating pussy.*

Had to keep your options open, didn't you?

*

It was all so easy.

Because she was usually the first one up, and because Ree always prepared the evening meal, she took over the role of making the morning coffee and putting breakfast on the table. Her first omelet was a failure, but all that cost her was a couple of eggs, and it didn't take her long to get the hang of it.

"We're getting so domestic," Ree said. "I think we're definitely lesbians. I think there's no question about it."

"I can see how upset that makes you."

"Plaid flannel shirts and cats," Ree said, "are just around the corner."

"We're lipstick lesbians."

"No plaid shirts, huh?"

"Not even to sleep in. And no cats, either."

"And no Chinese babies?"

"They're cuter than cats," she said, "and way cuter than plaid shirts, but not just yet, okay?"

"Okay."

So easy.


Later that day she was sitting on the couch reading, and Ree was doing a crossword puzzle, and their eyes met. That was all it took, really, and half an hour later they were lying side by side in Ree's bed in the shared afterglow.

And Ree said, "I guess I'm safe, huh?"

"Safe?"

"Well, nobody's ever safe. Like earthquakes and tornadoes and, I don't know, tsunamis? Not that I spend a lot of time worrying about tsunamis, but you never know, do you?"

Where was this going? "And there's always sinkholes," she said.

"That's right! No warning, nothing, and the ground just opens up underneath you. Gone, no forwarding. Just like that."

"But you guess you're safe."

Ree was looking off to the side. "What I figure," she said, "is if you were going to kill me, you'd have done it by now."

"Ree!"

"Well, you killed everybody else you ever slept with. Kimmie, I knew you weren't planning to do it, but suppose you couldn't help it? Suppose it got under your skin, and you couldn't rest as long as I was alive?"

"That only happened with men."

"You've killed women."

"My mother, and I explained that to you. And I never had sex with her, anyway. It was just—"

"And what about Angela?"

"Angela."

"She picked you up in the dyke bar, and her husband was hiding in the closet—"

"Oh, Angelica."

"I was close."

"And his name was Brady. He wasn't in the closet, he was hiding behind a Japanese screen."

"Thanks for clearing that up, Kimmie. The point is you slept with her and you killed her."

"Yeah."

"Strangled her with a scarf or something."

"A silk scarf."

"Herpes, I think you said."

"Hermés."

LAWRENCE BLOCK

"I know, silly. Ehr-mehz. Poh-mahr."

"Ree, they were going to murder me. He wanted to do me just for the thrill of it, and she loved the idea."

"I know, you told me."

"She was one vicious cunt. She brought me home so her husband could rape me, and when I turned out to be eager and willing, they decided the only way to keep it interesting was to kill me. She had it coming."

"I know."

"And how could I let her live once I'd killed him?" She frowned. "Okay, I have to admit I enjoyed it. Doing her with the scarf, feeling her squirming underneath me. But it's the way I'm hard-wired, Ree. Killing gets me off. I can't help it."

"Kimmie, it's one of the things about you that gets *me* hot."

"I would never, ever, hurt you. Not for anything."

"But how could you know you wouldn't feel the need? The only woman you ever went to bed with wound up with a scarf around her neck and her eyes bulging."

"That's not true."

"It's not?"

"Boise."

"Huh?"

She took a breath. "After Provo," she said, "I went to Boise. That's in Idaho."

"And?"

"All I wanted," she said, "was to come here. To you. But I couldn't do that if it meant putting you in danger. So I had to find out."

"How could you do that? What would—oh, you slept with a woman! In Boise? They have girl-girl bars in Boise?"

"Well, they had at least one of them. They made it hard to find,

I'll give them that. But I went there and I found a woman to go home with."

"And you had sex."

"Uh-huh."

"And she's still got a pulse?"

"Unless she stepped in front of a bus."

"You didn't mention it."

"No. I thought you might be jealous."

"Seriously?"

"Well, yeah. Or that it might trivialize what we've got, or something. Stupid, huh?"

"So how was it?"

"A successful experiment, because I had absolutely no desire to hurt her. Not at the time and not afterward. I didn't want to see her again, either, but I had, like, warm feelings toward her."

"What was she like?"

"I don't know. Late thirties, dark hair. A little dykey, I suppose."

"Was she better than me?"

"Absolutely. That's why I spent the rest of my life in Boise and never gave you another thought."

"What was the sex like with her?"

"Sort of vanilla. Kissing, touching. You really want to hear this?"

"Of course."

"Let's see. She went down on me and I came. Then I went down on her, and she couldn't come."

"With that magic mouth of yours? That's hard to believe."

"She said she's pretty much non-orgasmic. Her big thing is getting her partner off. Which she managed twice, because I came again while I was eating her."

"Just from doing it?"

"I was touching myself at the same time. And beside that—"

"What?"

"Well, I was thinking about you. That's what I did while she was doing me, too. Thought about you, made believe it was you I was with. Jesus, Ree, you honestly thought I was going to kill you?"

A shrug. "I thought there was a chance. But I figured it was worth the risk."

She reached out, took Ree's hand in hers. She was at a loss for words, but that was all right. She didn't need to say anything.

# THIRTY-THREE

"So I'm Luke," the fellow said, "and this is my buddy, Gordo. His folks named him Gordon, and he had the nickname for years before he found out it means *fat* in Spanish."

"By then it was too late," Gordo said. "So I'm at the gym five days a week, making sure the name never fits."

"So why don't the four of us take a booth? It's hard to hear in the crush at the bar. Like, I didn't manage to catch your names."

"You guys get the table," she said, "and we'll join you in a minute. Right now, nature calls."

"The only thing men can do and women can't," Gordo said, "is go to the bathroom alone."

"It's true," Ree admitted. "We need company."

And in the bathroom she said, "What do you think, Kimmie?"

"I think they're morons."

"But are they morons we want to fuck?"

"I don't know. Which one would you want?"

"No, you pick."

"I can't. I don't want either of them."

"Then let's get out of here, Kimmie. I know another place."

Two nights before, after dinner at the Thai place and an hour of HBO, they'd gone to bed. And after an hour or so she'd said, "The strap-on's nice."

"I know! It doesn't matter which of us is using it. It's nice."

"But so is a real cock."

"You know, I tried to buy one online, but—"

"What I mean is we may be lesbians, but that doesn't mean we don't enjoy fucking guys."

"I know. We talked about that. Do you want me to go out and get a guy? And then tell you about it?"

"I was thinking we could go out together."

"And bring some guy home?"

"Or two guys."

"Oh, wow. I'm just thinking of the possibilities."

"Uh-huh."

"But Kimmie? What about afterward?"

"Afterward," she said, "you and I'll go home together, and talk about all the fun we just had. Incidentally, I don't think we should bring them here. We'll go to their place, so we can leave when we want to."

"And so that this place is just for you and me."

"Exactly."

"But Kimmie, what I meant about afterward. If you're with a guy—"

"Yeah?"

"Well, won't he be on your list?"

She considered this. "I can't be positive," she said, "but I have the feeling I'm done with that list. I crossed off the last name, remember."

"With the proxy marriage in Provo."

"Right. Something changed that day, Ree. Something shifted. You know it was all about my daddy."

"I know."

"I kept fucking him and killing him, over and over. Not consciously, but let's face it, that's what I was doing. And I think he's finally dead, you know? And I'm finally at peace with it. You know what else I think?"

"That you had to be done with all that in order for us to be together."

"Yes! And we are, and I am." She frowned. "At least that's what I think. Ree? What do *you* think?"

Ree was silent for a moment. Then she said, "What I think is I'm picturing you on your back with your legs spread, and this guy's on top of you, and while he's pumping away at you, I'm doing him in the ass with a strap-on."

"That's what you're thinking."

"Yeah."

"And if it's two guys?"

"Oh, I didn't even think of that. Where would the second guy fit in?"

"I suppose I could always blow him."

"Sure," Ree said. "That'd work."

The Cascadilla Lounge was in downtown Seattle, tucked in between a pair of four-star hotels. The lighting was indirect and subdued, and a piano trio supplied soft jazz. The clientele ran to men in suits.

"Business travelers," Ree said. "Some of them are here for the drinks and the music, but most of them are looking to get laid."

"Just like us," she said.

They found room at the bar, and got a thoughtful look from the barman who filled their order for two glasses of white wine. "He's trying to figure out if we're hookers," Ree told her. "Like the red-head at the end of the bar. I've only been here two or three times, but she's always here, and always on the same stool."

"She's cute."

"You don't want to—"

She shook her head. "The Blue-Plate Special tonight is dick," she said. "Besides, you're the only woman in my life."

"I wonder if anybody's gonna hit on us. Those guys before, Luke and Gordo—"

"They were assholes, Ree."

"Yeah, I know. But they were ready to go, Kimmie."

"Hot to trot."

"You bet. By now we'd be switching partners for a second go-round, and in another hour we'd be back home doing each other and talking about what jerks they were."

"Instead of drinking wine we paid for ourselves and waiting for someone to make a move. Unless we're the ones who make the first move. You see anybody you like?"

"There was a guy who was sort of cute. I don't know where he went."

"Those two have been giving us the eye. At the table to the right of the piano player."

"We could give them the eye right back. Except—Kimmie, you know who they remind me of?"

"Luke and Gordo."

"Uh-huh. Luke and Gordo, plus twenty pounds and fifteen or twenty years."

"So let's not give them the eye."

"No, let's not."

"Ree, are we being too fussy? We're not gonna marry these guys. We're just gonna fuck their brains out."

"If we could even find their brains."

"We could go home."

"I was just about to say that. But, you know, we just got here."

"I know."

"Not that we couldn't have a perfectly good time by ourselves, but—"

"I know."

She picked up her glass, held it to her lips without sipping from it. The pianist was playing something she liked, something she'd heard a million times, but she couldn't identify it. She frowned, concentrating.

"Gloria!"

The male voice boomed in her ear. She turned and saw its source, a tall man in his early forties, wearing a dark suit with a chalk stripe. Whoever Gloria might be, her name had triggered something in her own memory. "*Laura*," she told the man. "Thanks, I was going mad trying to name that tune."

"Ah, *Laura*. But she's only a dream, right? But you're Gloria, aren't you? You've got to be, 'cause I never forget a face."

Who was he? And when had she ever called herself Gloria?

"Especially a face as beautiful as yours," he went on. "I guess you don't remember me."

"There's something—"

"What?"

"Familiar about you." And there was. The voice, for one thing, deep and resonant. The jawline, the sculptured brow, the blue eyes. She tried to coax the memory out into the open, and her effort amused him enough to make him smile, and as she registered his smile, the door in her memory slammed shut.

"I'm sorry," she said. "I can't quite place you."

"Don't apologize, Gloria. We knew each other very briefly. Ran into each other in a bar in downtown Philly. I don't even remember where it was, but—"

"Race Street."

"Yeah, that sounds about right. By God, you *do* remember!"

"But your smile is different."

He grinned, once again showing her two rows of perfect teeth. "Miracles of modern dentistry," he said, and tapped his upper incisors with his forefinger. "Chipped a tooth, did a real job on it. My guy capped it and the one next to it, and while he was at it he got rid of the gap between them. Up until then I never knew it bothered me, but afterward I had a lot more self-confidence. Started going to the gym, keeping a year-round tan. Taking better care of myself generally."

"That's great, Sid."

That brought the smile back. "That's right, I was calling myself Sid a lot in those days."

"Your name's not Sid."

"Well, no. It's Kendall, actually, which was my mother's maiden name. Ken's what people call me."

"And you're not from Philadelphia."

"No, did I say I was? I'm from Tulsa, I've lived there all my life. I was in Philly on business."

"I guess I knew that."

"And now I'm in Seattle on business. But I'm not working tonight. Gloria, we only had the one night together, and I'm not sure how much of it you remember, but I have to say I've thought about you often."

"Really?"

"Absolutely. And they've been good thoughts. I had a great time with you."

His hand was resting on the bar, and she laid hers on top of it. "Me too," she said.

"And here we are, running into each other after all these years."

"Quite a coincidence, Ken."

"It is, isn't it?"

"And an opportunity."

"Just what I was thinking."

She rubbed his hand with hers. "The only thing is," she said, "I'm here with my girlfriend."

"That would be the lady standing next to you? The one who's being very careful not to pay any attention to our conversation?"

"Her name's Ree."

"Rhea? That's a pretty—"

"No, just Ree."

"Even better. I think your friend is beautiful, and I bet it wouldn't be hard for me to find a gentleman here who agrees with me."

"You're probably right."

"And I'm staying right next door at the Alexis, and they went and upgraded me to a suite. Plenty of room for four, and a lot more comfortable than this joint."

"I'll tell you what," she said. "Let me take Ree to the ladies, and we can freshen up and talk things through. You'll be right here when we get back, won't you?"

"I'm not going anywhere."

"Because it took us long enough to find each other," she said. Her hand dropped to his groin, and she watched its effect reflected in his blue eyes. "I wouldn't want to let you get away again, Ken. Not after all these years."

Ree said, "Sid from Philadelphia!"

"No wonder I couldn't find him," she said. "His name's not Sid and he's not from Philadelphia. And what I remembered was his pasty complexion and the gap between his teeth, and now his teeth are capped and he discovered tanning beds."

"Isn't he worried about skin cancer?"

"He won't live long enough to get it."

"Kimmie—"

"I did him once," she said. "By proxy. Kellen Kimball died for his sins. Ree, if you want to split, just take the car and go home. I'll catch a cab or something."

"What are you talking about?"

"Oh, sweetie, I've got to fuck this guy. I mean I've just got to."

"So? Why can't we share? We both fucked Kellen. Why can't we both fuck Ken?"

"Ken and Kellen."

"I love how their names go together."

"Except it's actually Kendall, and that's even better. Kellen and Kendall. As in Ken Doll, and isn't that the perfect name for him?"

"And we can do him like Barbie never did."

"Oh, yes. With the strap-on, and everything we talked about. Ree, I don't want to leave you out of it."

"That's a good thing, because I wouldn't let you."

"And afterward you can slip out, and, I don't know, wait for me somewhere. Because you know what I have to do."

"You have to kill him."

"I do, I really do. The bastard is still on my list. His name's crossed out, but there's an asterisk next to it in the record book. He's unfinished business."

"I know."

"But just because I have to do it doesn't mean you have to be there when it happens."

"Maybe I want to."

"You think?"

"I don't know. Maybe I want to see you do it. Maybe not. All I know is I'm wet just picturing you with the knife."

"Shit, I didn't bring a knife. Or anything, really. I didn't think I was going to need anything. I guess I'll think of something. Ree, you can always slip into the other room."

"I know."

"Or not. Whatever. Come here. Jesus, you really are wet, aren't you?"

"Sopping."

"Well, let's go find our Ken Doll," she said. "Let's let him know just how lucky he is."

"So what we were thinking," she told Ken, "is Ree and I both think you're awfully cute, and I know how much fun you are to party with, so what do we need with another guy?"

"Because as far as we're concerned," Ree said, "three is not a crowd. Unless you feel differently."

"Not me," he said. "I think three's a terrific number. I mean, think about it. It's the very number God picked when he was deciding how many people to be."

"But there are a couple of things you ought to know. First of all, you know how you told me your name was Sid, but it's not?"

"Hey, I'm sorry about that, but—"

"No, it's cool, but the thing is my name's not Gloria."

"So Sid and Gloria are actually..."

"Ken and Kim."

"Kim," he said, and looked her over, and nodded. "Works for me. Ken, Kim, Ree—three people, three letters each. Keeps the typesetting costs down."

"Except sometimes Ree calls me Kimmie."

"Kimmie. Well, that works, too. If that's all I need to know—"

"One other thing," Ree said, "is neither of us has any pubic hair. See, Kimmie went and got herself a Brazilian, and I liked it so much I went and got one for myself."

"And that leads into the third thing you should know," she said, "which is that Ree and I are kind of into each other. So if that's something that turns your stomach—"

"Turns me on, is what it does."

"Then maybe we should all go inspect that suite you mentioned."

The suite was luxurious, the bed king-sized. When he finally excused himself to go to the bathroom, Ree said, "You know what I almost forgot?"

"How much you love cock."

"Yeah. He's got a nice one, too."

"You like him, don't you?"

"Sure. He's a nice guy. Oh, like maybe I don't want to go through with it? Kimmie, he's the guy. That means there's only one way this can end."

"I wish I'd brought a knife."

"Tell him you're hungry. They've got twenty-four-hour room service, don't they? Order a steak, they'll give you a steak knife with it."

"Maybe. You know what? I bet he'd let us tie him up. Once he's tied up there's a dozen different ways I could do it."

"Tie him up with what?"

"The cord from the window shades. No, we'd need a knife anyway just to cut the cord. Oh, the tie-back sashes! Like to hold the drapes in place. That would work."

"Are there enough?"

"Two pairs here, two in the living room. That's eight, that's more than enough. Once he's tied up you can just wait in the other room, and—"

"No way. I want to see it."

"Are you sure?"

"The whole idea is so hot. I might even want to help."

"You think? Shhh, here he comes. Ken, Ree and I were beginning to think you fell in."

"Oh, I figured I'd give the two of you a chance to do some more of that girl–girl stuff."

"Without you watching and joining in? Where's the fun in that?"

"God," he said, "how'd I get so lucky?"

And Ree said, "Seriously, Ken, you were gone a long time. Do you feel okay?"

"You want to know how I feel? I feel like I died and went to heaven. What, did I say something funny?"